DUBLIN DEVIL

A DARK MAFIA ROMANCE

EMERALD ISLE MAFIA SERIES
BOOK TWO

JENN MADORE
CAROLINA MAC

DAUNTLESS

Dauntless Publishing Inc — 1st ed.

ISBN: 978-1-998372-29-4

CONTENT WARNING

Dublin Devil is intended for mature readers. It is a spicy Dark Mafia M/F Romance full of heat, betrayal, violence, and survival.

Possible triggers: kidnapping, gang/mafia violence, arranged marriage, murder/death, assault, betrayal, blood, gun violence, nightmares, hostage situation, sexually explicit scenes, and mentions of sex trafficking.

Tropes: enemies to lovers, arranged marriage, forced proximity, forbidden love, on the run, starting over, touch her and die, over protective MMC,

Each book is a connected standalone with a completed story and HEA.

DEDICATION

To our new fans joining Mom and I as we embrace love stories in the real world and our diehard fans who followed us from Paranormal Romance and Urban Fantasy (JL Madore/ Auburn Tempest) and Pulp Fiction/Crime/Thrillers (Carolina Mac). We are ever grateful for your trust in our storytelling. Thank you for coming on the ride.

CHAPTER ONE

Piper

*T*his is my big night, and it's going perfectly. After nineteen years of being babied and treated like I have nothing to offer the family business, tonight I'm finally making inroads and proving to my father and my brothers that I deserve a place at the table.

My rightful place.

I'm a McGuire, the youngest of seven, and the only daughter of the biggest crime family in Dublin. I'm just as savvy and strategic as my brothers, and tonight I'm showing them I'm an asset to the McGuire empire.

Sitting in the private dining room of the NYX Hotel Dublin Christchurch, I put on my best smile as I shift my napkin from my lap and lay it on the table. "It's been a wonderful evening, gentlemen: great food, engaging conversation, and now, I'm sure you'll find the executive suite my father booked for you just as pleasing."

Vladimir Volkov, the younger of the two Russian Bratva representatives I'm schmoozing this evening, is the cousin of the big boss, Anton Volkov. He's the man to impress in St. Petersburg and told Da that if Vladimir is happy with what he sees here in Dublin, he'll consider establishing a business arrangement with my family.

Vladimir runs fat fingers through his chaotic beard. "Everything is wonderful, Miss McGuire. Your father is wise man. Giving you to us. Good for business."

I chuckle. "I'm glad you enjoyed my company. Come, I'll show you to your suite."

The other man, Arkady Sidorov, grunts his approval and buttons his suit jacket when he stands. He carries the same jacked-up, muscled frame as his partner, but with a much stronger stalker vibe.

He has eyed me up and down all night like *I* was his dinner instead of the four-hundred-dollar wagyu steak he ordered and inhaled.

But I grew up around dangerous men, so, while they intimidate me a little—the Bratva are violent and deadly—it doesn't stop me from doing my job.

All evening, I've smiled and played the part of the perfect hostess—the task my father assigned to me.

The hotel lobby is busy, the murmur of voices carrying from the reception desk and seating areas all the way to the restaurant entrance.

I gesture to the main doors as we walk toward the hotel lobby. "If you gentlemen would like to try your hand at roulette or blackjack, I can arrange a private table for you at the casino down the block. A quick taxi ride and you'll be all set."

Arkady purses his lips. "Nyet. Up to room."

"Of course. I'm sure you're tired after your travels. This way." My Louboutin heels clack out a steady rhythm on the polished marble tiles as I lead them to the bank of elevators.

Da has them set up in one of the top-floor suites overlooking the River Liffey. He mentioned that he's arranged female entertainment for them this evening as well. Men like this expect those kinds of business gestures as complimentary perks.

That's beyond my scope of the business, but I know my brothers often discuss the new girls they've got in town and what they'll be able to charge for them.

I don't judge.

A woman's body is a woman's choice.

When the elevator door closes behind us, I tap the key card to the sensor and push the button for the top floor. In the reflection of the mirrored walls, Arkady is checking me out. I discretely tug the hem of my short skirt down my thighs.

Da instructed me to wear something sexy to schmooze his Russian guests while I soften them up for the pending gun deal. He hated what I picked out and made me change three times until I put on this red sheath dress.

It's more wild night at the club than dinner with business partners, but he's the boss and I wasn't about to argue.

So, for the last three hours, I've made nice and done everything I could to put our family in a favorable light. I glossed over the recent trouble with the rival mafia family on the north side of the river, downplayed the trouble the Quinns are causing us, and even held it together when they brought up how our enemies recently killed my brother, Declan.

Apparently, the Bratva are very interested in how my father intends to respond to the killing of my brother. The Quinn's enforcer killed Declan over the betrayal of a woman they were both sleeping with.

I didn't have the answer, but assured him that the McGuires command everything south of the River Liffey with an iron fist. Retaliation will be brutal.

Personally, I'd like to know what will be done to the woman, because Siobhan Daley caused that situation by being a lying, spying bitch.

I don't get to ask such things—not yet, anyway.

But if tonight ends on a high note, like I think it will, Da and my brothers will take me more seriously.

The elevator doors open on the top floor, and I lead the way up the corridor.

Escorting these two to their suite is my grand finale. Then, I'll report back to my father that I nailed it and that Sidorov and Volkov are both happy and well fed.

I can't wait.

The carpet is soft beneath my heels, and our procession is quiet as we move past the doors to the three other suites on the floor.

Behind me, Arkady says something to Vladimir in Russian and the two laugh gregariously. I'm not as naïve as they might think. I know he likely commented on my ass in this dress or something, but it doesn't matter. Once I get them in their suite and settled, I'm off the clock.

I'm half expecting to find Da's female entertainment in the suite when we step inside, but no, it's empty.

I'm not sure when they're set to arrive, but I don't want to bring it up in case something unexpected happened and it might make Da look bad.

"Welcome to your home away from home, gentlemen." I lead them through a grand foyer and past the round glass table with a giant display of orchids. "Anything you order up to the room is covered, and over on the bar, you'll find a case of vodka Da brought in direct from Moscow."

"Wonderful," Vladimir says, heading straight for the bar. "A toast to Irish business."

I chuckle. "Just one. I had enough wine at dinner that I'll likely have a headache tomorrow already. But I'll toast to Irish business."

Arkady and I join Vladimir by the bar and I accept the splash of vodka in the bottom of a crystal tumbler. Holding it up to toast, I give my last effort at making this negotiation a success. "To a long and profitable arrangement between our organization and yours."

I swallow the vodka without choking, but it's a close call. The burn of it going down my throat is awful, and I blink quickly to get it down.

"Good." Vladimir tips his glass back and refills it. "To lovely McGuire daughter and business deals."

Arkady holds out his glass for a refill and throws that one back just as quickly. There's no world in which I could drink with two Russian Bratva and come out of it unscathed. I saw how much they can eat. I don't even want to imagine how much they can drink.

"And this is where I say goodnight, gentlemen. It's been a pleasure meeting both of you, and I hope you enjoy your stay in Dublin. My father will be in touch with you in the morning."

"What about our lady for staying night?" Arkady asks.

I set my empty tumbler on the bar and take my phone out of my purse. "Da mentioned he arranged for some female company for you. I'll call him and find out about that right away. You two relax and enjoy your vodka. I'm sure someone will be here shortly."

With another painted-on smile, I give them a nod goodbye and walk briskly toward the door. They're following me, looking annoyed, but if the Russians end up angry about there being no prostitutes here, that's not on me.

I've done my part.

I stop at the table in the foyer and set their room cards on the glass surface. "You're all set."

The few steps to the door seem like a mile, at least until the cool metal of the door handle is in my palm. Pushing down, I release the door and pull to swing it open.

A meaty hand brushes past my head and slams it shut. The

boom of my exit being denied has my heart hammering as I turn to face an angry Arkady. "No. Not all set."

Vladimir is there too. He's taken off his jacket and is unbuttoning his shirt. "No. Mattie says daughter for the night. His treat."

"As your hostess and dinner companion." I shift away from Arkady so that I have the foyer wall at my back. "I'm not your sexual companion for the night. Da has girls for that. They're obviously just running late." I lift my phone and hit my contact list to call Da. "Let me find out when they'll be arriving."

Vladimir grabs my phone and drops it in the vase for the orchids. "No call whores. Father promised me good girl. Virgin daughter is mine."

My face goes numb as all the blood rushes out of my head. *My father wouldn't have said that.*

"You misunderstood. I, uh...the language barrier confused you. He meant for dinner. I was your hostess for the evening."

Arkady grabs me, his fingers digging into my arm as he spins me and pulls me against his chest. Gorilla arms wrap around me from behind and pin my arms at my sides. "No misunderstand. He signed contract. We fuck you as part of deal and Vlad keep you for back home in Russia."

I kick backward, hoping my heels will stab him in the shins, but I only manage to lose my shoes.

"Settle, little wolf. I show you." Vladimir pulls a folded document out of his inside pocket and points to a section on the second page above my father's signature.

It's a contract binding me to an arranged marriage with Vladimir Volkov. And it's signed by my father.

He's lost his mind.

My stomach rolls and there's a good chance I'm about to throw up on my pervy Russian fiancé. I can't believe my father would do this to me.

He said he finally saw me as an asset to the family business. I thought he meant he saw my value as a contributor—he meant my value as a commodity.

Tears burn behind my eyes. I looked up to him. I waited for a chance to show him what I could do. What kind of man does this to his daughter? Does my mother know I'm part of the gun deal?

I don't want to fail my family, but I'm not marrying Vladimir, and I'm not having sex with two Russian brutes.

"Guns or no guns, I'm not for sale. My father should never have promised me as part of the deal. You need to let me go right now."

Vladimir chuckles, a cruel smile twisting his ugly face. "No play game. You are mine. I have papers. Come, we have father's vodka to celebrate."

Vladimir moves to go back into the suite and Arkady tightens his iron grip on me to drag me back as well. He has my arms bound, but not my feet.

I lift my hips, plant my feet against the wall and push backward with all my strength. He grunts as we go over backward and curses in Russian when we crash through the glass table and onto the floor.

The table and the vase shatter. Then the two of us are twisting on the marble floor, wrestling in broken glass and orchids.

And my *phone*.

I grab my cell in one hand and a large shard of the vase in the other. Wheeling back, I use all the strength I can and ram it into Arkady's thigh. With any luck, I hit his femoral artery.

He curses and kicks me into the back of the door. The hit dazes me. It may have even knocked me out because the next thing I know, Vladimir is helping Arkady up and they turn toward me.

I scramble to my feet, my legs shaky and my vision blinking

in and out. With a hand on the wall, I run for the stairwell, my sights locked on the metal door.

"Come back, little wolf." Vladimir shouts from behind me and I throw a quick glance back to find him chasing me down.

Arkady is leaning on the doorway to the suite, a growing patch of blood staining his right pant leg.

Good. I hope he bleeds out.

"You are mine," Vlad shouts at me. "I have papers."

"Fuck your papers." I burst through the metal door to the stairwell and grab the rail, racing down as fast as my bare feet can take me.

Vladimir is right behind me, and I know I'll never make it down three more flights without him catching me, so I grab the door to the fourth floor and change course.

I could bang on doors and yell for help. He wouldn't make a scene with other guests, would he? I'm about to find out. There's a group of people waiting for the lift, and I squeeze in the moment the doors open.

The tourists look alarmed when they see me, but I don't have time to worry about it. "Get in! Get in! Hurry."

Pressed at the back of the elevator car, I stare at the corridor and hold my breath as the guests get in and press the button for the lobby.

Vladimir doesn't appear. Instead of that making things better, it just freaks me out more.

Maybe he doesn't want to make a scene.

I catch a glimpse of myself in the mirrors, and it's not good. Between the fall, the glass, and getting kicked into the door, I look as beaten up as I feel.

"Are you okay, miss?" a guy asks me. "Do you need us to call someone for you? The police? Or a friend or someone?"

I hold up my phone. "I'll call my brother. Thanks though."

With the people in the elevator politely trying not to stare, I hold it together the best I can. When the doors open on the main floor, I scan the lobby as the elevator unloads, and then I head for the nearest exit.

The night air is cool, cooler still because of my wet dress and the warm blood gracing my skin from several lacerations. I run down the sidewalk a little, staring out at the lights shining on the surface of the river.

Numb and not knowing what to do, I lift my phone to call my brother Ryan.

My phone is dead. *Right.* It took a swim in the orchid vase. A taxi then. I'll grab a taxi...

I realize my mistake the moment I hear the thundering footfalls of angry men approaching. In a state of sheer panic and shock, I lingered outside the hotel for too long.

Vladimir and Arkady are racing down the sidewalk and are almost upon me. I run as fast as I can for several blocks, not knowing where to go.

I can't go home. My father expected me to obey his wishes. He gave me to the Russians.

Da is a brutal man when people within the organization don't do as he orders. I thought I was immune to his cruelty, but I'm not.

I'm not safe and won't be safe as long as I'm in Da's territory. I need to leave the city and give him time to calm down.

I'll make him understand somehow. Mam will understand. She'll know what to do—

The hit comes hard from behind. I'm knocked forward and the concrete of the sidewalk rushes up to meet my face. My collision to the ground is indescribable. The world goes black... and fuzzy.

I'm dazed.

The first kick catches me in the side. I scream and curl up like a shrimp. The second connects with my shoulder and rolls me onto my back. Arkady leans in and grabs me, hauling me to my feet.

I spin, trying to claw his beady eyes out with my fingernails, but he outweighs me by a hundred pounds.

He punches me in the face and my head snaps back as pain explodes in my right eye. I can't breathe. The pain is so intense it's like I'm drowning in it.

Vladimir catches up and joins the beat-up-Piper party. He reaches across his body and backhand slaps me. Then again with his open palm. Then the backhand. My head cranks to the side, the Volkov family ring he bragged about at dinner cutting my flesh with each assault.

Dizzy and disoriented, I throw up. Wagyu chunks fly and Vladimir steps back, cursing in Russian. When the second round of vomiting starts, I turn my head and spew at Arkady.

He has the self-preservation to shove me away, and the moment I'm free, I run.

The hotel is only a city block inland from the River Liffey and now that I see the bridge spanning the waterway, I know where I'm headed.

My only chance of surviving these two is to leave my father's territory and hope they know enough about the Quinns to not follow me.

My lungs burn for oxygen as I run across the bridge. Too dizzy, I pay little attention to the horns honking at me to get off the road and out of the way.

The Russians shout behind me.

More horns honk and a couple of vehicles swerve and barely miss me. Brakes screech and I scream as I cut through traffic to get to the other side.

A siren sounds in the distance, but I don't think it's for me. And if it is, that's fine too.

I've done nothing wrong.

I did everything right and yet, here I am.

I cast a frenzied glance over my shoulder to see if they're still after me. I don't see them, but I can't see much. Between my vision fritzing in and out and the blood-matted hair in my eyes, they could still be there.

My footing is sloppy by the time I make it to the north end of the bridge and cross the road to the sidewalk. A long row of shops on the far side might offer me some shelter.

It's late and raining and there are no pedestrians.

No one out for a stroll.

No one to help me.

With my strength flagging, I collapse. My body is shaking uncontrollably, and my legs will no longer hold me. I give up and give in.

I lay there on the damp pavement, listening through the rush of my pulse in my ears as my consciousness fades. If the Russians find me...will they kill me or drag me back to the hotel?

I don't have the energy to care.

CHAPTER TWO

Sean

*O*ne furtive glance cast towards the gavel resting close to my left hand and my men stop their smart-assing and pay attention. They've been with me since Tag and I began this MC five years ago, and they know my intolerance for interruptions during church.

Since the inception of the Devils, I've built the club up steadily and now we're more than one hundred strong.

We rule the north side of the river for ourselves and in support of my brother, Tag.

Tonight's meeting isn't a regular one where I require a full table. Special circumstances have forced an emergency gathering of the club executives to catch them up on the mayhem that went down at the hand of Gareth Campbell's men.

"It was an overt act of aggression," I tell them. "Tag and his girlfriend were leaving the street fair. Campbell's men prevented him from getting into his truck and jumped him."

Keefer Gallagher, my club VP, pushes his dark hair away from his face, his silver and black spider rings catching the light.

"Since when do the Campbells have the balls to do something like that?"

"That's the million-dollar question. Either the Campbells have an alliance with one of the major families or they need a reminder of who the Quinns are."

"Then it's time for retribution."

My twin brothers, Brendan and Bryan, both nod. Of course they agree. There's nothing the Quinn twins like more than mixing it up in a bloody brawl.

"Do you think this is part of the blowback from the McGuires?" Kieran O'Brien, my Sergeant at Arms asks.

I take a swig of my Guinness and swallow. "It could be. Aiden threw us into a blazing fire when he killed Declan McGuire. They were already pushing against the truce. I don't see it lasting much longer."

"What does Tag say about that?" Gallagher asks.

"He wants the truce in place for the good of the citizens, but realizes that might not be possible going forward."

"What about Aiden?" Kieran asks. "As Tag's right hand, Aiden killing the son of an enemy has to be addressed."

I shrug. "Thankfully, that's not my call. I've told Tag where Aiden is holed up to recover from his injuries. It's up to him to decide what to do with that information."

"What about Siobhan? That bitch played Aiden and Declan against one another. When does *she* get what she deserves?"

"The minute one of us gets our hands around her traitorous neck," Bryan says.

Brendan nods. "Fuck, I hate that bitch."

I set my pint of Guinness down next to the gavel. "Things are going to get dicey for the next weeks, lads. Let the men know to be ready for anything, day or night. If issues crop up on our side of the river, come down fast and hard."

"What about the other side of the river?" Gallagher asks.

"The McGuires have been making it their business to fuck us over."

I shake my head. "For now, we're not antagonizing the McGuires. Stay clear of them and don't engage. We don't want any more trouble with them than we already have."

The meeting adjourns, and the lads rush off to complete their tasks. I help myself to another pint from the fridge and look around our new and improved clubhouse.

We hadn't started off in surroundings as pleasant as this, but the recent renovation gave us a soundproofed meeting room, a kitchen, two bathrooms, a small room with two cots, an office for me, and a lounge area with a flat screen, music, a fully stocked bar, two pool tables, a poker table and two regulation dart boards.

The boys love to hang out. Many of them never had happy homes and found brotherhood belonging to the Devils. And it's often a fact that lads who come from the worst possible circumstances are the most loyal and dedicated to the club.

It's a good fit for me.

After closing up for the night, I stand on the long porch of the clubhouse and have a smoke while I consider where to go next.

I could go back to the compound and check on Tag, but it's late and hopefully he's asleep. I could go grab a pint at Jimmy's, but honestly, I'm too tired.

I need sleep.

I finish my smoke, pull out the keys to my ride, and straddle my Harley. On the second try, my contrary girl starts with a low growl, and I'm glad of it.

The weather took a turn during our meeting, and a chilling drizzle is pissing down from the heavens. I ease my bike out toward the street, lock the fence surrounding our yard, and note how wet and slick the pavement seems.

There's no traffic coming my way, so I give my baby some gas and test the traction.

Rain runs down the visor of my helmet and I squint to see the road ahead of me. A couple of loud bangs crack over the rumble of my bike and I slow to an idle to listen.

Were those gunshots?

I wait, but don't hear anything more. Letting the clutch out, I give it some gas and start moving up toward the bridge. The hair at the nape of my neck prickles as I glimpse something in the shadows.

It's an ominous gray and dismal night, but am I seeing a girl lying on the sidewalk?

Can't be.

Fog is drifting in from the River Liffey, creating a shroud of shadows along Ormond Quay. The turn to my place is up ahead on Arran East, but with what could've been gunshots, I pull over to the curb and set the kickstand.

My boots beat out a steady rhythm in the darkness and the closer I get, the surer I am.

Fucking hell. So much for sleep.

I take a quick look at the body lying next to a craft shop just on this side of the bridge. A homeless person? We have shelters in Dublin, many of them supported by my family and our charitable efforts.

Staring down at her through the rain and fog, she appears young and barely dressed. No, she *is* dressed, but her wee red dress is ripped.

I kneel to check on her and find dozens of fresh cuts marring her skin. "Who the fuck did this to you?"

A moan comes from deep inside her and when she sees my face, she skitters back. "Don't kill me."

Do I look like I'm going to kill her? Well, not her, but probably like I'd kill the person who did this. I raise my palms. "You're safe now, lass. I won't hurt you."

"I don't want to die."

"I'll do my best to honor that wish, but you have to let me help you."

She turns her head, and I get my first look at her face. My heart picks up the pace and I curse. A second look, ignoring how her cheek has been altered by red welts, swelling, and blood, confirms it.

Piper McGuire.

So much for staying clear of the McGuires. This is Mad Mattie's only daughter, and she's beaten and bloodied on our side of the river.

Fucking hell.

Tag and I grew up getting into schoolyard brawls with Ryan and Declan McGuire, and while we were never friends, we knew their little sister.

She was just a baby then, but a cute little thing. And with Da's views on family, the preservation of innocents, and the protection of women and children, we knew she was out of bounds.

Then, I saw her a couple of years ago at a charity event and she stole my fucking breath. Piper McGuire grew up well, and any man with eyes would agree with me. The fact that someone beat the shit out of her doesn't bode well for whoever did this.

"Let me help you, lass. Can you sit?"

I grip her under her arms and tug her off the wet concrete. The wall of the craft shop is sturdy behind her back, and I prop her up. The awning above our heads shields us from the rain, but the odd cold drip runs down my neck and makes me shiver.

"Piper, do you recognize me? It's Sean. Sean Quinn. How badly are you hurt, lass? Do you need a hospital?"

I glance around to be sure nobody sees me bent over a battered Piper McGuire. That would complicate things not only for me, but for Tag as well.

I'm trying to be a Good Samaritan—nothing more.

This girl belongs on the south side of the river, but I can't very well send her back looking like this. Mattie will take one look at her and declare an all-out war.

Aiden killing Declan was bad enough, but that technically wasn't family business and everyone who witnessed it knew it was about them both fucking Siobhan.

This would be entirely different. "How did this happen? Where were you, beautiful?"

"Hotel."

Hotel? That's not much to go on. I sit back on my heels and look around. There are no hotels on this stretch...but there are on the south side...and the Grattan Bridge is steps away.

But if she was beaten on the south side, why would she come here? Surely, she'd be safer in her father's territory. Wouldn't she?

Piper moans, and her head flops to the side.

Well, whatever the reason, she's in no shape to get home on her own and us hanging around out here is just getting us both wet. I'll have to take her with me.

I straighten and frown at my Harley. *Not ideal.*

"Hey, Piper, do you think you can sit up and hang onto me if I put you on my bike?"

She extends her hand and reaches for me. I'm not confident that she's got the strength to sit upright, but the longer we stay here, the greater the chance that this will blow up in my face. "All right. Let's try it. At least we can get out of this rain and have a cup of hot tea."

I lift Piper and cradle her against my chest. She can't weigh more than a hundred and ten pounds soaking wet—and she *is* soaking wet—so my estimate could be accurate.

It's awkward to get her secured on the back of my bike. Her bloody, bare feet slide off the passenger pegs, so it takes a bit to get her positioned to ride. She sways when I let go of her and I grab her, thinking she's going to fall off my big decker.

Shit. Falling off and hitting the pavement will do more damage than she's already suffering from. I don't know what damage that is and won't until I get her wet clothes off and I have a look.

The thought of Piper McGuire naked creates way too many visuals in my mind. I give myself an inward shake and remind myself she's almost ten years younger than I am. On top of that, she's vulnerable, and is a McGuire, *annnd* touching her in any way is a death sentence waiting to be handed out.

Right. I am simply helping an innocent woman.

With one hand pressed against her sternum, I slide my leg over the seat, reach back, and wrap her arms around my waist. "Hold on, Piper. You gotta help by holding on."

Her arms tighten around my middle, and I exhale.

This is going to be one long ride home.

Giving it a little gas, I release the clutch and start off rolling along at a snail's pace. My Harley gives me a throaty rumble and, since things go okay, I give her a little more gas.

Puttering along, I make the turn onto Arran, but at the last minute, decide to pass my place and not go there. Instead, I continue until I take a right onto Little Strand and pull into the driveway of one of the Quinn safe houses.

Lifting Piper off the bike, I carry her to the porch and set her down on the steps. The boys razz me about the weight of my carabiner, but what can I say?

I'm a man who holds a lot of keys.

It takes a minute and a few tries, but I find the key that fits this house. The lock clicks open, and I give the door a push.

"Come on. It's dry inside and I'll put the kettle on."

"I shouldn't be here...not with you."

No shit. "Would you rather be lying alone on the sidewalk near the river?"

"No."

"Then here we are." I lay her on the sofa and then stride into the little kitchen to put the kettle on. She's shivering badly and I don't know if it's the chill of the night, shock, or internal bleeding. "I'll find something dry for you to wear and call our doc to have a look at you."

"Please don't." Her voice cracks on the breathy plea. "It might get back to my father."

Something about that terrifies her. Is this the work of a piece of shit boyfriend she doesn't want her father and brothers to go after?

I'm no fan of Mattie McGuire, but I would stand in the front row to see him flay whoever did this to his daughter. "Don't worry. Our guy is discreet. He won't say a word to anyone. Relax and I'll be back in two."

I take the stairs two at a time and check the dresser drawers for anything dry Piper could wear. Tag keeps the safe houses stocked with the basics and though there's not a lot to pick from, I come away with a gray sweatsuit and a towel from the bathroom for her hair.

Then I grab a stack of clean cloths and a massive tackle box filled with first aid supplies.

Next, I pull out my phone, call up Doc Kelvin's contact info, and send him a situation update and the address. Then, I copy the message and send it to Tag. My brother is a newlywed, so he's not likely to be paying attention to his phone this late at night, but he'll get the message and come when he can.

When I get back to the sitting room, Piper is curled up on the sofa, crying.

"Is it the pain? What can I do?"

She gasps a few unsteady sobs and accepts the towel. After wiping her tears, she looks up at me with the saddest ice-blue eyes I've ever seen. "I messed up. Da and my brothers will be furious with me."

I don't like the sound of that but can't help but throw the girl a lifeline. "Tonight, let's worry about patching you up. Once we know you're okay, we'll work on fixing things."

She drops her head and closes her eyes. "There's no way I can fix it."

"Then there's nothing that can be done about it tonight. You might as well focus on yourself for the moment." I set the clothes on the coffee table and the first aid kit beside them.

The keening whistle of the kettle draws me into the kitchen. I drop a couple of tea bags into the Brown Betty sitting on the counter and then pour in the contents of the kettle. I save a bit of the boiling water to pour into a steel pot.

While the tea steeps, I take the pot and set it on the coffee table next to the rags. "I need to clean off some of this blood so I can assess the injuries we're dealing with. Will you let me do that?"

She blinks, her tear-filled eyes piercing me right to the depths of my dark heart. "Why are you helping me?"

"Because you're a young lady who needs help. Regardless of your last name, you ended up in our territory and have been through something bloody and violent. I can't ignore that and leave you to fend for yourself."

"But our families are enemies. Surely your Quinn Laws don't apply to me. Honestly, my father would shit a red brick if he knew I was here with you."

I laugh. "Well, thankfully, *my* father had philosophies about how business was to be run and how people are to be treated. The Quinn Laws apply to anyone within our territory and beyond, if we have any say about it."

She frowns down at herself and the tears well once more. "I don't understand how any of this happened."

I take one of the cloths off the top of the pile and dip it into the boiled water. It's still hot, but I douse it and then wring it out, so I can start tending to the dozens of scrapes and gashes on her legs. "Were you rolling in razor blades?"

"I was fighting…and we fell through a glass table and the vase of flowers shattered too. There was a struggle."

I keep my head down and dab at the cuts. "Well, you fighting is the most important part of that story. You fought, and you made it here. You're safe now."

Most of the damage I can see is superficial—likely from wrestling with her attacker in the debris of a shattered glass table.

When I have her legs wiped down enough to be certain nothing vital is bleeding, I rinse the cloth and lift her leg to set her foot on my knee. "I take it you lost your shoes pretty early in the fight? It looks like you ran across the city in your bare feet."

She hisses when I swipe the damp cloth under her foot, and I lean in to find a shard of glass. "This might hurt, but it needs to come out."

She draws a deep breath. "Aye, I'm ready. Do it."

With a careful pinch, I pull the shard and greet the gush of blood with the warm cloth. While I put pressure on the cut for a moment, I try again to find out what happened. "You mentioned a hotel. Was that on your side or our side of the river?"

Her gaze meets mine and I'm happy to see a little fire sparking behind her icy blue eyes. "Our side."

That's a relief. The Quinns don't need to be tied to any more violence involving the McGuire children. Declan being dead is bad enough—fuck you very much, Aiden.

"And when things got bad, you crossed the bridge to escape?"

A knock on the door pops the bubble of our private moment, and Piper's look of terror returns. I hold up my hand to keep her from bolting and drop the bloody cloth back into the pot. "It's either Tag or the Doc. Those are the only two people who know we're here."

She swipes at the tears now streaming down her blood-soaked cheeks. "Take your gun out. Be ready, just in case."

She's serious. Who the fuck spooked this girl bad enough that she thinks they'd follow her into our territory, and I'd need to shoot them to stop them from getting at her.

Still, there's no harm in humoring the girl.

Reaching to the small of my back, I slide my hand under the fall of my leather Devils cut and draw my SIG Sauer. When I show it to her, she relaxes a little.

Not a lot of the girls I know would have that reaction to me carrying, but I suppose Piper McGuire isn't like many other girls.

Another knock rattles off the door and I hustle over. A quick glance out the front window tells me it's Doc Kelvin. I holster my gun and let the good doctor in.

"Hey, Doc. Sorry about that. Our patient is a little jumpy."

Kelvin finds Piper on the sofa, and he lets off a long whistle. "Shit. They really did a number on her."

"Yeah. Look, she's understandably shaken up, but you need to assure her that no one will hear of this."

He pegs me with a look. "Since when has that become a concern with me?"

"It hasn't. I just want you to assure *her*."

That settles him down a bit, and I walk him over. "Piper, this is the Doc I told you about. He's good people and you can trust him."

She frowns. "I told you I don't need a doctor. I'm fine. I just need to be left alone."

Kelvin offers her a sympathetic smile. "Sweetheart, maybe you don't realize how bad off you are. You've been beaten, and by the look of things, the guy wore a ring. Your arms and legs are diced to shit—"

"She went through a glass table," I say.

"And by the way you're curled to the one side and holding

your ribs, I'm going to guess you took a couple of blows there too."

"He, uh... kicked me a few times."

Fucking hell. The thought of this sweet young thing falling prey to that kind of violence makes me homicidal.

"Hey, Sean." Kelvin's tone breaks through the rush of fury buzzing in my head. "Could you put that away and give us some privacy?"

I follow the doc's gaze to where my gun is clenched in my hands. Wow. Okay. Truly homicidal. I didn't even realize I'd drawn it from my holster.

"Uh, yeah. I'll be in the kitchen making everyone tea. Let me know when the coast is clear."

CHAPTER THREE

Piper

*S*ean leaves me with the Quinn doctor, and I try to reason with him and stop what I know is coming next. "I really am fine. I'd tell you if I wasn't. Sean shouldn't have bothered you."

Kelvin runs a hand through his ginger beard and sits on the coffee table opposite me. He's got a smattering of freckles covering his nose and cheeks, and kind eyes filled with understanding and a fair dose of pity.

"I understand that having me examine you is at the top of the list of things you don't want to do, but I answer to the Quinns, not you. Sean asked me to check you out, and that's what I'm here to do. Now, the quicker you let me do my thing, the sooner it will be over and I can give you something for the pain."

"But I don't want this—not any of it."

The doc sighs. "Aye, that's no surprise, but I promise I'm only here to confirm there's no internal bleeding or serious concern. The cuts and bruises don't worry me. You dying tonight in your sleep is more of a concern. What do you think it would do to the state of tension between the two families if the Quinns end up with Mattie McGuire's daughter dead in one of their safe houses?"

"It would start a bloodbath."

"Aye, that's the truth of it. And the people of Dublin deserve better than that—especially if it's preventable."

Well, I don't want to be responsible for that.

"You're a real doctor, right?"

He dips his chin. "Got the diploma and everything."

"And you can help with the pain?"

He winks and pats his bag. "I'm ready for anything."

It doesn't look like I have much of a choice. Still, I'm not sure how long Sean will wait in the kitchen, and I don't want him to see me in my underwear, all broken and bloody. The way he was clutching his gun a moment ago made me think he might stalk the streets of the south side looking to kill my attackers.

I can't let that happen.

Vladimir and Arkady are representatives of the Bratva. Me refusing sex with them is one thing. If they get gunned down in my father's territory during their stay, my entire family will be wiped out.

I need to diffuse this situation and the only way Sean will be satisfied is if the doc assures him I'm okay. I close my eyes and inhale a deep breath before nodding my consent. "All right, then. Make it quick. And I don't think I can raise my arms to get my dress off."

"That's fine. I'll cut it off and get you set up in this snazzy sweatsuit when we're done."

Despite my doubts, Doc Kelvin is remarkably professional. He probes my side, listens to my chest, examines all my gashes, and then wipes most of the blood away before helping me into an ugly gray tracksuit.

JENN MADORE & CAROLINA MAC

Moving around is hell, and by the time it's over, I'm sweating, dizzy, and ready to collapse.

Doc Kelvin gives me some space and goes over to push the kitchen door open. "Sean, the patient is ready for her tea now."

Sean returns to the sitting area carrying a tray of mugs and a creamer and sugar set. If I wasn't ready to pass out, I would make fun of the mean MC gang leader hosting a tea party.

"And here's your reward for being a good patient," Kelvin says, putting two white and one blue tablets into my hand. "These will ease the pain and help you sleep through the night so your body can heal."

"Thanks, Doc."

He winks at me and smiles. "Glad things weren't worse."

Sean hands me a cup of tea with milk and then focuses all his attention on Kelvin. "She's okay, then?"

"For the next week or two she'll have to accessorize to match black and blue, but she'll survive. The swelling to her face will likely get worse before it gets better, but her ocular bone is intact, and her vision doesn't seem compromised. A couple of her ribs are bruised, but I don't think anything is broken. Without x-rays, it's impossible to know for sure, but she would be in much greater pain and the treatment would be the same."

Sean offers the good doctor a cup of tea, but he declines, saying he's got a busy day tomorrow and should get some rest.

I swallow down my medication and lay back against the arm of the sofa. "Good night, Doc."

"Good night, sweetheart. Have Sean call me if anything crops up and you feel worse."

"Aye, thanks again."

Sean walks him to the door. The two of them share a few whispered words of goodbye, but I don't care. The tea is warming my insides, and the pills will soon drag me into a blissful slumber.

Then I can wake up and this will all be a bad dream.

If only that were true.

When it's just the two of us once again, Sean locks the door and turns off the overhead light. It's late and he must be as exhausted as I am. But when he moves to the fireplace to poke the flames and set another log on the fire, I realize he's not ready to call it a night.

Shadows light up his face as the flames dance, highlighting his powerful jaw and the scar that trails from the bottom of his cheek bone through his lip. His hair is the same ebony black as all the Quinn brothers, but his is the longest. It goes well with his gang leader persona.

As he crosses the room toward me, my gaze tracks his confident gait, the way his muscled chest fills out his leather vest, and how his ripped jeans hug his hips. He's hot, but more than his looks, his presence consumes the air around us.

When he sits in the chair opposite me, I give myself an inward shake. Why the hell am I checking out a man who is the sworn enemy of my family instead of trying to escape? Maybe I took one too many hits to the head.

"I'm glad you'll heal up." He claims his mug and sinks deeper into his chair. "Now, I need you to tell me who laid the beating on you."

"Why?"

"So I can handle them."

His gaze is stern and unapologetic. He doesn't even try to mask that when he says 'handle' them, he means by cutting off their balls or dropping them into the sea. But if the two Russians meeting with my father go missing, it will be my family that pays the price.

"Sorry. I don't need your help."

He arches an ebony brow, and I try not to get swallowed up by his bright green eyes. All five of the Quinn brothers are heart-stoppingly handsome, but Sean isn't the pretty boy that

Tag and Finn are. And he isn't a pumped up beast out for blood like Brendan and Bryan.

He's dangerous—that's a given—and looks even deadlier because of his glare and that scar. He leaves his hair long to hide it, but I've always thought it was sexy.

Not that he ever noticed me. He's ten years older than me and at the few events where we crossed paths, he usually called me kid or told me I looked cute.

Fingers snap close to my face, and I blink.

"Earth to Piper."

"Sorry, the pills are really kicking my butt. Did you say something?"

"You were about to tell me who did this to you."

Nice try. I'm not that out of it. "Muggers." My eyes drift shut as a yawn escapes. "I met friends at the old Hard Rock Hotel. It was bought up by NYX and has been remodeled. We had drinks, then when I left, I got jumped."

He frowns. "You left the hotel alone? I don't believe that for a moment. There's no way your father let you go out wearing a dress like that and didn't have someone on you."

Right. I forgot he knows all about how crime families work. "Ryan had to go and left one of the new guys to bring me home —I forget his name—but he kept his distance to let me have fun and then, when I went out to look for him at the end of the night, I didn't see him."

"Uh-huh. So, you walked out of the hotel alone, and you were mugged?"

"They must've been waiting in the shadows by the parking lot. They were brutal and left me lying on the pavement after they took my money."

"I see. And where did they go? Did they jump into a truck, a car? Did you get a plate number?"

"I didn't see. I never moved until they were gone."

"Didn't anyone see you there? Other people in the car park? That's a busy hotel."

"No. I didn't want to be seen. I thought they might come back, so, when I could breathe again, I ran across the bridge."

"And that's when I found you?"

"Aye, it is."

"And that's the whole story?"

"Aye, that's right."

He tilts his head and chuckles. "Not a bad lie for the spur of the moment."

"What? That's what happened."

"No, it's not, but I'd rather we stop talking about it if you're going to lie to me. You were mugged, but you have your purse. You were outside the hotel, but you went through a glass table. You thought they might come back, but you didn't contact your father or any of your brothers—the men who own that entire territory."

Ugh...my mind is so fuzzy from pain, exhaustion, and the pills, I can't even think. "I can't tell you what really happened, Sean. I just can't."

"That's fine. Come, I'll carry you upstairs and we'll figure out your next move in the morning. You're done for tonight."

Sean is incredibly gentle as strong arms scoop under my knees, and he lifts me off the couch. He holds me close as he carries me up the stairs, and the warmth of his body seeps into mine.

I lay my cheek against his chest and close my eyes. He smells like leather and that expensive tobacco he was smoking earlier. "Thank you for being kind to me, Sean. I know it isn't good for business, but I truly appreciate the save."

He lays me on the bed and helps get the duvet over me. "I'll leave the bathroom light on down the hall. If you need anything, just holler. I'll crash in the room across the hall. And don't worry, Piper. Whoever did this to you, won't get near you again. I've got you."

Despite Doc Kelvin's hope that the meds he gave me would help me sleep, every time I move, my ribs cry out, or the torn flesh of my cheek presses on the pillow. There are also moments when I wake up screaming.

I cut off the panic as soon as I realize I'm not actually being sold to the Russian mafia. Then I remember—I am.

My father threw me in as an incentive for a gun deal.

Aside from his betrayal gutting me—that can't be legal. Not that legalities hold any importance when dealing with crime families. Still, I'm almost twenty years old and I have rights. I'm an adult.

I get a say in my life, don't I?

Why would I think that when I've never had one yet?

So, here I am, lying in a strange bed, in the house of my father's enemy, beaten and broken by two men my father traded me to. I can't tell Sean any of it because I know better than to betray my father.

Except...he betrayed me first.

I don't know how to fix this, but confiding in the Quinns and accepting their help would be considered unforgivable. Not that I'm in any shape to refuse Sean's help. Ugh, it's an impossible situation.

The gashes on my legs sting, my bruised ribs refuse to let me take in enough oxygen, my vision is wonky, and my mouth is foul with the taste of blood.

And I'm sure I look worse than I feel.

Muggers? Did I really think he'd fall for that?

I regret that while he was being kind to me, I lied to him in return. There's no way I could've told him the truth. The guns I was helping Da secure were to strengthen the McGuire position against his family.

What was Da thinking signing away his 'good girl'?

I wouldn't even be a twenty-year-old virgin if he hadn't been so controlling and insisted on one of my brothers escorting me on every date I've ever been on. Hell, not just dates, but every time I left the house.

Was he planning on this all along? Was he controlling my V-card to play it when it suited him best? I know that arranged marriages between mafia families strengthen alliances but that's so last century.

I'm his daughter, for fuck's sake.

How could he want that for me? He didn't even talk to me first. He just dressed me up like a sexy present and told me not to fuck up. He told me to make them happy and give them anything they wanted.

Anything they wanted.

My stomach rolls, but I fight the nausea. I'm in no shape to be running down the hall to throw up. Still, I can't stop the tears.

Why should I worry about betraying Da when he betrayed me in the worst way possible? How will I ever look at him again? What kind of man gives his daughter away like that? As if I'm nothing more than a pawn for him to use in his games.

My brothers were brought up to run the family business and my mother has always held my father's ear.

Is it so wrong that I wanted that, too?

Da believes there's no place for women when running a business like ours—too much emotion. He totally dismissed that I'm smart and capable and strong enough to be equal to my brothers.

I doubt I'll ever get that chance after last night.

And certainly not if anyone finds out I'm here.

Not making a sound, I creep out my bedroom door and

glance up and down the hall. Sean left the bathroom light on for me, so it's not hard to find my way there. After the drinks at dinner and then tea to take off the chill, I'm desperate to pee.

The door across the hall is open a crack, but I fight the urge to peek in and see if Sean's sleeping. I need to pee and get home before Da sends my brothers out searching for me.

They may not think to look on the north side of the Liffey but if Vladimir and Arkady tell them I ran across the bridge to get away from them, they'll find out.

Sean has been decent, but there's no guarantee Tag or the other brothers will be. I'm no safer here than I would be back home.

Not that I can go home.

After what happened, Da will be furious. There's a good chance I blew the gun deal and that will fall at my feet. The sad thing is, given the choice, I would do the same thing again.

Not that I can tell him *that*.

What *can* I tell him?

"Sorry, Da, I wouldn't lay down and open my legs for two ugly brutes who think they own me. Get the guns some other way."

Da would beat me for disobeying him. A beating on top of a beating doesn't appeal to me.

I wince and hold in a whimper as I bend to sit on the toilet and can barely believe that the hip and legs I'm looking at are mine. Last night, I didn't even feel the damage to my legs, but this must be from when I crashed to the floor after going through the table.

Wow, fear and adrenaline really kept the reality of my injuries at bay.

It's a struggle to get up, but I grip the vanity countertop on one side and the towel rail on the other. Biting back the pain, I manage to get to my feet.

I'm upright, but I won't be winning any races today.

I finish in the bathroom, my mind spinning in circles as I

step back into the hallway. Sean is there, shirtless, unshaven and looking sleepy, with his ebony hair tangled and tousled, hanging to his shoulders.

Sweet Mother Mary, my ovaries have just exploded.

Sean is even more ridiculously hot than I imagined. In high school, when we read Romeo and Juliet in English class, I had a few Capulet and Montague sexual fantasies.

Tag was too intense for me, Finn was quiet and a bit sulky, and the twins, Bryan and Brendan, were sexy but too crazy. Sean always played the part of my Romeo.

He was older, broody, tattooed, and carried a scar on the outside while I always carried my scar within. He's dark and dangerous. The ultimate bad guy.

But that was a schoolgirl's daydream. There is no way I could fantasize about him in the real world.

Quinns are off-limits to me.

Still, I'm about to melt into a puddle at his feet. With no shirt, there's nothing covering the intricate fretwork of Celtic knotwork and fae gods covering his arms, chest, and back.

Does the masterpiece continue below the boxers?

"Are you all right?" His voice is graveled and husky with sleep. He runs his hand over his abs, scratching at the dusting of ebony hair trailing beneath the waistband of his boxers. "Did you get any sleep?"

I snap my attention back up to his face. "A little. I'm sore and feeling pretty rough, but I'm alive, thanks to you. And don't worry. I was staring at the ceiling, thinking of where I can go, and I have a plan. I'll be out of your hair first thing in the morning."

He frowns. "Where you can go? You're not planning to go home to your father?"

"No."

His gaze narrows. "Why did you flinch when I mentioned

going home? Did your father do this to you? Is that why you crossed the bridge?"

I swallow and stare at the carpet runner on the floor. Damn. He sees too much and when I look into his emerald eyes, I say too much. "No. Da didn't beat me."

But he might as well have.

"Was it one of your brothers?"

I meet his gaze. "They would never. My brothers might be rough around the edges, but they love me. They'd never hurt me."

"Yet you didn't say the same to defend your father. Why? What did he do, Piper?"

I push past him and shuffle down the hallway. "Nothing. My father loves me. I'm barely awake. I didn't mean to imply differently."

CHAPTER FOUR

Sean

*S*he's lying to me again. Not a good start to the day, but I'm getting closer to the truth. She's afraid to go home and Mattie McGuire has something to do with her ending up beaten and fleeing his territory last night.

It's obvious, if I push too much, she'll bolt.

I catch her elbow at the top of the staircase. She's favoring her right leg and shuffling along like she's ninety. The stairs are going to be hell for her in this condition.

"All right. I'll stop asking questions for now if you let me make you something to eat. It'll give you a chance to wake up and I'll know you aren't going to keel over at any moment."

"You don't have to."

"I know that, but I also know that if you hustle out of here in this condition, you're asking for trouble. Let me take care of you for a bit and then you can come up with a plan after a cup of coffee. Do you drink coffee?"

"Got any vanilla hazelnut?"

I make a face. "Do I strike you as a vanilla hazelnut type of man?"

That, at least, gets a giggle out of her. "Whatever you have will be fine. Thank you."

When she attempts the first step and winces, I slide around her side. "I've got you. Between the leg and those ribs, you really need to take it easy for a few days."

She reaches behind my neck and lets me pick her up without argument and that's either a good sign that she's beginning to trust me or a bad sign and she's hurting worse than she's willing to admit.

Still, I'll take it as a win.

I try not to overthink how good it feels to hold her in my arms or how naturally her soft and tender bits melt against my hard, chiseled ones.

At the bottom of the stairs, I consider putting her down, but I don't. I'm not ready to let her go and use the excuse that she's injured to take her all the way to the kitchen. Once she's settled in one of the four little chairs, I turn my attention to feeding her.

"We've got nothing in the fridge. There are some frozen juice containers in the freezer. Several boxes of cereal, but no milk. Oh, and a couple of boxes of berry Pop-Tarts."

"Pop-Tarts and juice for the win," she says. "Assuming you have a toaster."

"Ah, good point." I open a few of the cupboard doors and pull one out. "We do. Pop-Tarts it is."

Honestly, it's lucky I don't have to cook because breakfast in the clubhouse consists of steak and beer, and breakfast at home is prepared by Cora.

I'm a lot of things—culinary isn't one of them.

The two of us talk about nothing important as I start a pot of dark roast, make the juice in a glass jug, and start popping down our breakfast.

"I heard your brother has a new, American girlfriend. That must be exciting. What's her name?"

"Madelaine, but she goes by Laine."

"And do you like her?"

"I don't know her that well, but yeah, she seems nice. The important thing is that Tag likes her—and he does. They seem good together."

I set the juice and her plate of frosted pastry down for her and go back to get my coffee. "I'll call Finn and have him run to the grocery store for the essentials. Is there anything you want him to grab specifically?"

She swallows a sip of juice and pegs me with a look. "I can't stay here, Sean. Da probably has Billy out there searching the streets for me. And when he realizes I crossed the bridge, all hell will break loose."

I scoff. "I can handle Billy Gravely. Your father's enforcer is all brute and no brains. He doesn't scare me."

"Well, he scares *me*." It's obvious by her expression that even the mention of Gravely terrifies her.

Why? "Did Gravely have something to do with you ending up like this?"

She frowns. "You said you'd stop asking questions, but no, it wasn't Billy."

"Sorry, I really am just trying to help."

"That's why I need to go. I need to get south of the river before this blows up and is worse for everyone than it already is."

I take a sip of my coffee and let the bitter bliss take hold. "All right. Let's say you walk out that door. Where do you go from here? Home?"

There's no mistaking the tightening of her expression. "That's where I *should* go."

"But?"

"But nothing. My family is likely worried sick."

JENN MADORE & CAROLINA MAC

"You could call them."

"I can't. My phone got dunked. I'll need to let it dry out before I phone anyone." She eyes up the pantry cupboard. "Do you have a bag of rice?"

"No idea, but we can look." I set my coffee down and find a box of minute rice. Ripping the top open, I point to her ruined, red velvet clutch on the table. "Is your phone in there?"

She finishes her second Pop-Tart and rolls her eyes. "Like you don't already know that."

"How would I know that?"

"I'm sure the moment I was occupied with the doc last night, you went through my purse."

I consider lying, but she was raised in the same environment as I was and would smell the bullshit. "Fine. I did. So, do you want me to shove it in here?"

She chokes and her cheeks flame the cutest shade of pink. "I'm sorry, what? What are you offering to shove in where?"

My brain fritzes out for a beat.

Is she flirting with me, or does she think I'm flirting with her? Damn it, she's way too young and innocent for me to hang around.

Too cute too.

I cough to clear my throat and will my stiffening cock to stand the fuck down. "Your phone, Piper. We were talking about your phone. Should we put it into the box of rice to dry out?"

She blinks and there's a flash of disappointment in her gaze. "Oh, aye. Right. That would be grand."

What was that disappointment about?

I'm Sean-fucking-Quinn. I'm the enemy. A ruffian. An MC president and killer. Why the fuck is she biting her bottom lip and batting her lashes as if I'm playing the part in her bad-boy fantasy?

"Piper, you understand we live dangerous lives on opposite sides, don't you?"

She rolls her eyes at me, and it's way too fucking adorable. "That's why I keep saying I need to go."

"But go where? You were beaten up for a reason, Piper. I don't know what the reason is because you're not sharing, but I know that your father is involved and you can't just take an Uber back to the McGuire compound. You're in trouble and I'm trying to help."

She hands me her iPhone. "You've done what you could. You scooped me off the street and had me patched up, but that's where your involvement ends. I need to get home before Billy finds me here."

"Why are you so worried about Gravely? Does he threaten you?" I wait for an answer but don't get one.

A moment later, the door opens in the front room and then slams shut. "Sean? Where the fuck are you?"

"Kitchen," I shout back.

Seconds later, my older brother is standing in the kitchen doorway glaring at our guest. After a beat, his heated gaze shifts to me. "What the fuck were you thinking? Get her out of here."

I stand. "I was thinking that the daughter of our enemy was lying beaten and bleeding on our side of the river. If something happened to her in our streets, it needed to be addressed. The last thing we need is for her to be over here, playing on the other side of the tracks and for her to get assaulted by one of ours."

Tag's expression darkens. "Is that what happened?"

"No. This is somehow tied to Mattie and whatever happened in a hotel on the south side."

"Problem solved," Tag says, flinging his arm through the air with a fierce wave. "Call a cab and send her across the goddamned river. Let her family take care of her. She can't be here, Sean. After the Aiden clusterfuck, we don't need more bad blood with the McGuires."

"It's more complicated than that."

JENN MADORE & CAROLINA MAC

Tag doesn't seem affected by my words. "Then explain it to me quickly because we've got a busy day."

I take a couple of steps back and lean my ass against the countertop. "I can't explain it because she's not talking. I don't fucking know what happened."

"Then how is it our problem?"

"It's not," Piper says. "And as I told Sean, as soon as I finish breakfast, I'm out the door."

"No. You're not." I hold up a finger to keep her from arguing with me. "Your father either had you beaten or allowed you to be beaten to within an inch of your fucking life. You crossed the bridge last night to flee his territory, deciding that the Quinns were a safer bet."

"Well, she was wrong about that," Tag snaps. "Because if her Da is abusing her, she can go to a fucking woman's shelter. She can't be here."

"And I'm not shipping her off without knowing what kind of trouble she's in. Christ, Tag, she's an innocent in this. She's a young woman I found battered in our streets. Do our laws only apply if she has the right last name? Da wouldn't think so. That's not how he ruled."

Tag stiffens at the low blow of throwing Da in his face, but it doesn't make my comment any less true and he knows it.

He turns to face Piper, and I hate the way she shrinks away from his ire. "What did your father do, Piper? If you tell us the truth, maybe we can keep you safe. But you'd need to tell us the entire fucking story."

She shakes her head. "I can't tell you."

"No. You *won't* tell us," I correct.

"Semantics. Look, Sean, you helped me and I'm grateful for the kindness, but if I tell you my father's business, I'll be a traitor as well as a disappointment. I'll be cast out of my family."

Honestly, I don't see that as a big loss, but that's me.

Tag looks at me and shrugs. "Then there's nothing we can

40

do. She won't tell us and it's not our problem. Every moment she stays here puts the truce, the people of Dublin, and our family in greater danger. Send her south and be done with it. And do it within the hour."

He dips his chin, holding me in his gaze, and I can't get over how much like Da he is. And like our father, Tag is in charge of the Emerald Isle Mafia.

He's the boss and if Piper won't help me help her, then what am I sticking my neck out for? I don't like it but she's not giving me much of a choice.

"Fine. I'll take care of it."

Tag leaves and the walls of the house rattle when the door slams.

"Why would you start a fight with your brother over this? I'm not worth it. Just call me a taxi and send me back. I'll figure something out. I have friends."

I laugh, pulling out my phone to text the twins. "Right. And I'm sure your father put every one of them under surveillance the moment he learned you were missing."

"Probably not. I'm pretty sure he'll know I crossed the river by now. And if he does, he'll never expect me to come back and stay with one of my friends."

Bryan texts me back, saying they're on the way. Good. I have a few things I need to take care of and don't trust Piper to be left alone.

"We can agree to disagree on that."

She feels she can't tell me what happened. I get that. But that doesn't mean I can't figure it out.

"The twins are coming over to watch you for a bit."

She sighs and gives me a pleading look. "Just let me go, Sean. Billy is probably milliseconds away from burning this house down with us in it. Don't put your brothers in danger."

I laugh at the thought. Brendan and Bryan live for danger. They're seekers of bloody chaos. "Let Billy Gravely set foot on this property and he'll be missing his fucking head."

She groans. "It's a deadly mistake to underestimate Billy."

"Please. It's a deadly mistake to underestimate *me*. I run the Dublin Devils and have a crew of more than a hundred men who will do anything I tell them."

She sinks back in her chair. "You can't keep me prisoner, Sean."

"You're not a prisoner—you're my guest. Having you stay here is for your own protection and your father's."

She frowns. "How do you figure?"

I grin, letting her see just how serious I am. "Because if you go home and he lays one fucking finger on you, I'll rip his fucking hands off. I'll cut him up and leave his body for his precious Dobermann watchdogs to snack on. No one hurts you, Piper. No one. Not ever again."

CHAPTER FIVE

Sean

I leave Piper in the care of my younger brothers, knowing she'll be safe and there when I get back. Brendan and Bryan are like rottweilers. They're tough, loyal, and nobody with any sense will mess with them or they'll get their balls chewed off.

If Tag calls either of the twins to confirm that I've sent Piper south, they'll cover for me—at least unless our big brother returns in person and horsewhips them.

The odds are in my favor, though.

He said he has a busy day and that will keep him out of my hair for at least a few hours.

I lean into the right-hand turn, the morning breeze pulling at my hair as I give my girl more gas. The rumble of the engine between my thighs is almost as good as having a woman there.

Almost.

What's even better is being on my bike *annnd* having a woman there. It's another kind of ride altogether. Or getting ridden might be more accurate.

Images flare to life in my mind. Piper riding my cock while I straddle the black leather seat of my bike. Me bending her over the tank as I run my hands over her naked ass...

Man, I gotta get a handle on that because I'm stiff behind my fly for like the third time this morning. It's ridiculous. She's not even twenty and I'm almost thirty.

When I was sixteen and cock deep in Peggy O'Reilly, Piper was only six and playing with dolls.

No. This isn't a romantic thing. This has to remain about men praying on innocent women and me standing up to say it's wrong, regardless of who they are or what side of the river they came from.

And that's why I can't let this go.

One of our guys from the station of Garda Síochána, Seamus Peterson, is meeting me at Dinky's Diner. I asked him to look through the traffic cam footage from the bridge last night and to track the battered woman in the red dress back to whatever hotel she came out of.

He assured me he could get it.

I think the part of Piper's story where she said she was in a hotel and smashed through a glass table was the truth. She was in shock when she told me that and it slipped out.

The other stuff about muggers was bullshit.

The way Piper reacted to mine and Tag's questions makes me sure it was McGuire business. Family business she shouldn't have been part of and, unless we missed something along the way, hasn't been part of before now.

The hour of night and her sexy red dress makes me think she was dressed to impress.

But impress who?

And why would Mattie wave his nineteen-year-old daughter in front of anyone in our business?

Maybe she was telling the truth, and she was out with friends when she got recognized.

Maybe a transaction went sour because of something she said or did?

She's holding a lot of guilt over whatever happened. She said she couldn't stand to be a disappointment as well as a traitor. How could her getting beat up ever make her into a disappointment?

I just don't understand her fucking family.

And what about making the man who beat her up pay? She doesn't seem in the least bit anxious for revenge. If that were me, I'd be gunning to make them pay.

Why isn't that a consideration?

I park my bike out front and spot Seamus in a back booth. Dinky's is a favorite local breakfast place downtown, but it's nearly eleven on a Thursday, so there aren't many other diners.

"Hey, thanks for meeting me." I slide into the booth opposite him and smile at the coffee and the piece of apple crumble waiting for me. "You're a good man, Peterson."

He chuckles. "If my superiors knew I trade favors with the Quinn boys, they might disagree."

I scoop a large forkful of apple bliss and shovel it into my mouth. "There's a certain give and take to keeping the peace. We do our best, as do you, and it works out well for both of us."

"Aye, it does at that."

"So, were you able to backtrack the footage of the girl I told you about?"

Seamus cues up a section of video and turns his laptop around so I can view the screen. "It started at the NYX."

"Where the fuck is the NYX?"

"It's the Hard Rock Hotel. Newly remodeled but still with some of the same rocker vibe. Anyway, I wound the footage back, and this is where we first see the girl in the red dress."

I lean in and watch as Piper rushes out of the old Hard Rock Hotel, looks around like she doesn't know what to do next, and

JENN MADORE & CAROLINA MAC

then, when two men step out of the hotel, she staggers down the sidewalk into the shadows.

The footage follows her as she limps down Exchange Street, across Essex Gate, and then onto Parliament with those same two men chasing her.

"Who the fuck are those guys?"

"I'll tell you in a minute. Watch."

I watch as one of the bearded brutes catches her from behind, and she goes down hard. Her face smashes into the concrete and she's out cold for a few seconds.

"Fucking hell."

"She wakes up fighting like a wildcat, though."

One guy grabs her in a caveman hold and drags her into the shadows by the hair. Then he tosses her down and fucking kicks her.

Piper wakes up screaming, but a second kick to her shoulder knocks her onto her back. Then the one with blood staining the front of his leg grabs her and hauls her to her feet.

Despite the size difference and the fact that Piper has likely never made a fist, she launches at him and makes a damned good effort of clawing his eyes out.

"Well done, beautiful."

The fatter, older one catches up and slaps her across the face. The force of the blow has her head spinning and my heart pounding. Two of them. Two grow men put a beating to her and she's still alive to tell the tale.

Or not tell it, in Piper's case.

"This is my favorite part," Seamus says, pointing to the action on the screen. "Wait for it."

Heaving forward, Piper spews all over the one who kicked her. The guy is obviously revolted and when he shoves her away, she runs again—this time, over the Grattan Bridge.

"I knew it was bad, but fucking hell." I lean back and run my fingers through my hair. "Who are they? I take it you ran their faces through recognition software?"

Seamus ends the street footage video and pulls up black and white photos of the two men we just watched beating the hell out of Piper.

"Vladimir Volkov and Arkady Sidorov."

"Russians?"

"Aye. Known representatives for the Shadow Sickle Syndicate out of St. Petersburg."

"Bratva? What the fuck are they doing in Dublin?"

He shrugs. "I just report the news. I don't try to make sense of it. How delicate is this information to you and yours?"

"Why do you ask?"

"Well, now that I've seen them here, I could get into a lot of trouble if I don't tell the guns and gangs boys."

I sit back in the booth and consider the facts. "If Bratva are making dealings with the McGuires, that can only mean one thing—guns."

And guns are *our* territory, not theirs.

"Once again, Mattie McGuire is breaking the terms of the truce and thinking himself above the territorial agreement he made with our father."

Seamus curses. "Then I really need to bring this to the right people. But how do you know they're here for the McGuires?"

"Because the woman in the red dress is Mad Mattie's daughter, Piper. He must've enlisted her to show the Russians a good time, and then something went sour."

Seamus slides a thumb drive across the table and closes his laptop. "If you get wind of guns coming our way, I'd appreciate a heads up. No one wants more guns on our streets."

"Aye, if I hear of anything, I'll give you a ring."

Seamus extends his hand, and I meet the guy palm to palm. "Give my best to Tag and your brothers."

"I will. I'll also tell them how you helped us out on this one. They'll appreciate it."

Before I leave Dinky's, I text Finn:

> Drop everything and hack into the NYX Hotel's computer system. Find anything tied to the McGuires, Vladimir Volkov, or Arkady Sidorov. Then widen the search and see who we're dealing with.

Then I phone Tag. The call goes straight to voicemail, so I leave him the highlight reel at the beep. "Things are happening, brother. I have the full story and it's not good. I'm headed back to our guest now. Come as soon as you can."

CHAPTER SIX

Piper

*L*ying in the guest room in the Quinn's safe house, all I can think about is my father selling me to the Russians as a bonus for closing the gun deal. Does he think I'm one of his whores? Is that what he was thinking when he picked my dress last night? I thought his obsession with keeping me away from boys was a father being overly protective.

Was this his plan all along?

Using my body to broker an alliance and close a deal isn't the part I wanted to play in the family business. I wanted to be respected and trusted with important tasks like my brothers have been since they were old enough to drink.

It's why I've been studying PR for the past two years at uni. My father has a reputation for being unhinged and erratic. I intended to help with the optics of our family and swing public opinion in our favor like the Quinns do with their Quinn Laws.

Apparently, Da puts more value on my intact hymen.

Does Mam know? Is she worried because I didn't come

home from last night's meeting? Will she stand up to Da or will she stand by his decision?

I know the sickening truth without having to ask.

Samantha McGuire is the backbone of our family organization. She's the strategic one—not Da. If Da came to this idea of offering me to the Bratva, it likely wasn't his idea. It could've been Billy's.

In that case, maybe she didn't know.

Da has been acting crazy for ages now. He hates the reputation of being Mad Mattie, but he's earned it.

There are some days I swear he's fucking nuts.

A door slams downstairs and then the murmur of male voices drifts up through the floorboards. I can't hear what they're saying, but by the tone and the rising volume, it doesn't sound good.

Is Tag back? Did he come back to make sure that I've been sent home and realize I'm still in his house? What will he do to me? Probably carry me to the Liffey himself and toss me into the icy cold water.

What will he do to Sean for disobeying him?

Why *is* Sean disobeying him? I may have been raised on the south side, but everyone knows that the Quinn brothers stick together. Sean and Tag are the oldest and they are known to be really close.

Why would Sean ignore his brother's wishes and keep me here? It's not like I want to be here.

Well, there's a part of me that wants to stay here a little longer, to hide from the mess I've made until I'm stronger, until I have a plan.

If I'm being honest with myself, I like the way Sean cares about my well-being. I know it probably has more to do with not having another dead McGuire on their hands than actual affection, but it doesn't feel like it.

I close my eyes and exhale. I don't have feelings for Sean Quinn. I *can't* have feelings for him.

There is no mixing of Quinns with McGuires.

Oil and water.

Kerosine and flame.

A wild, unbridled flame with panty-dampening tattoos and a scowl that makes me want to climb him and bite that scarred lip of his.

I give myself an inward shake.

That's not helping.

Tag wants me out of his house, and I don't blame him. My brothers would never protect a Quinn. If they found one bleeding in the gutter, they'd shoot him and leave his body in the street to rot.

There are no McGuire Laws of conduct.

Maybe that's the problem.

Maybe if my family had a code to live by, they'd actually have some ethics.

Knuckles tap gently on my door and Bryan sticks his head in. "Sean brought lunch. Are you feeling well enough to join us?"

"Aye, I am. Thank you."

"Do you need help on the stairs? Sean said you were having trouble this morning."

"No. I'm sure that was just morning stiffness. I'm fine, thanks. I'll meet you down there."

"Alrighty. If you need a hand on the stairs after all, just holler."

I listen as Bryan's footsteps retreat, and he goes back downstairs. Why are Sean and his brothers so nice to me? Honestly, they're nicer to me than my own brothers.

It's tough to get up with my ribs aching the way they are, but I roll onto my other hip and use the end of the bed to pull myself onto my feet. Once I'm upright, the pain eases off a bit.

Straightening as much as my side and my hip will allow, I

glance in the mirror. I'm a hot mess. I look like I should be on a poster for domestic abuse. There's not enough coverup and foundation in the world to erase the purple of my cheek and the scabbed hamburger scrapes where Vladimir's ring cut me.

Why should I care what I look like? It's not like I'm here to impress anyone.

I step into the upstairs hallway and shuffle toward the top step. Gripping the railing, I push my hair out of my eyes, so I won't fall.

"Holy fuck. That's brutal." Brendan's voice drifts up to me and I pause.

"We can't let shit like that stand, Sean," Bryan adds.

"Och, we won't, little brother. I promise you that. These fuckers will bleed. Strike for strike. Punch for punch. Kick for kick. They'll wish they never set foot in our city."

I ease down the stairs, step by tortuous step, being careful with my footing.

"As soon as Tag gets here and gives us the go, we'll school these fuckers on how things work in Dublin."

I wonder what they're talking about. Maybe that's how I redeem myself. Would Da forgive me if I brought him something juicy from behind the Quinn curtain?

Possibly. It would have to be good, though. Like who they're planning to go after and why.

I shuffle into the kitchen and find Sean and the twins at the table. The three of them are bent forward, staring at the screen of a laptop. "Sorry. I didn't mean to interrupt. Should I leave?"

Sean's gaze meets mine and heat hums over my skin. His twin brothers look up at me, too, their gazes intense.

"Why do I feel like a bug under a microscope?"

Before any of them answer, Tag comes striding in behind me. "All right. I'm here. What's this about?"

Sean turns the laptop toward us and my breath catches. It's me on the screen and I'm getting beaten up down by the river last night. "Mattie McGuire is negotiating a gun deal with the Russians—more specifically, with representatives of the Shadow Sickle."

Tag scowls. "Bratva? What the fuck is he thinking? We don't want those crazy fucks in Ireland."

Sean straightens and runs his fingers through his long hair. "No. We don't. But that's how Piper got beat up."

All eyes turn to me, and I take a couple of steps to get away from Tag. My butt bumps against the counter sooner than I like and I realize I can't get any further away from him.

Tag shakes his head. "Your father is fucking reckless. We were coexisting under a truce that has done us well for almost three decades."

"Guns are our territory, not his," Brendan snaps.

Tag nods. "Our fathers divvied up the business arrangements, and it's worked well for years. Your family gets hard drugs, hit men, and sex trafficking, and we deal in party drugs, restaurants and night clubs, and guns. Everything else is fair game. Why the fuck is he so power hungry now that he wants it all?"

I shrug. "I don't know. I'm not involved in the business."

Tag scoffs and points to me in the company of Vladimir and Arkady. "Apparently, that's not true."

"But it *is* true. I've wanted to be involved. I've begged my parents for years, but Da said I had nothing to offer." Hot tears sting the cuts on my cheek, but there's no stopping them.

"Nothing until he dressed you up and set you up with two Bratva animals," Tag snaps, pointing at the laptop.

"I didn't know what he had planned." My breath gets tighter with every passing second. "He asked me to charm a couple of out-of-town big shots. He said to meet them for dinner and then escort them up to the suite. I didn't know he told them they could have me as part of the deal."

"He did *what?*" Sean and Tag shout at the same time.

53

JENN MADORE & CAROLINA MAC

I'm sobbing now and can't bear to look at them. It's disgusting and so incredibly humiliating. "He told them I'm a virgin and said they could do what they want with me to sweeten the deal."

I'm surrounded by swearing on all sides.

"They need to die," Sean says. "I'll send a few of the boys over the river and take them out in their suite. Leave the bloody mess on Mattie's doorstep."

"Fuck yeah," Brendan says.

Tag slams a hand against the wall and curses. "As appealing as that is, we can't. If two Bratva representatives end up dead in Dublin, we'll have the fury of the Shadow Sickle Syndicate raining down on our streets. No. We need to think of something else."

"We need to sour the gun deal and send them home," Bryan says.

Tag turns to him. "Aye, Bryan. That's good."

"How do we do that?" Brendan asks.

Tag's gaze snaps to me. He picks up the paper takeout bag and one of the drinks, then tilts his head toward the sitting room. "Excuse us for a moment, will you, lass? I'm sure you understand."

"I do. I've been shooed out of the room my entire life. I know the drill." Taking my lunch in hand, I leave the Quinns to plot their counterattack.

Shit. Shit. Shit. Da is going to lose the gun deal because of me. The Quinns will ruin his plans, and he'll think I gave it up and betrayed our family.

Billy Gravely will hunt me down and kill me for sure.

I have to get out of here. I've got to go home and explain to Da what happened. I would never betray him or my family no matter what.

Setting my lunch on the coffee table, I cast one last look toward the kitchen before heading to the door. I've stayed too long. If I tell Mam what happened, and explain to her that those men started hurting me and I didn't know what Da told them...

I grab the doorknob, and it doesn't turn. That's when I see the push button security box on the wall beside the door. There's a lock to get out of the house and one to get in? Seriously? I flip back the curtains and check the living room window next. It's locked shut, too.

I really *am* their prisoner.

Before they catch me trying the door, I return to the couch like a good little hostage and see what Sean brought me for lunch. There's no sense starving myself. I need to heal up and get strong in case I get the chance to leave. If so, I gotta be ready to run.

It's almost dark when a knock on my bedroom door wakes me from my afternoon nap. "May I come in? Are you decent?"

I adjust the blanket over my body. "You saw me all but naked and bleeding last night, Sean. I have very little modesty left, but aye, I'm decent."

He opens the door carrying a cup of tea.

I chuckle and accept the offering. "Who would have thought that Sean Quinn, mafia son and President of the Dublin Devils, would be so invested in making tea for me? This is getting to be a regular thing."

He makes a face. "Is it weird? Sorry. Mam used to say a cuppa is the first step to healing all wounds. When she got sick, Da was forever bringing home different flavors and making them up for her. It always put a smile on her face and made her feel better, so I guess I thought you might feel better, too."

My heart. He may be hard on the outside, but Sean Quinn has a gooey center.

"It's not weird. Thank you. I appreciate the gesture. I appreciate everything you've done for me."

His gaze narrows. "Why do I hear a 'but' in that comment? What aren't you saying?"

"I noticed this afternoon that there is a security box keeping me locked in. I feel like a hostage. Despite everything you've done for me, I won't be your prisoner to be used against my father."

He stiffens. "You mean the father who whored you out and signed you up to be raped by two criminals?"

I take the hit and find that some of the desperate disappointment and hurt that's been aching inside me is turning to anger. That's good. I've cried too many tears in the last twenty-four hours already.

"Take my father out of the equation. I don't want to be kept hostage."

He shrugs. "I'm sorry. With what we found out today, you're stuck with me for the foreseeable future. We need to protect our edge, and I want to make sure someone is dedicated to protecting you."

"My family can protect me. I truly don't believe my parents would've sent me out with those men if they knew how brutal they could be."

Sean frowns. "They're Bratva, Piper. Everyone knows how brutal they can be. I'm sorry. It's unforgivable, but your father chose a business foothold over you. That's the truth. It's vile and hurtful, but it's the truth."

"I know it is, and it sticks like a dagger in my heart. But maybe, this is my first big lesson in being part of the family business. The 'blood in' moment of initiation. Do you think?"

Sean's eyebrows arch and are lost behind his ebony hair. "Are you fucking kidding? No, Piper, I don't think. That's mental. No one initiates their daughter by setting her up for that kind of abuse."

I suppose he's right. Although, my father has made crazy decisions before. Could I forgive him if he truly is losing his grip on reality? Still, if that were the case, why didn't someone else step up and stop him?

Da doesn't make decisions in isolation—he always likes an audience. Someone else knew of his plan and didn't care enough about me to warn me.

I push that thought away for now and focus on my current untenable situation—being the house guest of Sean Quinn.

My tea is warm and has a lovely berry flavor with a hint of vanilla. And when I swallow it, I can't help but smile. "Your Mam was right. Tea does help."

We sit quietly until the room grows dark and Sean reaches over to turn on the bedside lamp. "I'm still surprised that you didn't have protection on you. Even if his plan was to give you to the Russians, why didn't your father have someone watching you?"

"Ryan was supposed to be there. When we came out of the restaurant, I was surprised to find he wasn't. I thought he might've been outside in the car, but when I ran out of the hotel, I was on my own. That's another reason why I need to go home. Ryan is probably in terrible trouble."

Sean doesn't look convinced. "Your energy is better served to worry about yourself, not your brother. Mattie used you as a bargaining tool and when you ran, it made him look bad. He'll take that out on you to save face. Like it or not, you're not safe from your family right now."

I hate what he's saying, but part of me knows he's right. If I get caught on the south side of the river, Billy Gravely will kill me.

He hurt me before and that was when I was 'Da's little girl'. What will he do now? Now that I've fallen from favor, there's nothing to stop him.

The mug trembles in my hand and I take a long sip to keep from spilling it.

"I realize this is hard for you to accept, but your family isn't a safe option for you. Whether they're angry about you fighting with the Russians or that you're here or that we figured out about the gun deal and are about to squash it, you're in a dangerous position."

I groan. "But none of that is my fault."

"That changes nothing. You need to stay here, rest, and in a day or two, we'll sort things out for you. By then, you'll be recovering and feeling stronger."

Sean is a growly biker with long hair and a scar that gives him a bit of a perma-sneer, but when he looks into my eyes, I see the man beneath the violence. His tough exterior likely serves him well while he's torturing and killing people, but there's another side to him.

The man who scooped up a beaten woman in the street and, despite who she was, offered her kindness, protection, and honesty.

I look away and focus on the darkening Dublin sky. Nothing in my life is what I thought it was. Was I too naïve to see, too eager to please, or too complacent to ask questions?

Doesn't matter. That's over.

Piper McGuire's eyes are wide open now. "If I ask you a question, will you answer me honestly?"

"If it's something I'm free to talk about, of course."

Fair enough. "In the kitchen, Tag said my father deals in hard drugs, hit men, and sex trafficking. Is that true?"

"Among other things, but those are the three areas of focus for your family's business. Why do you ask?"

I hear the truth in his words and another piece of what I believed my life was about chips away. "And your family controls party drugs, real estate, and guns?"

"We do."

"Why those things?"

"That was what our father believed we could dominate, while still keeping the streets of Dublin safe. This city was his life, and he believed its citizens were his to protect regardless of us living outside the law. He drew up the truce agreement with your father in a way that allowed both territories to thrive and not to compete overtly with one another."

I don't remember life before the truce with the Quinns, but I've heard my older brothers talk about it sometimes. It was a violent and scary time.

"And my father chose what he wanted to control?"

"Aye, he did."

"And he chose sex trafficking?"

Sean frowns and I can tell what he thinks of that decision. "I suppose there's a lot of money in it, but our father had no interest in the exploitation of innocents."

"But your family has prostitution. I've heard my brothers talk about how your brothels are bad for business."

Sean scoffs. "Bad for McGuire business, maybe."

"So you admit that you do have prostitution. Isn't that exploiting innocent women?"

Sean shakes his head. "Not even a little. We own several gentlemen's clubs where women are free to work. We provide a safe location, security, and access to all medical needs to ensure the girls are clean and able to care for themselves. They run their business. They choose their clients. And yes, they pay us for the use of the space and the services we provide, but they keep the lion's share of their earnings. We're only there to assist. It's good business."

I draw in a deep breath. That's not at all how my brothers talk about the 'whores' they run. They laugh at the Quinn Laws and say how stupid they are. But I don't think they're stupid. I think they're commendable.

In a violent, criminal world, they're trying to do right by the people as they make their money.

"My father only cares about power and profit."

The mattress dips as he sits on the edge of the bed. He sends me a compassionate smile and then he gives my hand a squeeze. "You can't help the family you were born into and aren't responsible for the choices they make. You are your own person."

"Am I? I've always been a McGuire. I was proud of being from a powerful family, but if my reality is sex trafficking and a father who offers my virginity to Bratva brutes, what is there to be proud of?"

Saying it aloud makes the horror of it too much to bear. Another round of tears falls, and I clench my eyes shut to stop from falling apart. "I hate this. I hate all of it. All I wanted was to be valued by my father and to be given the same respect my brothers have. Now I feel like I'm about to shatter into a million pieces."

Sean brushes a finger beneath my chin and lifts my teary gaze to meet his. "I won't let you shatter, Piper. And if you do, I'll pick up every wee piece and help you pull yourself together again. I promise."

Man…why does he have to say things like that?

I can't fall for a Quinn.

Sean tugs me forward and wraps his arms around me. His embrace is strong and warm, and the scent of his leather MC vest fills my senses.

I don't care why he's being so kind to me. At least there's one person who cares if I'm holding it together after the worst night of my life.

Sean's hand brushes up my spine and clasps the back of my head, holding me against him. There's nothing tentative about the way he handles me. He's confident in how he touches a woman. How many women would it take to be this comfortable with this kind of closeness?

A dozen? A hundred? More?

He's almost ten years older than me, so there's no telling what experiences he's had.

And I've had none.

Still, his arms are around me tonight and not another woman. That's all I need to focus on. That and how safe and cherished he makes me feel, despite the situation.

"Now that you know the truth about your father, you can make your own choices—informed choices—about what you want your life to look like going forward."

I don't want to go forward. Sitting here, wrapped in his arms, I want to stay like this forever. When was the last time anyone hugged me like this?

Has anyone *ever* hugged me like this?

I can't think of a single instance. My mother is a tough love kind of parent, my father is more of a pat on shoulder kind of man, and my brothers are more likely to punch me affection-ately—or not—if they are expressing themselves.

This closeness is something I didn't even know I crave until this minute.

Too soon, he releases me from his embrace and eases back. "Hey, I've got to meet Tag and take care of this Russian guns thing. Get some rest. Finn is downstairs and I've got a couple of Devils watching the house. You'll be safe and I'll be back as soon as I can."

The idea that Sean is going to meet up with Vladimir and Arkady twists the knot in my stomach. "If you get the chance, feel free to cut their balls off."

Sean doesn't laugh as I expect. Instead he leans in until we're nose to nose. "Tonight, we need to build a relationship with the Bratva. After that, I will make them pay for what they did to you —I swear it."

The fury in his dark eyes should terrify me. It doesn't.

Sean makes me feel safe.

Standing up, he presses his lips to my forehead and steps away from the bed. "Rest. I'll be back before you miss me."

I doubt that's possible. I miss him already.

When the latch of my door clicks into place, I lay back in the bed, the ache of disillusionment and betrayal hot and piercing in my heart while the wonder of new beginnings wars with everything I've ever known.

Was it better when I didn't know the details about my father and our business? Do my friends know what my family does? Did Sean Quinn just kiss me? Sure, it was on my forehead, but his lips touched my flesh. What does that mean?

I stare out the window, the city now swallowed in full darkness. Informed choices...

I knew my family dealt in ugly business, but I never took the time to question why. Da chose those business ventures. That's the kind of man he is. Does that mean that's the kind of men my brothers are?

Maybe Da selling me off was the wake-up call I needed. What would he do to me if he got his hands on me? Would he add me to his next sex trafficking order to punish me?

I honestly don't know what he's capable of.

My brothers talked about the girls they had coming up, and I always thought they were talking about dancers or call girls. I never imagined sex trafficking.

That's my legacy.

I'm a McGuire.

And for the first time in my life, I wish I wasn't.

CHAPTER SEVEN

Sean

The back of the delivery van is quiet as we approach the NYX Hotel. Quinns don't breach the territorial lines and go to the south of Dublin. It's a tenet we've lived by for over twenty years.

Tonight, we make an exception.

It's becoming more and more obvious that Mad Mattie doesn't respect the terms of the truce between our families, so why should we?

"You okay, boss?" Kieran's curious gaze meets mine as he slides his lighter into the pocket of his MC cut. "You look weird."

"Have you looked in the mirror lately?"

He chuckles. "Touché."

I check the tranquilizing pistol and make sure I'm ready in case this goes sideways. "Just going over things in my head."

"Fucking Bratva," Brendan scoffs. "Mad Mattie's living up to his name these days."

"I'm thinking he's got a fucking brain tumor or something," Bryan adds. "He's fucked in the head, for sure."

No argument. How could a father do that to his child? I try not to think about the heart-wrenching sight of Piper's world shattering, but being sucked into her glassy eyes nearly did me in.

I shouldn't be so drawn in by her disillusionment, but there's something about her... It's like I have a pathological compulsion to protect her, to keep the evils of her life at bay until she gets back on her feet.

Not that her being with us is much better—the Quinns are no saints—but we're a fuck-ton better than the McGuires.

Usually, being out with the boys clears my head and gives me singular focus. Tonight, all I can think about is that video of those Russians taking the boots to Piper in the street and the fact that I can't avenge her.

At least not yet.

I'll save that torture until the time is right.

"This is a straight snatch and grab, boys. Kieran's contact will let us in the side door and give us a door card for the elevator and the suite. We go up, we tranq them, we leave the same way we came."

Brendan chuckles. "These tranq guns look crazy real. We should play a game of Quinn Tranq Tag one night when we're drinking. Last man standing wins."

"I'm game." Bryan grins.

I meet Kieran's gaze and roll my eyes. "My brothers are eejits."

He holds up his palms. "What you five do on your own time is your business. I'm just thinking that it would hurt. These tranq darts are wicked sharp."

The truck's brakes are wet and let off a whine as the truck rolls to a stop. Gallagher sticks his head into the opening of the window from the cab and grins at us. "Last stop, the NYX Hotel. Everyone out."

Five on two are good odds and I'm not a bit worried that we'll be out-manned. I watched the video of the two Russians attacking Piper a dozen times and while they were sent here as representatives, they are the big man's cousin and his bodyguard, not true Bratva killers.

The area around the side door is dark, the light over the door conveniently turned off. Kieran sticks his mug in front of the glass sidelight of the door and the metallic clunk of a push bar opens.

As we shuffle inside, Kieran meets our contact with a clasped hand and then gestures down the hall for him to get us moving. "Where are we headed, sham?"

He strikes off down the carpeted corridor with the five of us in tow. "The top floor has eight extensive suites, and the one the McGuires rented is 604. You'll need this key card to get the elevator to move, and it'll open the door for you as well."

The guy is wearing a NYX polo shirt and, by the tool belt hanging around his hips, I'd guess he is a maintenance man of some sort.

"You'll be quiet and careful, won't you?" He turns a worried look on us as he calls the elevator.

Sure, five tattooed guys with long hair and wearing leather look threatening, but what did he expect? We're a fucking motorcycle club run by a mafia family.

It would be even worse for him if he saw the weapons we're carrying.

Still, he's Kieran's contact and we try never to burn our eyes and ears on the south side, so I field his question and draw an X over my heart. "We'll be as quiet as Mary's little lamb, I swear."

Brendan chuckles, but a look from me quells his amusement. "We appreciate the help, mate, and will do our best to ensure nothing blows back on you."

The doors of the elevator slide open with a mechanical whoosh, and we get in. Kieran does the honors of pressing the buttons and we begin the climb to the top floor.

"For your troubles." I hand the guy five hundred bucks folded into a neat wad. "All you need to do is hold the elevator for us while we secure the Russians, so we can get gone fast."

His eyes blow wide. "Me? I thought all I had to do was get you in."

I hold the bills when he reaches for them, assuring that I have his attention. "You're almost done, kid. Don't freak out on us now."

"He's not going to freak out." Kieran faces the guy and squeezes his shoulders. "They won't be conscious, so they won't see your face. I give you my word. This is going to be fine."

Kieran isn't big, but he's wiry and lethal. I'm not sure if the reassurance makes the kid less afraid of the Russians or more afraid of crossing us.

Whichever it is, it seems to work.

He swallows and gives me a nod. "I'm good. I'll be here, holding the elevator."

"Good man." Kieran pats his arm, and I release his payment.

When the elevator door opens, we rush out. The five of us beat feet up the hall, moving quick and quiet. Outside the suite, Gallagher and I pull our tranq guns, Brenny and Bryan roll their shoulders ready to muscle us in, and Kieran stands beside the door with the key card and a stupid grin on his face.

We haven't had this much fun in a while.

With a nod from each of us that we're ready, Kieran does the honors. The green light signals that we're a go. Brenny and Bryan ease through the door without making a sound and we follow.

A bulky Russian wearing boxers is in the sitting room on the phone. He's ordering from room service and facing out the window. He's the one who kicked Piper in the ribs when she was down in the street.

The other isn't in view.

Brendan and Bryan press back against the foyer walls and Gallagher raises his tranq gun. It's as easy as that.

Until the fucker falls and takes the desk chair and the lamp to the floor with him.

The clamor brings the other guy rushing out of one of the bedrooms, gun raised. He's fat and slow compared to Brenny and Bryan, and they're on him in a flash.

My two little brothers tackle the guy and take his gun out of the equation. I move in fast and when they're clear, I pump two shots into him—chest and thigh.

"Two?" Gallagher takes the cable tie handcuffs out of his bag and tosses me over a pair. "Doc Kelvin said one would do it."

I hand the cuffs to Bryan and point as Brenny rolls the fat guy over. "Our guy is twice the size of yours. Twice the size, twice the tranq darts."

Gallagher chuckles. "Fair enough."

With both Russians out cold and with hands bound, I leave my crew to get them on their feet. While they do that, I take a look around.

They're slobs, but that's not helpful. The bedrooms have their personal stuff, their clothes, phones, guns, and some porn magazines.

I grab the phones but leave the rest where I found it.

In the sitting room, I lift the desk chair and set it back on its wheels. Then I grab a laptop, a folder with a rundown on the McGuire organization, and a stapled wad of what looks like a legal agreement.

"What the actual fuck?" I scan the contract and skim through the dirty details. "That motherfucking prick."

Gallagher comes over with the bag and starts sliding our takeaways inside. "What is it?"

I fold the contract and slip it into my back pocket. "More incentive to kill Mattie McGuire. Come on, boys. Let's get north before anyone knows we were here."

Tag is waiting for us behind the bar at the MC clubhouse when we arrive. He's pouring himself a dram and when he holds up the bottle, Brendan, Bryan, and I go over to join him. He looks past us to Kieran and Gallagher. "Take our guests into the boardroom, gentlemen."

I point to a couple of the other lads. "Give them a hand. And remember, for the moment, they're to be treated well."

"And after that?" Micky asks.

"We'll see how things go." I want to tell them to sharpen the sheers because I'm going to be making these two assholes into eunuchs, but that little nugget is private and can stay that way.

If I say it, my brothers will wonder why I'm so invested and there's no way I can answer that question without Tag getting mad. If he even suspects I care about Piper, he'll order her away from me.

If I play it cool, it might buy me more time.

"So, how'd things go?"

"Like clockwork." I accept the tumbler and throw the amber liquid back in one gulp. When I set the empty glass down, I tap the rim for a refill.

"Any problems?" Tag tips the bottle and sets me up.

"Not a one." Brendan takes a drink, and I realize the three of them are staring at me.

"What?"

"You have that homicidal gleam you get when you are envisioning dismembering someone," Bryan says.

I focus on my second glass and take a normal, calm drink. "Well, if I do, it's justified."

"How so?" Tag's question sounds casual enough, but he knows me and he's reading my reaction.

It's his fucking superpower, and it's annoying as hell.

"This stays in the vault, got it?" I stare down the twins, to make it clear I'm speaking to them. "Not a word to anyone."

Brendan shrugs. "Sure. Whatever."

"Cool. Got it." Bryan climbs onto one of the bar stools. "The secret is in the vault."

I pull the folded contract from my back pocket and hand it to Tag. "Mattie actually signed away Piper to sweeten the gun deal. He offered her virginity to them during negotiations and then, if the fat one likes her, he can take her home as a parting gift."

That earns a round of cursing and what the fucks.

Bryan scowls. "I told you. He's fucked in the head."

Tag frowns. "I don't even know how to process this."

"It can't be legal, right?" Brendan looks between us. "I know arranged marriages can be legal, but Piper is nineteen. She's an adult."

"I can't see how it could be legal." Tag hands it to Bryan. "Go make a copy of this, and we'll take it home to Laine. She'll know better than we do."

That's a good idea.

A lot of loud Russian cursing booms from the back room, and Tag finishes his drink. "All right, boys. Looks like the meeting is in session. Let's go find out what kind of deal Mattie McGuire made with the Bratva, how we can break it, and then what we can do to send them home happy so they stay the fuck out of our city."

I finish my drink and fight the urge to bring the bottle. As much as I'd like to take the edge off my homicidal gleam, as Bryan called it, if liquid sedation lets my guard down, I'll likely put two plugs in their skulls.

And that will piss Tag off.

CHAPTER EIGHT

Piper

I wake screaming, and when I jolt upright in bed, my cries of panic turn to pain. Agony grips me, the sudden movement of my bruised ribs stealing my breath.

Heavy footfalls precede the darkness of the room being broken. The door swings open and light from the bathroom silhouettes Sean racing toward the bed.

"You're all right, Piper. You're safe. I've got you. I won't let anyone hurt you."

His arms come around me, and I cling to him, the terror of my dream still suffocating me. "There's a contract…" I gasp, envisioning Vladimir waving those papers in my face. "My father gave me to them."

"Shh… Piper. Don't think about that. You're here with me and you're safe. There's no way I'll let your father, or those Russians take you back. You're safe."

I push the covers out of my way and crawl into his lap. My breathing is shallow and quick. There's not enough oxygen in the room. "I can't breathe. I'm dizzy. What's wrong with me?"

Warm hands clasp the sides of my face as he bends to meet my gaze. He presses our foreheads together, his emerald green eyes all that I can see before me. "You're in a bit of a panic, but it'll be fine. You just need to look into my eyes and trust me. Do you trust me?"

Do I? "Aye, I do."

"Good girl." He takes my hand and presses it on his bare chest, right over his heart.

In my mind's eye, I envision the elaborate Celtic cross he has inked there. It's bold and sexy and thinking about touching it steals my breath even more than my nightmare did.

"Piper, close your eyes and feel me taking deep breaths. When I breathe in, you do it too. When I breathe out, you'll do the same."

Another time, another place, or even with another man, I would feel stupid doing this. But this is Sean. He's become my haven over the past two days.

"Breathe with me."

I close my eyes and do as he says.

Matching his breathing isn't as easy as it sounds. My heart is racing, and my breathing is rapid and shallow.

"From here, Piper." He places his hand across my tummy, right above my navel. "Let your breath fill all the way down to my hand."

I try my best, and after a while, the room stops spinning. I'm not sure how long it takes for my heart rate to slow, but eventually, the world doesn't seem so scary.

It's still dark out, but the dim light from the hall silhouettes his frame enough for me to realize he's only wearing boxers. He's got an amazing body and even in the shadows, I see the cut of his abs and how those Celtic tattoos melt into the night, darker than dark.

"That's it." His voice is deep, and the calmness in it seems to hang in the air. "Now, just relax. We'll stay like this for as long as you need."

I focus on my breathing, on how the icy chill of panic is being chased away by warmth. It's radiating from Sean's hand, resting over my diaphragm, up into my chest and down to the crux of my legs.

The heat blooming low in my belly is delicious, and I keep my eyes closed. Between the darkness and the silence of the house, it feels like we're hiding away in a bubble where no one bad can get us.

I swallow and press my hand over his. It's still resting above my navel, and I fight the urge to guide it lower.

Neither of us move for a long time and after a while, I feel braver. "Sean, can I ask you something?"

"Anything."

"Will you stay with me? Every time I fall asleep, I'm sucked into the violence of fighting off those men. Having you here makes me feel safe. Will you sleep with me?"

There's a moment of silence, and then he exhales an unsteady breath. "That's not a good idea, Piper. I've already crossed a lot of lines getting involved in McGuire family drama. You're young and feeling vulnerable right now. It would be too easy to—"

I shake my head and climb off his lap. "Forget it. If you're telling me I'm too naïve to understand why you're here, you're no different from my family. You can go."

He straightens. "Don't compare me to your family. I would never do what they did. I care about you. Keeping it simple is simply the wisest choice. You're young and—"

"—We should have sex."

"*What?*" Even in the darkness, I see his eyes bulge wide. "Why would you want that? You were just assaulted."

"Because my father sold me off as a good girl virgin. If I

sleep with you, I'll be damaged goods. That might kill the arranged marriage idea in the eyes of the Bratva."

Sean curses and moves to shift away.

I make a bold move and reach through the darkness, grabbing his stiff cock, boxers and all. "I'm not so young and inexperienced that I didn't notice how your body reacted to me sitting in your lap."

His hand grips mine, but I don't allow him to pull away. Instead, I squeeze harder, and he lets off a hiss. "Fucking hell, Piper. That's biology. You're hot and only wearing my t-shirt. You were sitting in my lap, and we shared a moment."

"So, let's share another moment. It's win-win. We'd both enjoy the sex, and my market value will suffer."

"Don't talk about yourself like that. It's fucked up." He grips my hand and tries again to remove my hold.

I use the friction to give his erection a couple of firm strokes. "If it's just biology, then fine. There's nothing wrong with having our biological needs met."

He grunts and moves to scooch back on the mattress. I grab his hand and press it against the crotch of my panties. The cotton is damp and warm because he's not the only one having a biological reaction.

He groans and I grind against his hand. "I'm not twenty for another month, so what? I know my mind and body. I also know you understand my world better than any guy from school I could call up to get the job done."

"You're not calling a random guy to come and fuck you."

"Why not? It's just biology, right?"

He runs a rough hand through his hair. "Your first time should be memorable."

I laugh and rub my thumb over the engorged head of his cock. Pre-cum has seeped through his Denver Hayes and my mouth waters just thinking about what he tastes like. "I have a feeling Sean Quinn is a memorable lay."

"You're killing me. You know that, right?" His voice is growing deep and husky, as his hand presses up against my clit. "Tag will fucking kill me."

"Your brother doesn't have to know. We'll do the deed, burn off the crazy attraction arcing between us, and go back to our lives. No one will be the wiser."

"Unless you get pregnant, because this is a safe house. Tag doesn't supply condoms in the bedside table."

I roll my eyes in the dark. "I won't get pregnant. My mom has taken me for birth control shots since I was fifteen. I've got that covered. You haven't got any gross STIs, do you?"

"What? No. I'm clean, but that's not the point."

With the two of us on our knees facing one another, I edge closer and slide my hand down the back of his boxers. His ass is toned and when I give his cheek a squeeze, I press my lips to his jaw. "Please, Sean. I want it to be you. I want you to be my first. I trust you."

He tilts his head back as I nip my way across the tender flesh of his throat. "This is such a bad idea."

"No, it's not. It's a fantastic idea."

"I'm almost ten years older than you, Piper. You'd be young for Finn and I'm five years older than him."

He's spinning his wheels now and we both know it.

I use both hands to shove the waistband of his boxers down his muscled thighs and his cock springs free. "If you tell me what you like, I've always wanted to suck cock."

His cock bobs forward in a pulse.

"Liked the sound of that, did you?"

Sean curses and then eases back. "You're not sucking me off on your first time. If we do this, it's all about you."

"Then help me get naked and treat me right, Mr. Quinn, because I have a long list of firsts that need to be crossed off."

Sean

She's gonna get me killed. There's no way this works out in my favor, but there's also no way it's not happening. I've always thought I'm a strong man who could handle any conflict that came my way.

I was so fucking wrong.

I'm weak. With Piper McGuire offering herself up to me—demanding I take her virginity, there's no way I can say no.

I don't *want* to say no.

"You're still really beaten up, so I'll be gentle." I ease the t-shirt she's wearing up her tender side and over her head. Her ebony hair falls free from the collar and rains down around her shoulders. It falls to cover the milky skin of her collarbone and brushes her naked breasts.

Damn, she's fucking perfect.

I tried my best not to look while I scooped her off the sidewalk and got her changed into the sweatsuit, but I may have noticed a few of her highlights.

Now, being able to look at her without guilt or self-loathing, she takes my breath away.

"You are so fucking beautiful."

She snorts. "Easy on the flattery, Quinn. I look like roadkill and I'm a sure thing. No need to sweet talk me."

I can't hold back the grumble that rumbles from my throat. "That's not false flattery, Piper. It's a fact. From the sleek ebony of your hair, to the soul-shattering ice blue of your eyes, to the little dimple that shows up in your right cheek when you smile, you're a stunner."

I stroke my hand over her hair as I kiss each of her eyelids and then move to press my mouth on her cheek. "And yes, you've got a mouth made for sucking my cock."

I claim her mouth and while I want to spend hours

exploring her lips and tongue, I'll have to circle back around to that in a bit.

"And then there are your tits."

"Which are small and unimpressive," she says.

I frown, wishing it was light enough to show her how wrong she is. "They are not. Granted, they're not as round and heavy as some, but they're impressive in their own way. They're a happy handful and sit perfectly in the palm of my hand. Look. See how beautiful they are?"

She laughs. "A happy handful? You do remember you're a dangerous mafia killer, don't you?"

I lay her back on the mattress, kick off my boxers, and continue my inventory. "I'm a complex man. Sure, I can be brutal, but I can also be gentle. Especially when faced with nipples like these."

She giggles. "Are my nipples happy, too?"

"No. They are resplendent."

I stroke over the peaked tip on her right breast while I suck her left nipple into my mouth. Her body bucks and I smile as I flick my tongue. Taking my time is no hardship, but when I've tortured her enough, I release my suction with a wet pop and prop myself up on my elbow. "Tell me about your list of firsts. Am I getting close to ticking anything off?"

"No way. I'm not disclosing my schoolgirl fantasies. This is just biology, right?"

Not even close. That was the only thing I could think of to justify me getting what I want—what I've wanted since the first moment I held her in my arms.

I lave my tongue over the heated peak of her breast and then blow across the skin. It's too dark to see, but I feel when her skin blooms in goosebumps and I smile against her heated flesh.

As I move my kisses down her body, I pay careful attention not to hurt her ribs.

While rough play can be fun, pain isn't. And tonight already has a bit of pain awaiting us. But once I claim her virginity, it'll be nothing but pleasure.

I'll make sure of that.

I drag my tongue in a line from her belly button piercing down to her manicured mound. I'm not one to care about shaved, trimmed, or natural, but it's nice to get to know a little more about her.

"Has anyone ever gone down on you, kitten?"

She chuckles. "Never a man."

I lift my head, glad she can't see me because my eyebrows have likely arched up to my hairline. "You enjoy girls?"

"I enjoy orgasms, and my father and brothers wouldn't let a boy anywhere near me, so I experimented."

"Resourceful girl."

"I thought so."

"And? What did you think?"

"About being with a girl or having orgasms?"

"You've already stated you are pro-orgasm. How did the experiment turn out?"

"I have nothing against girl on girl, but it didn't do it for me. I learned that I'm all about the man parts."

"Good to know." I shift to settle between her thighs and lift her knees to make more room for my shoulders. I love that this is uncharted territory for her, but somehow, her experimentation eases my guilt a little.

She says she knows her mind and isn't as naïve as people think she is. Maybe that's true.

I kiss the tender flesh at the crux of her body and nuzzle her moisture. When she pressed my hand to her underpants, she was already hot and wet.

Biology, right?

We both knew that was a lie. There's been a tangible sexual energy arcing between us since the beginning. I thought my protective wires had gotten crossed at first, but she felt it too.

She admitted as much when she said that us claiming this moment might work it out of our system.

I don't believe it will.

I'm afraid sinking inside her and having her heat welcome me will make me want her more.

Too late now.

I drop my mouth to her core and pull my tongue through the heat of her folds. She's soft and slick and cries out, arching her back off the mattress. I press a gentle hand on her mons to hold her in place and rub her clit with my thumb while I tongue her.

"Sweet mercy," she purrs, grinding against my mouth. "Don't stop. Don't ever stop doing that."

"Trust me, kitten. I'll be here a good long while. We need you languid and relaxed before I fuck you."

She tastes like sunshine and salty bliss, and I forget about all the reasons we shouldn't be doing this and lose myself in devouring her.

Her body is hyper-responsive, and she orgasms twice before I even consider coming up for air. Piper doesn't have to worry about me stopping because, given the option, I'll never let her get out of bed.

"Fuck, you taste good." I swallow and the taste of her coats my tongue and the back of my throat.

"Cock, Mr. Quinn. I want your cock."

I chuckle at the breathy plea and bring my fingers into play. "You've got one more in you."

"Who knew you were such a cock tease?"

I laugh. "I'm not sure you used that right, but it doesn't matter. I'm not teasing. Your first time will hurt, and I want you ready for me."

"I'm ready." She gasps as I ease my thumb into the first inch of her entrance and work to stretch her.

Damn, I feel like a sixteen-year-old kid again, but this time, I have way more respect for a woman's first time and way more stamina to do right by her.

I work her over with my mouth, and when her body shatters again, I climb up the mattress. She's still breathing hard when I prop myself up on my elbows. "You doing okay?"

"Amazing," she breathes.

My hips are cradled between her thighs, the head of my cock poised at her core. "Last chance to call it off," I say, my need for her building to dizzying heights. "Be sure, Piper. If you're not, we stop now. No hard feelings."

The moon has shifted in the night sky enough that I see her expression as she responds. "I'm sure, Sean. Take me, please. I want you inside me."

I slick the crown of my erection through the moisture we've made and then breach her entrance. "Hold onto my shoulders, Piper. Big breath in."

I thrust forward and lock my hips as she lets out a throaty gasp. Her eyes go wide and water, but she forces a smile. "I'm good. I'm fine."

I wait until she catches her breath and then I ease back and push forward again. "How are you doing?"

"It's a strange sensation. Invasive. I actually feel your cock sliding inside me."

"Aye, that's kinda the point."

She grins. "I'm not sure I can orgasm again when it's so tender, but you do your thing. I want to feel you moving inside me while I watch you lose it."

I said it before...this girl is going to kill me.

"It won't take long. Your body's been through a lot. I don't want to hurt you."

She bites her bottom lip. "You'd never hurt me, Sean. I trust you."

CHAPTER NINE

Piper

$\mathcal{I}$'m not sure what time it is when I wake up next. The gray haze of daylight is edging its way into the night, and I'm sad to see it go. Locked in the shadows of darkness, the two of us shared something—something more than biology.

It might be impossible for a Quinn and a McGuire to make something of their feelings, but I won't pretend I don't have them—at least not to myself.

I acknowledge that he's the enemy.

I acknowledge that he's a decade older than me.

I acknowledge that he's a dangerous man who has tortured and likely killed dozens of people.

But with me, he's just Sean—my black knight. My protector. The man who scooped me off the wet and bloody cement to take me out of the rain and save my life. And in no way do I think that's dramatic.

If he recognized me, someone else could have, too, and not been so kind. Or the Russians could've followed me and found me. Or I could've lain there bleeding in the rain and caught pneumonia. Or a drunk passerby could've found me barely dressed and unconscious and continued what the Russians started.

No matter how I look at it, Sean saved me and I'm glad he was my first lover.

I close my eyes and let the memory of last night wash over me. He was thoughtful and careful about everything. And after he came inside me, he got a warm cloth and cleaned me up.

The blood was a little unsettling, but he didn't bat an eye. He cleaned us up, made sure I took my painkiller, and then snuggled in behind me.

Sean Quinn is a snuggler. Who would've guessed?

"Everything all right? Any regrets?" Sean's gravelly sleep voice is super sexy.

"Everything's grand." I wriggle back to increase the connection of him spooning me. His morning wood meets the crack of my ass, and I wonder if I can convince him to play house with me a few more times…and maybe a few after that. "Although I have ideas about how things could be even better."

I grind against him and groan as my hormones kick in and I'm warm and wet and wanton.

He chuckles, shifting his hips back to lessen the contact. "Created a sex kitten, have I?"

"Unleashed is probably more accurate. I've always had a healthy curiosity. Now I have an opportunity to bring my fantasies into reality."

He nuzzles into the back of my neck and kisses my shoulder. "Are we talking about your list of firsts? You'll have to show it to me, so I can make things happen."

I wish that were in the cards for us. But one amazing night of denial doesn't change our situation. "I was thinking about how different things could be if we were different people from different families."

JENN MADORE & CAROLINA MAC

He lets off a throaty grunt behind me. "Aye, I've thought about that, too."

"Really?"

He chuckles. "Piper, you're a beautiful woman, you understand and aren't afraid of or repulsed by my world, and the sexual chemistry between us is crazy. Of course, I've thought about it."

His words warm something deep inside me. "So, you'd keep seeing me, if you could?"

"Until you tired of my dark-hearted, broody ways and went looking for a hot, captain of the rugby team type."

I glance behind my shoulder and laugh. "That would never happen."

"No? How can you be so sure?"

"Because I'm a sucker for a broody bad boy and when you add in your whole alpha protector vibe, I'm a goner. Do you know how hot it is that you would literally kill to keep me safe?"

He laughs. "Other women might call that obsessive and unhinged."

"I'm not made like other girls, then."

"No. You're not. But as things stand, your father would burn down the city and Tag would lose his mind if they found out. Lives would literally be lost."

That's pretty much what I was thinking, too.

"But we have this moment." His hand is resting on my bare hip, and I shift it down to where I'm wet for him. "And unless you brought a nightstick to bed with you, it feels like you've got something I want."

He chuckles against my neck, the warmth of his breath making my nipples tighten. "Are you sure you're not sore?"

"I'm tender, not sore, and was raised never to waste an opportunity. So, if you wouldn't mind, Mr. Quinn, I'd like you to slide that lead pipe you've got back there inside me. I'm not sure once is enough to truly say I'm not a virgin anymore."

His hand bypasses my core and when he lifts my thigh to open my legs, he inches forward from behind. "I don't think there are degrees of virginity, my little sex kitten. But if it makes you feel better, I'm willing to put in the time until you're confident."

"Time is nice, but I'm more interested in you putting in your cock."

He chuckles. "Who am I to disappoint?"

He shifts behind me and grips my hip, careful not to touch my side. He slides through the heat he calls from me and presses forward. I am sore, but I won't waste any opportunity to feel him inside me.

In this position, he doesn't get as deep as he did last night, but I feel just as deliciously full.

"It's amazing how different it feels from behind."

"I wish you weren't hurt. I'd get you on your knees and really give it to you."

Images of that explode in my mind. Sean gripping my hips and slamming into me with both of us on our knees. Bracing my palms against the mattress, to take every thrust. The slap of flesh on flesh...

The muscles gripping him pulse in response, another rush of cream slicking his cock. "I want to try that."

"Not yet, kitten. There are so many ways I want to fuck you, but not with your ribs so sore."

"They are better every day." I close my eyes, my breath escaping as he brushes his fingers over my clit and through the moisture between my legs. "A couple more days and I'll be ready to take anything you give me."

He laughs. "Ribs can hurt for a month."

"I'm tougher than I look, and you have no idea how determined I am."

"I look forward to finding out."

His fingers rub over the sensitive bundle of nerves at my

core and my release builds. I arch against the slow and steady thrusts from behind and grind against his touch. "It feels so good when you touch me."

"Good. That's right where I want you to be."

Last night, I was nervous about how much it would hurt and how much I might bleed, but this is just nice. It's lazy and sexy and I can focus on how good it feels.

And wow, it feels good.

Sean is a powerful man, and he knows how to use his body. I'm quite content to lie here and be the recipient of all this attention.

"Fuck, you're tight."

"Is that good or bad?"

He grunts and shifts his hips for another luxurious in and out. "It's incredible. Your pussy is squeezing me so hard I'm losing my mind."

"Well, good. I want to leave a lasting memory."

"You do. And when you lose it, and your insides pulse and grip my cock, there's no way I'll be able to hold back. You feel way too good."

A guy like Sean is all about control.

I like that being inside me drives him past his control. He should be able to let loose once in a while. He's so serious and broody to the outside world, I love that I get to see him with his guard down.

Sean shifts his bottom arm beneath my head and bends it to cross my chest and pull me tighter against him. The added hold makes me feel even more pinned to him, and I love it.

"Open your legs more and throw your calf over my thigh. That'll give me more access to you."

I do as he asks and almost laugh at how exposed I feel. "Wow, if someone walked through the door right now, they'd get one hell of a show."

Sean grumbles in my ear. "I'd kill anyone who came in and saw you like this. Your pussy is mine, Piper. Mine to fuck. Mine to eat. Mine."

The possessive growl in his voice does something carnal to me, and my inner muscles throb and pulse around him.

"That's my good girl. You like being claimed by me? Do you want to be mine?"

I swallow, my orgasm building deep in my core. "Aye, I do."

His thrusts...

His fingers rubbing my clit...

His warm kisses along the column of my neck…

It's all too much and my body shatters.

I cry out his name with a rush of breath that tears from my chest. He is everywhere at once.

Touching me. Tasting me. Fucking me.

The waves of pleasure that pulse from within me steal my sanity. It's incredible. And even though I have little experience in this, I know that it's all Sean.

I don't even want to think about how he got so good at making a woman feel like this.

He follows me over the edge of bliss, and his hips lock behind me. With his bottom arm across my chest and his free arm gripping my hip, he pulls me against him with an almost crushing force.

I'll have bruises, for sure, but these marks I'll wear with pride.

"Fuck, you're addictive." His breath is ragged and has a sexy gravel to it.

"I'd say the same, but seeing as how your cock is still inside me, I might be unduly influenced."

He barks a laugh behind me. "Get used to it. I intend to have my cock in you for whatever time we have left to spend together."

I let off a contented sigh. "Let's hope it's long enough to check a few more things off my list."

"Count on it." He turns my head to look back at him and claims my mouth. "Now close your eyes. It's still sleep time."

Sean

I wake up next to Piper's beautiful warm body and we're both naked. Tag will kill me for this if he ever finds out. Our family has enough trouble keeping our business running smoothly without sparking a war with the McGuires.

Turning my head, I glance at her contented face and watch her sleep. She wanted to reclaim some control in her life and made a choice.

Was it more than that?

Did she want *me* or just to take her virginity off the table on her own terms?

It wasn't a hardship either way.

I slide to the edge of the bed, grab my boxers off the floor, and close the door behind me so Piper doesn't wake up. In the bathroom, I take a piss and hop in the tub to take a quick shower.

I'm wrapping a towel around my hips when my cell rings. #1 Brother comes up on my screen and I grab it off the vanity. "Hey, Tag. What's up?"

"I just got word our shipment arrived early. It's at the docks and will be unloaded later this afternoon."

"Okay, what do you need?"

"Well, with the McGuires gunning for us, I want to take every precaution. I need you and the Devils to oversee the unloading and escort the shipment to the factory."

"On it. I'll send a dozen of the boys there now and will join them shortly."

"Where are you? At the clubhouse?"

"No. Still at the safe house."

"Why do you sound funny?"

"No idea. I just got out of the shower."

"Late morning. Is babysitting making you lazy? You're not getting distracted, are you?"

I laugh. "Says the guy who's been sneaking home for afternoons in bed with his girlfriend."

"Caught on to that, did you?"

"Hard to miss. You've got a goofy 'just got laid' face you wear after a good workout. You've been wearing that face a lot lately, brother."

He chuckles. "I didn't know I had a tell."

"Fuck it. Happy looks good on you. Hey, did Laine have a chance to look at that contract, giving Piper to the Russians?"

"It's totally bogus. She's not sure what it'll mean to the Russians, but it won't hold water here. If Piper were younger or had consented or lived somewhere else, it could've gotten messy, but as it stands, it's a no-go."

"Good. I didn't think it would have any legs, but it's good to hear."

"Yeah. Mattie is seriously off his fucking rocker."

"There's nothing more dangerous than a desperate man, T. The other families have to see it, right? They must know he's losing his grip."

"I would love to say yes, but after the Campbells attacked me last week, I haven't got a fucking clue."

"Anything new on the aftermath of that?"

"Maybe. Andrew was going through the security tapes for the compound perimeter. A truck has been spotted across the road a few times and drew his notice. He's not sure, but he thinks someone's watching the house."

"That could be the Campbells or the McGuires."

"Assuming they aren't one and the same."

"You think they've made an alliance?"

"I'm not discounting it—especially after Laine and I were attacked."

Never known for minding his own, Gareth Campbell will be pissed that Laine shot one of his boys. It was totally justifiable as self-defense, but Old Man Campbell is a sewer rat. He's not big on facts.

"We've been so busy with the McGuires, we haven't properly addressed the overt act of aggression on you two. Maybe it's time for retribution."

"Yeah, I'm thinking so. If Campbell isn't with McGuire, it'll remind him of the hierarchy of power. If he is, it'll knock him down a peg."

In our line of work, payback is a fact of life...an inescapable facet of the business.

"I'm headed to the clubhouse now. I'll have Gallagher take a dozen boys out to remind Campbell of a few things and take Kieran and another group with me to set up protection at the docks."

"Sounds good."

"Can you send the twins over to stay with Piper?"

"Sure. How's she feeling?"

Better and better. "She's healing and getting stronger."

"I'm sorry having her on our side has taken over your life, but you were the one who dragged us into this McGuire mess."

"And if I hadn't, you wouldn't have found out about the Russians and Mattie brokering guns."

"Aye, that's true. I suppose Mam was right and everything happens as it's meant."

If that's true, I wonder what he'd think of me sleeping with the girl? He'd fucking hate it and pound the shit out of me. No question.

"All right. When the twins arrive, I'll head out."

"Good enough. I'll send them now and see you in a few hours."

The call ends and I frown at the closed bedroom door. Let's hope Piper has a good poker face and can keep our fucking around a secret. Otherwise, she won't be the only one sporting a shiner and bruised ribs.

CHAPTER TEN

Piper

*J*wake up alone in bed and the daylight coming in at an angle that tells me it's mid-morning at the earliest. Sleeping in has never been one of my strong suits, but I suppose a night of sex can do that to a girl.

Not that I have much to base that theory on.

Stretching, I reach my arm out, and my hand brushes a piece of paper. I grab the note on Sean's pillow and smile.

Morning, P,

Had to run to the clubhouse and then off to do some work for Tag. The twins are downstairs to keep you safe. I told them you need to heal and to let you sleep.

Looking forward to scratching more off your list.

Remember to keep private things private, take your pain pill, and eat something. You need your strength 😊

Back as soon as I can,

Mr. Quinn

I chuckle and read the note again. It doesn't say much, but it also says a lot. Folding Sean's thoughts into a small square, I tuck the note under my pillow and pull on the t-shirt of his I've been wearing as a nightie.

I'm alone upstairs when I poke my head out of the bedroom but hear the muffled timbre of male voices downstairs. I'm about to venture down in search of sustenance when I catch myself in the mirror.

Wow, is that really me?

Day three of the bruising isn't doing me any favors, and that's before the bedhead and looking like I was up all night giving away my V-card.

I step closer to the mirror. Will anyone be able to tell? Do I look any different?

Whether or not I look different, I certainly feel different. Last night I took my first steps to reclaiming my life. Up until now, I twisted myself into knots being who and what my mother wanted me to be, hoping she and my father would see my value.

Last night I chose me first.

I hold back the giggle trying to break free when I imagine my parents' faces when they find out I've been sexing with Sean Quinn.

Any Quinn would be bad, but Sean runs the MC and is the one who is directly responsible for ruining many of Da's plans lately. I've overheard how his motorcycle crew have intercepted shipments and burned down warehouses and have generally been a giant thorn in Da's side.

Yay, Sean.

With a smile glowing from within, I shower, brush my teeth and hair, and slide into the gray tracksuit for a third day. If my girlfriends could see me now, they wouldn't believe it.

I'm more of a designer jeans and cute blouse kinda lass, but here I am re-wearing one of Sean's t-shirts and a drab pair of oversized sweats for the third day in a row.

And I don't even care.

The only person I care to impress is the one who gave me these clothes. He's also the one who will be taking them off when he gets back from his errands for Tag.

With my hair still damp, I ease down the stairs. My girl parts are tender, but my descent is noticeably easier than it was yesterday.

Despite Sean's warning that I might not be up to some of the more aggressive sex positions he wants to show me, I'm determined not to let my ribs hold us back.

Maybe there are ways to heal things up faster.

I've heard castor oil wraps and heating pads can do amazing things. Would that help ribs?

"She's awake." Bryan raises his mug to me from where he's sitting, watching the window. "Good sleep?"

"Grand. I didn't sleep much at all the night before, so aside from waking up with a few nightmares, I slept like the dead and am moving better today."

"That's good to hear." Brendan sets his game controller down and turns off the console. Then he stands and gestures to the kitchen. "Come. Sean gave us strict instructions to make sure we feed you."

I laugh. "What does he think I've been doing for the past twenty years without him?"

Brendan shrugs. "He's always had a protective streak. When our Mam died, Tag had to help Da with work and Sean watched over us and Finny."

That doesn't surprise me at all. "Kind of ruins the whole Dublin Devil persona, doesn't it?"

Brendan laughs. "Oh, don't get me wrong. He's no pushover. He's just protective of those he deems worthy."

Something about that gives me a warm and fuzzy. Sean Quinn considers me worthy of his protection.

"Have a seat and I'll get you set up. What would you like? We weren't sure how long you'd be staying so we got a bit of everything."

"I'm not fussy. Do you have anything to make a sandwich? Or maybe some soup?"

"Soup and a sandwich, coming up."

"I said soup *or* a sandwich. I don't need both."

Brendan waves away my words. "Your body's been through a lot. You need to eat."

"You sound like your brother."

"I'll take that as a compliment." Brendan gets busy in the kitchen, and I go over to look into the top of the rice box. "How long does a phone need to sit in rice before it's dried out?"

"Generally, twenty-four to forty-eight hours. Why?"

I pull my sexy blue and silver phone out from the Minute Rice. "The Russians tossed it in a plant vase."

Bryan comes into the kitchen to join us and frowns. "Speaking of the two Bratva fuckers, can we just say how fucked up it was that your father did that to you? Sean told us not to bring it up, but fucking hell, tossing you in as part of an arms deal. That's fucking cold."

A knot tightens in the pit of my stomach, but I refuse to let it take hold. I stuff my phone back into the rice and leave the box on the counter. There's no one I want to speak to right now, anyway. "I appreciate that. Thanks."

Brendan twists around from where he's working at the counter to meet my gaze. "I'm sorry, Piper. But if it's any consolation, Laine looked at the contract and said that other than what it might mean to the Bratva, there's nothing to it. You're not tied to those bearded fuckers in any way."

I blink, not sure what to say about that.

Brendan must read something in my expression because he frowns. "What? You should be happy about that, shouldn't you?"

"I am. It's a relief to hear, but it's awkward that all of you know about it. How *do* you all know?"

Brendan sets a turkey sandwich stacked high with meat in

front of me and sets another one out for Bryan. "Well, without getting into specifics, we had a conversation with Vlad and Arkady last night."

"You did?"

Bryan nods and grabs three glasses from the cupboard. "Aye, we did. Tag made it clear to them that your father has no right to be making gun deals. Guns are our territory, and the McGuires importing would nullify our truce and create a direct power war."

I pick a slice of turkey free and eat it. "I never wanted that. So, will Tag fix it?"

Bryan swallows a large bite of his sandwich and shrugs. "He asked what the details of the deal were so he could find a solution."

"And what details did you find out, other than them getting me as a plaything?"

Brendan frowns. "Tag was hoping your father was only looking for a one-time shipment. If that were the case, he'd just buy the guns and be done with them."

"But that wasn't the case?"

"No. Apparently, your father was brokering an ongoing import of weapons through Galway and into Dublin. Now Tag has to figure out how to keep the Russians happy and not end up in bed with the Bratva."

"What was Mattie even thinking bringing the Russians into Dublin?" Bryan asks.

Brendan sets a hot pad down in the center of the table and then a steaming pot on top of that. "Russians are bad news. We don't want them anywhere near our citizens."

I take a bite of my sandwich. "That's the difference, though, right? My father doesn't care about Dublin or its citizens. He cares about McGuire power and money."

Brendan grabs a ladle and then starts dishing out bowls of

Campbell's chicken and rice soup. "It's only from a can, but it'll heal what ails you."

Bryan chuckles. "Chicken soup is for healing colds, not bones and bruises, dumbass."

Brendan shrugs. "Show me the studies where it says I'm wrong."

Bryan laughs. "Like you've ever read a study in your life. Now you're just showing off for Piper."

Brendan hands me a spoon and winks. "Is it working? I'm known to be pretty charming."

I laugh. "I thought Finn was the Dublin Charmer."

Bryan barks a laugh. "She's got you there, brother."

The three of us continue to share our lunch and I can't help wondering why I couldn't have been born into a mafia family like the Quinns instead of the McGuires. They actually seem to care about one another.

Wouldn't that have been novel?

Sean

When I arrive at the docks, I back my bike up to fall in line with Kieran's Road King Special and the other eight bikes beyond that. It's a sight that never gets old. There's nothing sexier than a row of Harleys and knowing that they belong to my MC and are ridden by my army.

Except maybe Piper shattering on my cock.

That was pretty fucking unforgettable.

And though I've got 'don't fall for a fucking McGuire' running on a constant mantra in my head, deep in my dark, selfish heart, I know it's too late.

I fell for her the moment I scooped her off the sidewalk, bloody and beaten. Because if that's what her family and her life did to her, she needs someone to watch out for her—to put her safety and happiness first.

My boots beat a heavy rhythm as I make my way over to where Kieran is overseeing the loading of the shipment into our trucks. He's standing far enough back to let the dock workers do their thing, but he's still got an open line of sight to everything being done.

Beside him, I pull a hand-rolled cigarette out of my pack. "Everything been quiet?"

Kieran gives me a quick nod. "The biggest drama was the seagulls swooping in and taking Frenchie's bagel right out of his fucking hand."

I look over to where the big black biker is scowling by the truck. "Did someone feed him? He's an asshole when he's hangry."

Kieran laughs. "Duke had a couple of granola bars in his tail bag, but I don't think they'll hold the big guy over for long."

I laugh. "It's a fucking soap opera some days."

"Just with more guns and leather."

"True story."

The forklift driver sets another pallet into the back of the truck and Frenchie uses the jack to move it deeper into the box.

"How much more do we have?"

Kieran checks the manifest he's holding. "Two more skids and we're gone."

"And who's at the warehouse?"

"Renzo and Deek are inside, and we've got two on the roof and four on the grounds."

Good. That's good.

Kieran and I shoot the shit as the dock workers finish the unloading and then Kieran heads over to give them each their thank you packages.

Supporting the local economy and treating Dubliners right is part of the Quinn business model. Well, that and making sure everyone knows what happens to them if they fuck us over.

My phone rings and I step away from Kieran talking with the workers and head back toward my bike. "Give me the good news."

Gallagher grunts at the other end of the line. "Do you think that actually works?"

"It was worth a shot. Are you saying you've got bad news?"

"Not exactly." There's a pause on the line as he takes a draw on his cigarette and then exhales. "The message has been sent to Campbell and his men that the Quinns are pissed."

"Good. And did anything come of that?"

"We found out that Campbell's not over Tag's woman killing one of his boys."

"Boo hoo. They were killing my brother."

"Just telling you what we found."

I take a long haul on my own smoke and exhale a cloud of sweet-smelling bliss. "Anything else?"

"I just got a call from Beau. The boys on patrol spotted Ryan McGuire, Billy Gravely, and a half-dozen McGuire boys crossing the Samuel Beckett Bridge twenty minutes ago."

"Coming to the north side in broad daylight?"

"Yep."

"Ballsy fuckers. Any idea where they're headed?"

"Nope. Docks. Clubhouse. Warehouse. Your guess is as good as mine."

"Thanks for letting me know. Anything else?"

"Do you need anything else to worry about?"

"Fuck no."

"Then you're good, because that's all I've got."

"Thanks, brother. Safe home." I end the call with Gallagher and stamp out my smoke.

Striding back over to where the truck is parked, I press my fingers under my tongue and let off a whistle. When the eyes of

JENN MADORE & CAROLINA MAC

my men are on me, I raise my arm and give the universal finger whirl that signals for them to wrap it up and get moving.

"What's up, boss?" Kieran asks.

"We've got McGuires on our side of the river, boys," I shout, loud enough so the boys within earshot will here. "Get the truck to the warehouse and phone ahead to Renzo and Deek to put them on alert."

"On it." Kieran jogs off to his bike, his cell at his ear.

"On your horse, Frenchie!" I gesture for him to get in the fucking truck and get it moving.

The rumble of the big diesel is reassuring, but then I turn and see two trucks baring down on us with men standing in the back, holding onto the headache rack.

Fucking hell. Striding across the concrete, I shout my orders. "Maxim, get the dockworkers out of sight. Drake, Micky, Tig, and Garret, get on your bikes and escort the truck. The rest of you are with me."

There's a moment of chaos as everyone runs to get it done, and I check the distance of the McGuire attack. There's barely time, but I pull my cell and send Tag a heads-up.

McGuire attack at dock.

With that, I pull my gun and get ready. "I'm told Ryan McGuire is with them, boys. You know the rules. We don't draw first blood on Mattie's family. Anyone else is fair game."

I've barely got the words out, and the trucks hit the brakes and find cover behind a freight container.

Then all hell breaks loose.

The good news is, they seem to be gunning for a fight and aren't out to take down our shipment. The bad news is, I don't want to go back to the safe house and tell Piper that Billy Gravely and her brother are on the north side.

"Are you lost, Ryan?" I shout, so he knows where to come if he's after a Quinn. "Because you're out of your territory."

Niall, Declan, and Ryan were born from Mattie's first

marriage and bear little to no resemblance to Piper. Where she has the straight ebony hair, icy blue eyes, and soft features of her mother, they have dirty blond hair, angled features, and a chip on their shoulders from Mattie loving their mother first and most.

Billy Gravely, on the other hand, is dangerous. That asshole is tough as the side of a boot, and as mean as the devil himself.

As Ryan storms toward me, I see that his hands are empty, so I holster my gun and get ready for the fistfight that's coming. "What's so important that you're willing to risk a clan war by coming here today, Ryan?"

"You've got my sister, you twisted fucks." Ryan comes in, fists flying and it's on. "You crossed a line, Sean."

I laugh and bury my knuckles into his ribs. "It wasn't me who crossed the fucking line. Your psycho father sold Piper's virginity to those Bratva fucks, and they didn't take it well that she didn't want to be their plaything. They beat her to within an inch of her life."

"That's family business. Give her back."

"You're not even surprised." I'm so stunned that he knew and doesn't care about the arrangement that I miss the left hook that catches me in the jaw.

Fucking hell.

"You knew about the approved rape party your father set up and did nothing to help her?" Rage ignites in every cell of my body at once and I fight not to kill him. "Did you know about the marriage, too?"

We exchange another few wild punches and he spits blood at me. "Alliances are made all the time."

"How can you not care that Piper was traded like a piece of chattel? She's your fucking sister."

"Yeah, and the bitch who fucked our family over. I need her back. There's a chance we can still fix things."

I see red. Fix things? They still plan on giving her to the

Russians? Only now they'll be out for revenge and to teach her a lesson.

Ryan is her family and should be looking out for her. Instead, he's here to find Piper and take her back to toss her to the Russians.

My fist smashes into Ryan's face over and over, and I don't even register the blood. My breath is heaving in and out of my chest and my arm feels like it might fall off.

The McGuires are all fucking nuts.

Possessed by the fury of seeing justice done for Piper, I lose track of the fight around me. I'm coldcocked from the side, and I go down hard.

Fuck, it's Billy.

The world spins around me. I scramble to get to my feet but end up back on the concrete dock. I swipe at the blood in my eyes, my hair thick and wet.

There's a rush of heavy boots to ground and then the grunt of a man getting tackled. Two of my boys have come to my aid and take Billy to ground.

Gunshots ring out on my left.

That's the signal to get on our bikes and get gone. We may have a strong hand in the policing force in Dublin, but there are a lot of clean cops and true believers that will throw our asses in the can without a second thought.

I want to get going, but Billy rung my bell so badly I can't stand up.

"We know you have her." Ryan grabs me by the front of my leather vest. "You don't think Siobhan gave us a list of your safe houses? We've got men searching for her now."

I fight his hold, but I'm seeing double. "Go near her and I don't give a fuck. It'll be open season on McGuires."

"Too late. It's already open season on Quinns." Ryan's words ring in my head as his blade sinks deep into my side.

I curse as he twists the blade, and then it stops with the crack of a gunshot.

Ryan McGuire's dead weight lands on top of me, and then more gun shots. I hear Billy Gravely call for everyone to get back to the trucks and there's a mad scramble.

A moment later, Tag and Aiden are above me and rolling Ryan's weight off to the side.

Tag's gaze falls to where the hilt of Ryan's knife is sticking out of my side. "Fuck. He stuck you good, brother."

"Get it out." I flail at my side with sloppy hands.

"No. Leave it the fuck in," Tag snaps. "If he hit anything vital, you'll bleed out before Kelvin can patch you up. Aiden, help me get him in the truck. We need to get back to the compound."

"No! Siobhan gave them our safe houses. We need to get Piper."

"Un-fucking-believable." Tag grunts as he, Aiden, and a couple of my guys hurry to get me in the SUV. "Let them have her. If protecting her is what gets you killed, let the McGuires deal with their own family dysfunction."

I'm about to lose consciousness, but I can't...not until Piper is safe. "Call the twins. Bring her to the compound."

"Like fuck. I'm not bringing her to our home."

I squirm in their hold and there's a round of shouting as they try not to drop me. I don't fucking care.

"Either you bring her, or I'll get her. If our safe houses are compromised, she won't be safe anywhere else."

Tag has his shirt off and is pressing it against my side. "You stubborn fucker. You're willing to die over this?"

"It's the right thing. No one has her six."

Tag curses. "Fine. I'll call the twins. Now stop squirming before you bleed out all over the back of my fucking truck."

They wrangle me into the oversized hatch of the SUV and lay me down.

"I'll do my best."

CHAPTER ELEVEN

Piper

The twins and I have a rather uneventful lunch and are cleaning up the kitchen when Brendan's phone rings. "Hey, Tag. What's up, brother?"

He tosses the dishcloth on the counter and shifts to look out the kitchen window. "No, nothing. Why?"

There's another long pause, and his easy smile morphs into a furious scowl. "How bad is he? Fuck. Okay, got it. We're on our way."

He hangs up the phone and meets Bryan's gaze. "Start the car. We're bugging out. Piper, grab what you need. We're blown. McGuires are on the north side. Gravely's coming."

"*What?!*" My heart races as I grab my pills, the box of Minute Rice, and my purse off the counter.

Brendan flashes me the funniest expression ever. "Really? I tell you the walls are closing in and the rice is what you choose in an emergency? You're an odd duck."

There's no time to respond because in the next instant, Bryan honks the horn of the car outside and Brendan escorts me through the safe house, out the side door, and practically wraps his bulk around me like a fire blanket until we're in the back seat.

"Go. Go. Go."

Bryan hits the gas, and we pull out. He takes the turn onto the street so fast I'm flung to the side and drop the box of rice.

Brendan catches me, sits me back up, and reaches over my shoulder to strap me in.

"Did you just spill something in my car?" Bryan's brows tighten in the rearview mirror.

"Nope. Nothing to see here," Brendan lies.

There's a mountain of white instant grain on the floorboard and a snowstorm of the stuff sticking into the black carpets.

Brendan makes a face and shakes his head. "Straight to the compound."

"You asked how bad 'he' is. Who's down?"

"Sean took a blade to the belly. They're racing him to Kelvin's clinic."

"Fuck. It must be bad if they're not going to deal with it back home."

My heart was racing about Billy Gravely coming to get me, but it shudders and misses a beat at the mention of Sean being stabbed."

"We need to go to the clinic. He's hurt."

Brendan shakes his head. "No. Tag was clear. You're to be taken to the family compound. Sean wouldn't agree to treatment until he promised we'd take you there."

What? Sean's been stabbed and, by the sound of it, seriously wounded and he's fighting with his brother to get me to safety? My resolve to not fall for Sean Quinn is quickly fading to dust.

Remember to keep private things private.

Sean's words echo in my mind, and I make a mental note to calm myself and keep my feelings more well-guarded. "Who stabbed him?"

JENN MADORE & CAROLINA MAC

"He didn't say." Brendan has his gun in his hand and is scanning the streets as houses and shops blur past.

"What *did* he say?" I hold up my hands, realizing how harshly that came out. "Sorry."

Brendan pats my knee. "It's fine. We're all on edge."

"We picked up a tail." Bryan's gaze in the rearview mirror narrows. "Blue pickup. Four cars back."

"Piper, lay down and face the back of the seat." Brendan slides to the front of the seat and unbuckles my belt. He makes room for me to lay down and I do as he says as quickly as my sore ribs will allow.

My head's spinning. "This is all my fault."

"We don't know that, sweetheart. No need to borrow trouble when we've got enough as it is."

He's just being nice. I know, to the marrow of my bones, that the attack on Sean and them saying the McGuires are on this side of the river are related.

"We gotta lose this asshole before I head to the compound," Bryan says.

The hum of Brendan putting down the window precedes him readjusting his bulky frame in the back seat. "Sorry, Piper. I don't mean to squash you."

"You're fine. I'm fine."

"Good girl. You're doing great. Just give us another five minutes and all will be well."

Five minutes? That seems like forever.

"Bren, I'm going to take us into those warehouses where Jimmy bought his kitchen equipment. It's remote, and the layout is fucked up. We can either lose them or you can get a couple of shots off without causing a huge commotion."

"Sounds like a plan, little brother."

Bryan snorts. "Two fucking minutes."

"That still makes me older."

Bryan makes a hard right turn and laughs. "You likely shoved me to the side so you could get out first."

"Are you saying a guy can't be assertive in the womb?"

I close my eyes. How can they joke when Sean's hurt and we're being chased through the Dublin Streets? The Quinns are a different breed of men, that's for sure.

"All right," Bryan says. "One more turn and we'll be there. You ready?"

"I was fucking born ready."

~

Sean

The ride to Kelvin's clinic is a shit show, and every bump seems to tear the hole in my side a little wider. Or, at least, that's how it feels.

Tag has the split seat down and is lying half in the back seat and half in the trunk. He's got one hand holding his fancy-ass designer shirt against my wound, and the other holding his phone against his ear. "We're coming in hot, Kelvin. Clear a path."

Oh, this is going to piss off the good doc.

Kelvin has a legit surgical practice and hates it when we interfere with the optics of him being just another Dublin doctor.

He's going to bill Tag a small fortune for showing up in his clinic.

The SUV makes a jerky stop, and I curse. "Fucking hell, Aiden. Easy on the fucking pedals."

But no one is listening to me.

Aiden is out of the front and opening the back in a split second. It's the first time I've seen him since the clusterfuck of him losing his head over Siobhan and killing Piper's brother, Declan.

A couple of weeks ago, I didn't understand how a woman could make him so volatile and reckless.

Now, knowing that Piper's in trouble, I get it.

Aiden reaches in to put pressure on my side and meets Tag's gaze. "I've got him, T. Go get the doc. A gurney probably wouldn't hurt either."

I must've passed out for a bit because the next thing I know, I'm lying on a cold, steel table and I'm being blinded by overhead lights.

"Shit, he's waking up. Sean, I need you to stay still. I've got my fingers in your side and I'm currently plugging a hole. Don't move. Nancy, give him another dose of anesthesia and send him back to dreamland."

I recognize Kelvin's voice, although his tone is more agitated than usual.

"Nancy's got the mask over your face. Deep breaths."

I take a couple of deep breaths and the world melts away.

CHAPTER TWELVE

Piper

*W*e arrive alive at what the twins called the compound and once Bryan parks the car, Brendan gets out and I have the space to roll away from where I've had my face plastered to the back seat for the last ten minutes.

"Easy, Piper." Brendan jogs around to the other side of the car and helps me get out. "Sorry about the rough ride. It sounds like your family's brute squad is out for blood today."

It's crazy to see my brothers and Da's men through the eyes of the Quinn family.

They think we're thugs bent on violence.

Isn't that normal? Isn't that what all crime families are like?

When I'm out of the car, Brendan takes a step back and I blink. We're parked under a covered porch in front of a beautiful stone castle on a giant piece of rolling green land. "Wow. Where are we?"

"This is our house." Bryan gestures for us to head toward the door. "Or, as we call it, the compound."

I chuckle and follow him, Brendan walking behind me as we go. Surely that's a coincidence and not them keeping me safe at their own home, right?

We step inside a grand entrance and I'm more confused than ever. "Why am I here?"

Brendan shrugs. "Tag said to bring you here, so here you are."

We're barely in the door when a woman with long, mahogany hair comes rushing down the stairs. "Thank goodness you're here. Did you hear about Sean?"

The panic in her expression makes my stomach flip. It also makes me wonder if anyone at my house looked this worried when they heard about me getting beaten and being missing.

The little girl in me hopes so, but I doubt it.

"Madelaine, this is Piper McGuire, youngest of the McGuire clan." Bryan gestures between the woman and me. "Piper, this is Madelaine, Tag's better half."

"By a long margin," Brendan adds.

Madelaine playfully smacks Brendan's arm. "I go by Laine, and you can ignore these two and their smart mouths. They adore their brother almost as much as I do. Come in. From what I've heard, you've had a rough three days."

Is that all it's been? Man, it feels like forever.

Laine's gaze falls to the box tucked in my arm and a smile plays at the corners of her mouth. She says nothing, so I figure I'll offer the explanation before the entire family thinks I have a strange fixation on rice.

Reaching in, I pull out my phone and show her. "It got dunked by my attackers and Sean said a couple of days in rice might dry it out."

"Ah, well, it'll likely also be dead. If you give it to Bryan, he can take it to the office and find you a charger."

The idea of giving them my phone—my only link to my

family—makes me uneasy, but I'm not even sure I would call them if I could.

Technically, I'm sure I could borrow a phone or use a landline if I truly wanted to speak to anyone.

I'm not sure I do.

"Or not." Laine raises her palm to Bryan who has his hand out waiting for me to hand over the rice and the phone. "You can keep it, but I can tell you right now, Tag won't be happy if you have it. He's protective of his family and won't like you having the opportunity to betray our kindness."

I straighten and hand Bryan both. "I would never do that. When I go home—*if* I go home—it won't be a secret or a strategic maneuver. It'll be because I have a plan and want to see my father's face when I tell him what I think about him and what he did to me."

Laine frowns. "I'm so sorry. The entire ordeal must've been devastating for you."

Words could never express how much, so I say nothing. I don't want to cry in front of Sean's family. They've been good to me—better than I imagined possible—but they're still strangers.

"I hate to be rude, but I'm not feeling up to much more. Is there somewhere I can lie down?"

Laine nods. "Of course. Cora got one of the guest rooms ready for you. Come. I'll get you settled."

I follow Laine upstairs, each step making it harder to lift my feet. Whether it's my injuries, the adrenaline let-down after the car chase, or worrying about Sean, all the life has drained out of me.

We get to the top of the steps and take a right. After passing a couple of bedrooms, Laine stops at an open door and gestures for me to go in first. "This is you. You have your own bathroom and there's a little terrace behind those sheers that overlook the pond."

"All I care about is that there's a bed."

Laine nods. "I remember that feeling all too well."

I'm not sure what she means by that, but I don't have the energy to ask. My feet are already shuffling toward the grand, four-poster, and I've never seen anything more inviting. "If you get any news about Sean, will you let me know? He's been so good to me. I hate the idea that he's hurt because of my family."

Laine steps toward the hall and reaches for the handle to close the door. "I promise. Now, get some rest. You're safe here, Piper. We've got you."

When the door clicks shut, I half-expect to hear a lock shifting into place, but the house is quiet.

So quiet, I don't even have time to pull a blanket over me before I'm out cold.

It must be hours later when Laine comes to wake me because it's dark out and my stomach is growling like a bear coming out of hibernation.

"Did you sleep well?" she asks.

"Too well. My father would smack me for letting my guard down and leaving myself vulnerable while behind enemy lines."

Laine shakes her head. "But you're not behind enemy lines, Piper. No one here faults you for the actions of your family. None of us controls the family we're born into. It's the luck of the draw."

I don't want to think about why fate gave me to people like Matthew and Samantha McGuire. It certainly wasn't to be loved. It's crazy but I've learned more about love and acceptance in the past few days than I did the twenty years of living with my family.

My stomach gives off a long cry for sustenance, and Laine chuckles. "How about we get you a quick sandwich before the boys get here? It'll take them a few minutes to get Sean upstairs and settled, anyway."

"Get him settled? So he's good?"

"The doc said surgery went well, and that the blade didn't perforate any vital organs. If he takes it easy for a few days and doesn't pull the stitches, he'll be back on his bike and tearing up the streets before we know it."

I press a hand against the lump in my throat and my eyes well up with tears. Staring up at the ceiling above the bed, I fight to rein in my emotions. "I'm so relieved. Brendan said Billy and his crew were here looking for me. If Sean died because of me, I would never survive it."

"Well, he's expected to make a full recovery, so you can let yourself off the hook."

I don't think I can, but I'm still relieved.

Sitting up, I give my side a moment to protest me moving around. Once the aches and pains ease, I slide off the bed and join Laine by the door.

It takes longer than I thought before Brendan comes to the kitchen to tell us Sean is settled. So long, in fact, that I've not only eaten my sandwich, but also two pieces of the most incredible raspberry mousse chocolate cake.

"I think I might explode." I pat my belly as Laine and I head up the stairs.

Laine laughs. "When I first arrived here last month, I had the same problem. Cora's food is beyond addictive."

"Last month? Oh, I thought...you seem so at home here. I thought you and Tag might've been together for a long while."

"Nope. It's just very easy to feel at home here. The Quinn boys are special. They accepted me into their home and I'm hoping that your time here will give you a different perspective than one you might've been raised with being isolated by your family."

It already has.

We arrive at a bedroom in the same wing as my room and my heart stops beating when I see Sean lying in the bed, bandaged and pale, with Tag and his brothers hovering over him.

"Sean, what happened?" Without meaning to, I rush forward, my eyes glassing up so badly I can't see Sean behind the wall of tears.

He raises his hand as I rush over to sit on the side of the bed. "I'm okay."

"I'm so sorry. This is because of me, isn't it? You got hurt because you helped me."

"No," Sean says.

"Yes," Tag snaps.

Sean gives his older brother a dirty look and Tag shrugs. "It's the fucking truth. If you hadn't taken home yet another wounded stray, Ryan and Gravely wouldn't have come gunning for us on the north side."

"She's not a wounded stray." The scowl Sean throws at his brother murderous. "Piper is an innocent woman who was hurt by mafia business as much as or more than a hundred citizens we've protected. Your only hang up is her last name, but that doesn't change the situation."

"Doesn't it?"

"No. It doesn't. And if that's the way you're planning on treating her, we'll fucking leave right now." Sean flips the sheets back and starts to get out of the bed.

All of his brothers curse and jump forward at once.

"Simmer down, killer." Brendan leans in and prevents Sean from getting up. "No one's going anywhere."

Finn nods at the end of the bed. "Doc Kelvin said no movement today, Sean. He wants you lying perfectly still until the stitches heal."

I stare at the wide swath of white gauze bound around his middle and wonder how bad the damage is. Usually, staring at his chest is hot and sexy because of all the ink. That's not the case now. "I'm so sorry."

Sean waves a weak hand in the air. "It's nothing to worry about and you have nothing to apologize for."

Tag frowns and takes off the long-sleeved shirt he's wearing. His arms and torso are stained with blood, and Laine gasps. "Dammit, Tag. You said you weren't hurt."

"I'm not. This is his blood. I used my shirt to pack the wound and because the blade was stuck into his side hilt-deep, we had to leave it there until we got him to the clinic. He's playing it off as nothing, but if I hadn't gotten there when I did, Sean would be the one dead."

The image of a knife sticking into his side to the hilt is sickening. That's really deep. I'm trying to push the visual of that out of my mind when Tag's words register completely. "The one dead? Did Billy Gravely do this? Is Billy dead?"

My mind spins with what that might mean for me and for my brothers. Da makes the calls, but Billy is the one who executes the horrors.

If Billy's dead, I would be safer, but my brothers wouldn't be.

It takes a moment for me to realize that everyone in the room has gone quiet and all eyes are on me. "What? Why are all of you staring at me?"

Sean squeezes my hand again and offers me a sad smile. "Do you remember when I told you we have a protection order out on all McGuires…that everyone in our organization knows not to draw first blood on your family?"

I swallow, but my mouth remains dry. "Of course. It blows my mind. My father would never give you guys the same consideration."

"No, he wouldn't," Tag snaps.

Sean flashes his brother a look, and my anxiety ratchets up a couple of notches. "Sean? Tell me what happened, please. All of it. The truth."

He nods. "We had business at the docks, and I got word that McGuires had crossed to the north side of the river and were incoming. Two trucks arrived moments later, and it was an all-out battle."

"Was it my fault? Did they come at you and your men because of me?"

"It's not your fault. Your father has been breaking the truce agreements more and more over the past months. But yes, Ryan was leading the charge, shouting about me needing to give you back so they could fix your mess."

"Fix my mess? Ryan thinks me fighting off pervy Russians and running for my life is me messing up? I really hoped my brothers would be on my side."

"I'm sorry, P. That's what he said."

"Okay, then what?"

"Then the docks exploded into a battlefield. Ryan was gunning for me, so I holstered my weapon. We went at it fist to fist and I was besting him."

Brendan grunts. "Of course you were."

"Gravely saw that Ryan had lost the battle, and so he clocked me on the back of the head and took me down." Sean turns to show me the back of his head and the blood matted into his hair.

I reach up and touch the swelling. "That's one hell of an egg."

"Aye. It hurts as much as my side does."

"So, Ryan was down, and Billy hit you. Then was it Billy who stabbed you?"

"No. My guys saw Gravely hit me and two of them rushed to help. I was dizzy and couldn't see…that's when Ryan tackled me and stuck me with his blade."

I'm following the story, and see the finish line coming. Even though I think I know what's coming next, I need to hear him say it. "You killed Ryan?"

"No, I did." Tag's admission hits me hard, but there's not one ounce of remorse in his gaze. "Our truce only goes so far. When I got there, Ryan had Sean down and was about to finish him. I stepped in and took the shot."

The news hits me like a physical blow to the stomach. I can't breathe. Another one of my brothers is dead at the hands of the Quinns.

Sean squeezes my hand again. "I'm sorry, Piper. Your brother is dead. It was him or me."

I pull my hand free and cross my arms. A crushing weight of guilt and disloyalty presses at me from all directions. I convinced myself that Sean and his brothers were a different kind of crime family.

But when it comes down to it, they're still the enemy.

I stand, unable to meet Sean's gaze. "If you'll all excuse me. I'd like to go lie down."

CHAPTER THIRTEEN

Sean

*P*iper's going to bolt. I see it in her eyes the moment Tag tells her he killed her brother. She pulls her hand out of mine and can't get away from us fast enough.

If I could manage it, I would chase her down the hall, but I won't be going anywhere for a few hours…maybe a few days.

I fucking hate being laid up, but with all the blood I lost and the crack to the head, I won't get anywhere. And me face-planting in the hallway won't improve my ugly mug any.

So, I do the only thing I can think of. I send Laine a pleading glance. "Can you please make sure she is okay?"

Her gaze is sharp, and I worry she sees too much, but I'm in no condition to front that I don't care about Piper. Of course I care about her—I rescued her and have spent the better part of three days with her.

Tag walks Laine to the door, whispers something to her, and then closes the door before coming back.

"What did you tell her?" I don't like the look he's pegging me with, and my instincts are screaming at me that I won't like what he says, either.

"I told her not to get too close to Piper. She's upset and Laine's pregnant."

I meet his stony stare with my own. "You think Piper will attack Laine? You're taking paranoia to a whole new level there, brother."

Tag shrugs. "Whether or not you acknowledge it, you brought someone into our home who is not only an unknown danger, but who also has a mafia family hunting for her."

"Well, that sounds familiar. Wasn't Aiden spewing those exact words at you when you brought Laine here? You knew her *one* day when you brought her home. And she had not only a Chicago crime family searching for her but a psychotic husband."

Tag's gaze narrows. "You'd be wise to leave Laine out of this."

"You were the one who brought her into it."

It doesn't escape my attention that Finn, Brendan, and Bryan have grown unnaturally quiet. *Whatever.* Tag may think Laine is the center of the universe, but her coming here was messy, too.

Still, they got through it, and it all worked out.

"At least we've known Piper her entire life and know what we're dealing with, right? There are no surprises, so we can plan for the fallout."

Tag frowns. "You say that like it's an advantage. Aye, we know her, but we also know how bad it will be if Gravely and an army of men come take her from us. Whether or not you want to admit it, her being here endangers Laine, our baby, as well as Cora and Connor."

I feel bad about that. Especially since Connor is still in a cast with a broken leg after being attacked by Laine's dead husband.

"Give me one night to rest and regain my strength. Tomorrow, I'll find a spot and move her somewhere you find more suitable."

Tag lets off a long sigh. "Fine. Tomorrow works."

When Tag turns to leave, I feel the anger and tension between us, and it doesn't sit well. "I'm really not trying to jam up the family, T. She was terrified to go back, and with Gravely closing in, I wanted her safe until she could make her own choices."

Tag dips his chin. "Until tomorrow, then."

Piper

Tears stream down my cheeks and drip to leave damp spots on the t-shirt I've been wearing for days now. It's Sean's, and the black fabric hangs to my mid-thighs.

When he first gave it to me to wear, it was gallant and the swoony girl in me softened to the man who was kind to me when no one else was.

And while I don't regret a moment I've spent with him, hiding from my family changes nothing. In truth, it's shifted the focus of my father and his men and got my brother killed.

The loss of Ryan so soon after Declan compounds the hollow ache in my heart. We weren't that close—given that there were almost twelve years between Declan and me and more than ten between Ryan and me.

By the time I was old enough to understand that I had six brothers, Niall, Declan, and Ryan, had already moved out to a flat of their own and were busy learning the family business.

Their mother was Aimee, Da's first wife, and when she died, the boys were only toddlers. From what people say, Da loved her with all his heart and after her death, he was never the same.

He married my mother a couple of years later and while it's never smart to judge the relationships of others, I'd say they have always been a smart match, but not a love match.

They are partners. They are aligned in focus. And they each do their part to keep the family strong.

It's not the kind of marriage I want.

I want passion, kindness, and for my children to know they are cherished for who they are—regardless of whether they are a boy or a girl.

Because in our household, the boys mattered. Period. End of story. I was always left behind and dismissed as being too young, naïve, or delicate to understand the cruel realities of our lives.

Niall, Declan, and Ryan were more like Da's favorite enforcers that came around the house for holidays. They escorted me to school at times. They intimidated boys who stopped to talk to me. But they never treated me like family.

Still, Ryan was my brother, and my mother loved him as if he was her biological son. She must know by now that he's dead and will be grieving.

It hurts my heart to know that while she grieves Declan and Ryan, she's likely also worried and hurting that I'm missing.

Does she know how badly Vladimir and Arkady hurt me? Would she ever have let Da promise me to them if she'd known the way they would treat me?

There's a part of me that is desperate to believe she wouldn't. That if she understood what it meant to be handed over to the Bratva as their party favor, she would've fought my father's plan tooth and nail.

And she would've won, too.

Da rarely goes against my mother's wishes.

Happy wife, happy life, right?

"Hey, are you all right?" Laine steps into the room with a box of tissues in her hand.

"Sorry. I can't believe everything has gone so wrong. Sean has been kind to me, and I returned that kindness by getting him stabbed and my brother killed."

Laine comes deeper into the room and sits on the edge of the bed beside me. "The boys don't share everything with me, but I've got a pretty good idea of what the past three days have looked like for you. One thing I know for sure is that nothing that happened is your fault."

"How can you say that? If Sean wasn't hiding me, Ryan and Billy wouldn't have come at him and been out for blood. Sean was attacked because of me."

Laine twists and slides her leg onto the bed to sit sideways, facing me. "This is 100% your father's fault, Piper. He made a horrifying deal with the Russians. He sent you into a dangerous situation unprepared. He made it impossible for you to feel safe in your own family territory."

"But maybe if I—"

"No, sweetie. Don't do that." Laine holds out the box of tissues and leans closer to meet my watery gaze. "Don't make the decisions of angry men your fault."

"But if I—"

She shakes her head. "Do you know I worked as a criminal defense attorney in the US until I came here a few weeks ago?"

I pull several tissues free of the box and blow my nose. "No. Sean's been very private about all of you."

"Well, I did. Since I graduated from law school, I have spent years defending criminals. I know what I'm talking about when I say they make their own decisions and are responsible for their own actions. Yes, you fled your father's territory, but he could've done a dozen other things than have your brother hunt you down and attack Sean. That was a brute response to a situation, and it reflects what kind of person he is—not you."

I dry my tears and wad up the tissues in my hand. "But I can't stay here and hide. Tag's not wrong to want me out of your family home. Me being here puts all of you in danger."

She pats my thigh. "All the Quinn boys have an alpha protector streak in them. Tag is worried and protecting his family, but that doesn't make Sean wrong because he's worried and wants to protect you."

"But he shouldn't have to protect me. I want to protect myself. I've told my father for years that I'm a McGuire and I can take care of myself. Then, the first time he gives me a job to do, I ruin all his plans."

Laine scowls. "You can't seriously be beating yourself up over the Bratva thing. Piper, that was disgusting."

"I know. Trust me, I know, but like you said, people are responsible for their actions. When cornered by those Russians, I chose to fight them, and then I ran to Quinn territory to hide for days. Maybe there were other ways to handle it. Maybe I should've stood up to them or confronted my father."

Laine sighs. "Given the situation, I don't think you had any choice. I've seen the video Sean has of what was done to you. It shows how strong and smart you are that you got away from them. There's nothing wrong with surviving to fight another day."

I look around the room, wondering what it would've been like to grow up in a family home like this. To have brothers who loved me and would kill to protect me instead of leaving me to a bunch of animals.

"I need to go home. I need to be there for Ryan's funeral and to look my father in the eyes and tell him that what he did was unforgiveable."

Laine dips her chin in a slow nod. "I understand where you're coming from—and I applaud your conviction—but why don't you give it a day or two? You're still recovering from your injuries and Sean just got home. If you leave, there's no way he'll lie in that bed and heal. It seems to me that you both need a day or two to heal wounds and regain your footing."

What she's saying makes sense—and not just because I'm terrified to face my family. Each day that passes, I feel stronger and more prepared to take on the next battle.

JENN MADORE & CAROLINA MAC

I envision myself going home to face my father. As long as he doesn't turn me over to Billy Gravely, I think I'd be all right. He won't add to my mother's grief. I could explain what happened, comfort my mother, and then, when he tells me I'm a disappointment and not fit to call myself a McGuire, I'll pack my things and leave.

It's not a great plan, but it's something.

I meet Laine's deep chestnut gaze and nod. "All right. I'll stay another day or two. Mam will have O'Reagan's handle the funeral, so once I find out about Ryan's service, I'll know when I need to go. Still, I got the feeling Tag wants me out of this house ASAP."

Laine pats my leg and gives me a warm smile. "You let me worry about Tag. A couple of days will give Sean time to recover and you a chance to get back on your feet. I think that's a wise decision."

I sigh. "That makes one of us."

Laine chuckles. "Come with me. If you're staying, you need something better to wear. No offense, girlfriend, but it looks like Sean dressed you out of a lost and found bin."

I look down at the gray sweatpants and Sean's t-shirt and laugh. "Yeah, this actually is pretty awful. Something to wear would be great."

CHAPTER FOURTEEN

Piper

I wake to the sound of car doors slamming shut below my window, and it takes a moment to remember where I am and why. Waking up in three different bedrooms in four days is disorienting.

Without my phone, there's no way to know what time it is, but by the angle and color of the light shining through the window, it's mid to late morning.

I'm not usually such a sleeper. Healing really takes it out of me.

Flipping back the covers, I visit the bathroom for a quick refresh, and then I'm padding down the hall.

I meet Doc Kelvin coming out of Sean's room. He closes the door behind him and gestures for me to walk with him down the hall. "I gave him something for the pain, but he'll need food in his belly, or the medication will make him sick. Can I leave that with you?"

"Aye, I'll make sure he eats. Is there anything in particular he should have?"

We descend the stairs together, and Kelvin stops at the bottom. "It might be good to stay away from fried foods for the morning, but other than that, whatever you can get him to eat is fine."

The two of us part when he heads to the front entrance, and I strike off to get food for Sean.

I do my best to backtrack the path I took with Laine to the kitchen yesterday, but Quinn Castle is big and has a maze of rooms and corridors. Between the main house and the two wings on opposite ends, it takes a bit of exploring and a couple of turnarounds, but I end up finding my way.

In the kitchen, I find a silver-haired woman wearing the traditional uniform of house staff. She's shuffling around behind a wide, marble island, taking the stainless-steel lids off serving platters.

She must sense my presence because she looks up and smiles. "Good morning. You must be Piper. I'm Cora. You missed the sit-down for breakfast, I'm afraid, but make yourself a plate and I'll heat it for you."

"Thank you. I'm actually here to make a plate for Sean. The doctor asked that I get him to eat, so his medication doesn't make him sick."

Cora grabs two clean plates from a stack by the sink and holds one out to me. "Perfect, then I'll make a plate with all Sean's favorites, and you make one for yourself."

That works for me.

Cora gestures to the serving platters, and I make my selections while she hums a cheerful tune and fills a plate for Sean. She skips over some dishes and scoops twice from others, being selective of what she chooses.

"How long have you been cooking for the Quinn family, Cora?"

"Och, going on thirty-five years now. Cormack hired me when he first got married."

"So, you've watched the boys grow up."

"Aye, I have at that. Been one of life's greatest joys for me and my man, Connor. We couldn't have kids of our own, so caring for these five has been good for our souls."

I finish my breakfast selections and hand her my plate to warm with Sean's. My brothers and I had a dozen different governesses and housekeepers over our lifetimes. None of them stayed long. I always figured they couldn't take my brothers misbehaving, but now I'm wondering if it was more about working for my parents.

Perspectives change as we get older and wiser.

"Good morning, ladies." Laine joins us, carrying a tea tray and a plate with a chocolate-covered croissant and a bowl of cut fruit.

"Och, lass, you must eat," Cora says.

Laine shrugs. "The peppermint tea is doing its job. I'll be able to keep things down in a few hours."

"Are you pregnant?"

My question seems to catch them off-guard, but Laine waves away Cora's concerned expression. "Barely. It's too soon to make plans or talk about it."

Cora scoffs. "Quinn babies are strong and determined. This babe will grow to run the halls and be a terror to us all, just like his Da and his uncles. You'll see."

Laine grins. "From your lips, Cora."

When a timer goes off, Cora sets both plates onto the tray Laine returned. Once she covers each of them and adds a couple of cloth napkins wrapped around cutlery, coffee, and two glasses of juice, she gives me the go-ahead. "There now. That should fill you both up."

"Is that for you and Sean?" Laine asks.

"Aye, Doc Kelvin asked that I get him something to eat so his medication doesn't turn his stomach."

"Excellent. I'll walk you up. Tag asked me to make sure he

125

JENN MADORE & CAROLINA MAC

was taken care of, but if you've got things in hand, I'm going to lie down for a mid-morning rest."

"Is the wee one keeping you up, luv?" Cora asks.

"No. Nothing like that. Tag's phone started ringing around four this morning and didn't stop. He and the boys have gone to handle things, so I'll take advantage of the house being quiet."

"Aye, do that. I'll plan for a light lunch then, shall I?"

Laine nods. "I'm happy to heat some of the soup you made yesterday. No need to go to any trouble."

"What about you, Piper?" Cora asks. "What do you fancy?"

I glance down at the tray of food in my hands and chuckle. "I doubt I'll be hungry anytime soon. If I am, I'm happy to warm up the soup, too. Thank you."

Laine walks with me, and with her guiding our path, I don't get lost and need to backtrack.

We arrive at the staircase without incident and before I know it, we're upstairs and she's turning the doorknob for Sean's room. "You two enjoy your breakfasts and take it easy. I'm going to lie down, but if you need me, don't hesitate to come find me."

"Thanks, Laine." When she steps into the hall, she closes the door behind her.

Being alone with Sean seems to settle the chaos warring inside me, and I take the tray over to set it on the dresser beside his bed.

"You clean up good, kitten."

I glance down at the sundress I'm wearing. "Laine is taller than me and a few sizes bigger, so finding outfits for me was tricky. Still, it's good to wear something that wasn't meant for men after a workout."

He lets out a long breath and looks sad. "I was worried you were going to bolt last night."

I remove the two covers and hand our plates to Sean before coming back for the cutlery and drinks. "I almost did."

"What stopped you?"

"Laine reminded me that Ryan's wake won't be for a few days, and that we both could use that time to heal and get stronger before facing the world."

"Laine's a smart woman."

I sit sideways on the bed to face him and reach for my plate. "She's also very nice."

"That's what the boys say." Sean hands me my breakfast and both of us start digging in. "Honestly, I haven't spent much time with her, but she brought Tag back to us and my younger brothers adore her, so that's good enough for me."

"What was wrong with Tag?"

Sean shrugs, pushing food around his plate. "Losing Da was hard on all of us, but having to take his place and fill his shoes every day was hard on Tag."

I can imagine.

Knowing that Declan and Ryan are dead hurts my heart and we weren't close. From what I gather, the Quinn brothers and their father were all very close.

How would I feel if my father was gone?

If I asked myself that a week ago, my answer would've been very different from what it is now.

"Wow, Cora is one hell of a cook."

Sean still isn't eating much. It's definitely not because of the food. That's for sure.

"What's wrong?"

He arches an ebony brow at me. "What's right? Your life is a mess. I'm down for at least a few days. There's shit going on with Tag and the business. And you're planning to go home because my brother killed your brother."

I take another bite of the breakfast casserole. "Granted, our lives have been a series of disastrous events for the past four days, but hey, we're still on the sunny side of the daisies, right?"

"That's true."

JENN MADORE & CAROLINA MAC

"And as long as we're still breathing, there's time to turn it around, isn't there?"

The smirk he gives me as he rolls his eyes feels like a win. "I suppose that's also true."

"So, eat. We both need to gird our loins and get ready for the next clusterfuck."

That earns me a full belly laugh. "Gird our loins? I don't think you have the loins in question, P."

I don't even care. The dark storm that was brewing behind his eyes when I got here a few minutes ago is gone. Now the spark of the warrior in him is back.

"I hate that you got hurt."

Sean makes a non-committal grunt and puts a forkful of food into his mouth. "It's not the first time and it sure as shit won't be the last."

"And as much as I hate that it came down to you or Ryan, I want you to know that I don't blame you or Tag for fighting to be the ones to survive."

Sean pegs me with an intense stare. "You sure about that? Last night, it felt like you might be worried that you're on the wrong side of the fight."

"Loyalty is a tricky thing."

"Aye, it is at that."

We both eat the rest of our breakfast without saying much more. What is there to say? My family wants his family wiped out. They have a stronger moral center and are trying to prevent a war from overtaking Dublin.

I admire what the Quinns are fighting for, but don't want my family wiped out, either. Rory and Brody aren't much older than me and haven't been involved in the business long. Do they deserve to die because of my father's greed and ambitions?

I don't want to see that happen.

Brody and Rory are the two brothers I'm closest to. If something were to happen to them, I would be devastated. The three of us have always been tight.

Sean's phone buzzes with an incoming text. He checks it and then sets it face down on the sheets. "How are you feeling today?"

"Better every day."

"Did you take your pain meds this morning?"

"No. I didn't think of it. I was more worried about you. Doc Kelvin asked me to get you food, so the pills wouldn't turn your stomach."

He pauses, with his fork hovering in front of his mouth. "Off you go. Get your pills."

"Seriously? Bossy much?"

He arches a brow. "Oh, kitten, you don't know the half of it. Where did you leave them? You remembered to bring them from the safe house, didn't you?"

"I did. They're in my room down the hall."

"Then off you go. They're to be taken morning and night. It won't be morning much longer."

I bite my bottom lip. "And what if I don't do as I'm told, Mr. Quinn?"

He sets his fork onto his plate and his plate on the bed beside his leg. "If we weren't injured, I'd show you, but since neither of us are up for any Dom discipline, I'll have to use emotional blackmail and refuse to eat."

I meet his stubborn smirk and chuckle. "Seriously? You're calling a hunger strike if I don't do as I'm told?"

Sean winks. "Be a good girl and humor me. I promise, I'll reward you for good behavior."

The electrical charge in the air between us crackles with sexual energy. And just like that, I'm ready to melt into a horny puddle. Until I take in the freshly changed bandages wrapping his torso.

"You're in no shape to make promises, Mr. Quinn."

He lowers the sheets, exposing his black boxers and how the cotton knit is straining to contain his stiff cock. "What's that, kitten?"

I shake my head. "There is no way Doc Kelvin would approve of us having sex with you like this."

Sean runs his thumbs under the elastic waistband and pulls the front of his boxers down to spring his cock free. "Never count me out of the game. Around you, I am always ready and willing. Now, go grab your pain pills. The sooner I see you take one, the sooner we can move from pain to pleasure."

It's emotional blackmail, but it's effective because before I can think of all the reasons it's a bad idea for us to have sex in his family home and in his condition, I'm rushing toward the hall to get my bottle of painkillers.

"That's my good girl."

CHAPTER FIFTEEN

Sean

*I*f I have to be sidelined and stuck in bed, I can't think of a better way to pass the time than playing house with Piper. Last night, when Tag told her about Ryan's death, she pulled her hand from mine and withdrew.

I thought I'd lost her.

Thankfully, a night's sleep has tempered her hurt with the reality that it was him or me. *'I don't blame you or Tag for fighting to be the ones to survive.'*

Her words chip away some of my sharp edges. How did I end up on the winning side? I didn't expect it, but I also won't question it.

No. For whatever time I get to have Piper in my life, I'll be greedy and enjoy every moment.

My phone buzzes with another notification, but I don't look at it. The MC has been blowing up my cell since four a.m. and there's nothing I can do about it.

If I could get out of bed—I would.

JENN MADORE & CAROLINA MAC

If I could ride to the burning warehouses and help clear out the contents—I would.

But all I could do was phone Tag in the bedroom down the hall and tell him either the McGuires, the Russians, or maybe the Campbells came after.

How did we end up with so many enemies all of a sudden? However it happened, three Quinn warehouses were mysteriously torched the night we killed one of the McGuire boys.

It doesn't take any stretch of the imagination to guess who lit the match. If there were something I could do—I would. Since there's not, I intend to distract myself.

Before Piper gets back, I tilt to one side, pull my underwear off my ass and then tilt to the other side to get rid of them.

Fuck, that hurts.

Which is why I have to get it done and be smiling by the time Piper gets back. It takes a couple of tries and a great deal of cursing in my head, but I get them down my thighs.

She can take it from there.

Piper shuffles back in and lifts the orange pill bottle in the air. "Mission accomplished. Did you miss me?"

With her swinging her hips and her dress swaying around those silky thighs, how could I not? And why the fuck didn't I think of picking her up a few dresses? Because this is a fuck ton better than seeing her in my old t-shirt and sweats.

Not that I don't love seeing her in my clothes—I do.

But this is better.

"Lock the door and get your pretty little ass over here. I'll show you how much I missed you."

She obeys without question, and it does my heart good to see her beaming smile as she hurries to get to me. When was the last time someone was genuinely excited to spend time with me?

The MC cut bunnies are a good workout when I'm stressed

132

or want to forget my troubles for a night or two, but I never go back for more than that.

I would hate to give any of them the wrong idea.

And there are nights I take the emotions out of things altogether and go to one of our gentlemen's clubs. Bride Nolan's girls respect our involvement in keeping their interests safe and are always happy to give a Quinn brother a little thank you perk.

But the way Piper's smile warms when she sees me is both endearing and terrifying. In my head, I'm pumping the breaks big time with this girl. In my heart, I've committed the greatest sin of all—hoping it can last.

Not that I'd admit that to anyone. Ever.

The click of the lock is like a Pavlovian trigger, and I lift my plate to hand it to her. "Let's clear the playing field, shall we?"

Her smile dims. "The deal was that if I got my pills, you would eat."

I flash her a lascivious grin. "Och, I intend to feast. Now, set this aside. There's a new bounty on the menu."

In truth, I'm still starving, but whatever. A man's got to have priorities. Orgasms first. Nutrition second.

"Take one of your pills and then come tend to the wounded, baby."

She makes a show of pouring one of the white tablets into her hand and washing it down with a swig of orange juice. "If I were tending to the wounded properly, I wouldn't be humoring your libido."

"Humoring my libido. Is that all this is to you? I'm crushed."

She rolls her eyes and climbs onto the bed. "I'm sure you are."

I pat the mattress beside my hips. "Come here. Let me get under that dress."

"Are you sure I won't hurt you?"

I toss the covers down my legs and give her the full show. "No more than I enjoy, I promise."

She crawls up the bed on her hands and knees, her gaze locked on my cock. Her tits sway as she comes to me and I'm practically done in. Then, she pauses and bites her bottom lip. "May I try something, Mr. Quinn?"

"Is it on your sex list?"

"Mm-hmm."

"Then yeah. Go for it."

She leans forward, gripping my shaft and drawing her tongue over the bead of precum escaping my cock.

I press my palms into the mattress and try to remember how to breathe. "How do I taste?"

She takes another lick and the pressure in my balls triples. "Like salty sin."

Her head drops again and her lips part over my crown as the sweet heat of her mouth sucks me in. My vision bursts into fractals of light and I close my eyes.

"Am I doing this right?"

It takes a moment to make words form in my mind, but I get there. "You're a natural."

"Really? I've always wondered what sucking cock would be like. It's sexy. Your skin is so soft, and it slides over the steel rod beneath."

She's killing me. Piper is literally going to end me.

"I'm pretty sure your cock is laced with some kind of addictive substance, because I'm hooked. I want to explore what it can do all day and night."

Oh, little girl. Be careful what you wish for. "I can make that happen—we've both been put on the sidelines for the next few days. Might as well make the best use of our time."

She glances up from my lap, her pale blue eyes dancing with mischief. "What about Tag? He won't be happy to find out you're sleeping with a McGuire."

"Who said anything about sleeping?" I reach down her side and slide my hand under the fabric of her skirt to pull her closer. I'm pleasantly startled to find nothing but warm, bare skin. "No underwear?"

"I took them off when I went to my room. I thought you might like the surprise."

"I fucking love it." I splay my fingers and run my hands over her bare ass. With a satisfied smirk, she drops her head and claims me with her mouth again.

As she entertains herself and finds her way, I do my best not to go off early and ruin her fun. It's tough, though, because I wasn't exaggerating when I told her she's a natural.

"That's my good girl. I swear, you were meant to suck my cock, Piper. It feels so good."

My erection is being treated to so much genuine appreciation it's incredible. When she finds a slow, sensual rhythm and starts to suck, my eyes roll back, and I swear I almost black out.

"If you keep doing that, I'll finish way too soon."

"Says you."

There's no mistaking the challenge in her voice or how greedy she's getting with her stroke and suck. "You deserve to be worshipped, too, kitten. In fact, I think you should be rewarded for the no underwear game and come sit on my face."

"Yeah?"

"Definitely."

She pops off the end of my cock and flashes me a wicked smile. "Rain check. I'm not done feasting on you. Besides, you took good care of me when I was hurt. I want to return the favor."

I see stars when she sucks me back into her mouth and then reaches lower and grabs hold of my sac.

Incredible. Piper may not have had a lot of experience, but what she lacks in finesse, she more than makes up for in enthusiasm.

Which is cute as fuck.

I drop my head back and shift my grip on her ass to slide between her legs. She's warm and wet and when my fingers slide into her heat, I match her efforts stroke for stroke.

If she doesn't want to give my cock up, who am I to argue? She's got a dominant side blossoming inside her and I'm so on board for that, it's crazy.

Whatever Piper wants to do with me—I'm game.

As she works me over, I rub her clit and wind her up like she's doing to me. It doesn't take long before she's groaning and grinding against my touch. "Come sit on me, Piper. Let me fill you up."

She shakes her head. "You're hurt. I don't want you pulling your stitches open."

"I won't be able to pound into you for a few days, but I'm capable of sitting here and letting you ride me. We're fine."

She chuckles. "Why do I feel like you'd say that whether it was true or not?"

Because she's an exceptionally intelligent woman. It's still true. "I'm taking it easy here and letting you get me off, but I can do more. I promise."

She considers for another moment before she shakes her head and resumes her fun. With her head down and her attentions locked, it doesn't take long for her to find her rhythm again.

And all I can do is enjoy the ride.

Fuck, when was the last time a woman was this focused on pleasuring me? A woman that wasn't an MC groupie or a professional, that is.

I can't think because Piper finds her stride and the pressure at the base of my balls is incredible. I don't want this to end, but there's no way I can hold back.

"Kitten, I'm going to come so hard, I'll be shooting straight into your stomach. If you don't want me in your mouth, now's the time to use your hand."

But she doesn't pop off and there's no holding back.

My release explodes out of me in hot streams as my hips buck and the world fractures around me. It's so good. I grind my teeth and try not to shout out and bring the household running.

Waves of pleasure pulse through me as I give her everything I've got. And through it all, Piper makes this feminine sound that's a cross between a purr and a groan.

"Holy hell," I grind out between clenched teeth. "You're going to kill me."

Piper freezes. "Oh, god. Did I hurt you?"

My eyes are clenched shut, and after a couple of calming breaths, I meet her panicked gaze. "No, lass, but you made me come so hard I'm still seeing stars."

"Really?"

"Really. Sweet mercies, Piper. You have no idea what you do to me, do you?"

"If it's anything like what you do to me, we might be in trouble."

I laugh. "We are definitely in trouble."

"But you liked it?"

"I fucking loved it."

She's all grins and glowing pride as she climbs up the bed and settles on the pillow next to me. "Do you know what I loved most?"

"Tell me and I'll make sure I never stop doing it."

She bites her bottom lip. "When you called me your good girl while I was having my fun."

I stiffen a little more. "You like that?"

Her ebony hair has fallen over her cheek, but it doesn't hide her blush. "Is that weird?"

"Not at all. One thing you learn when you have lovers, is that whatever happens behind closed doors between consenting adults is fair game. If it makes you feel good, claim it."

"Then yeah, tell me I'm your good girl." She meets my gaze, and I see her mind spinning.

"*Annnd?* Is there something else you'd like?"

"I'd like it if you wrapped my hair around your hand and pulled it a little, too." Her cheeks flush pink and I swear this little vixen is going to be the death of me. "Behind closed doors, right?"

I groan and wish for the thousandth time that the two of us were in full fucking form. "Behind closed doors, kitten. Anything you want. All you have to do is tell me and I'll make it happen. Now, let's take care of you."

The frown on Piper's face isn't what I expect, but then she lifts her hand from my side. "Sean. You're bleeding. Did I open your stitches?"

I frown down at the traitorous blood and curse my bad luck. The stain of scarlet is creeping forward, growing darker and spreading across the gauze. "No. You did nothing wrong. I'm fine."

She swings her legs off the bed and rushes to the bathroom to wash her hand. "We should call Doc Kelvin and get him back here."

"No. You should lift your dress and straddle me. That would do more to heal me than any stitches or pills."

"It's a solid no." She hands me back my plate and sits at the end of the bed with her back against the footboard. "Toss me a pillow."

I do as she asks, and she sets herself up, facing me with her legs stretched out beside mine. "Time for you to rest. I'll watch to make sure the bleeding doesn't get worse. Then, we'll see how things turn out after Kelvin checks you over tonight."

"You're worrying about nothing, Piper." I gesture to the bandages and scowl. "It's not even that much blood."

"No means no, Sean. Now, finish your breakfast or I'll go back to my room."

I arch a brow and flash her a smirk. "My kitten has a bit of wildcat in her."

She grins. "After the past four days, you might not realize I have claws, but I do."

I wave away her words. "Only someone with claws could've survived what you did. I imagine it took a lot of fight and strength to grow up in the McGuire household."

She grows a little sullen, so I focus on eating the rest of my breakfast and leave her to her thoughts. Laine was right when she said that a few more days would allow Piper time to grow stronger. And, with a nudge here and there from me, she'll leave here understanding how capable and valued she is.

The silence that follows is comfortable and I think she might doze off until she touches her cheek and bites her bottom lip. "What is it like having a scar so noticeable? Do people comment on it? Do they ask you where you got it?"

She's studying the scar that slashes down my cheek and cuts into my lip. It's a stark reminder of a terrible time that marked me when I was twelve.

"It changed how strangers saw me. Teachers and kids at school treated me differently. Like I was a tough kid, or a bit broken."

Piper's fingers trace the tender flesh of her cheek. Of course, she's worried about her scar—she's always been seen for her beauty, and now it exposes a vulnerability.

"It never changed the way people close to me treated me, though. The people who knew me saw past the damage. At home and with my truest friends, it was never an issue."

"It's earned you a reputation on the street, for sure," she says, offering me a sympathetic smile. "There are all kinds of local myths about how you got it."

I chuckle. "I've heard a few. The one about the crossbow and the clowns high on PCP is my favorite."

"But not the truth?"

I laugh again. "No. One of Da's competitors snatched me off the street after school one day when I was a kid. They meant to use me as leverage, but there was a spot where a vent cover was unscrewed in the room where they locked me up. I bent back the metal to climb free, but my face and my hands got sliced up bad."

She squeezes my thigh through the sheet and swallows. "I'm sorry. I shouldn't have asked."

"It's fine. It doesn't bother me. It was so long ago I'm over it."

"I can't imagine being over it. I'm terrified that I'll see it every time I look in the mirror and think about Vladimir attacking me and about my father throwing me away."

My chest tightens at her words, and more-so, the pain and fear laced through them. I run my hand gently up the inside of her ankle. "What was done doesn't make you any less beautiful."

"Liar."

I'm not lying—not even a little—but having been where she is, there's nothing I can say that will convince her of that. All she sees is the carnage of violence and betrayal. "Plastic surgeons can do incredible things. I bet they can erase the damage or make it so it's barely noticeable."

She looks at me, her gaze seeking reassurance.

I squeeze her ankle. "But even if you're left with a scar, it's okay. That scar, like mine, is a symbol that you survived the worst night of your life. It's proof of your strength, not a sign of weakness."

Piper's eyes glisten, and she draws in a deep breath. "Do you really believe that?"

I tap a finger against my lip. "Knowing my story, what does my scar signify to you?"

Her mouth eases up into a sweet smile. "That you were strong enough to survive even when you were alone, scared, and in danger."

"Exactly. And that's what anyone who knows you and loves you will see, too. If they don't, they aren't your people and they don't matter."

The moisture in her eyes brims over and I open my arms. She crawls up the bed and sinks against me, burying her tears in my chest.

Many men get put off by the tears of women—I don't. After I made it home from my kidnapping, Mam would cry often when she saw me. She used to hug me close and say that emotions build up in women the same way they do in men.

Tears are a woman's way of release and reset, unlike a man's need to punch his fist through a wall or start a fight. And given what Piper's been through, she can use me as her emotional outlet for as long as she needs.

"The mark on your cheek doesn't change how I see you, Piper. Not negatively, at least." I lean down and press my cheek to the top of her head. "To me, it tells a story about what a brave, strong, and unbreakably beautiful woman you have become."

I hold her while she resets, the world outside fading into insignificance. After a while, her sobs quiet and her body relaxes. When the soft in and out of her breathing tells me she's fallen asleep, I'm more content than I've ever been.

This.

If we weren't from opposite sides of a brewing war, I would claim this woman and keep her forever. It would be my greatest honor to protect her and hold her when the world becomes too much.

But we *are* on opposite sides.

No matter how much I wish it could be different, Piper isn't mine to keep. I need to stop pretending she is and get my head back in the game.

What happened between us over the past four days has to be about protecting an innocent, offering her a chance to heal, and helping a fellow human being.

Nothing more.

CHAPTER SIXTEEN

Piper

*a*fter having the house practically to ourselves on Sean's first day of recovery, it's a bit of a letdown on the next two days, having Finn and Laine home and Tag and the twins coming and going.

Even though they've been good to me, it's obvious I'm not welcome here. It's no secret that Tag wants me gone. It's also obvious when the others stop talking whenever I enter the room.

I understand why, but it's a bit unnerving.

What's even more unnerving is Sean.

I'm not sure what changed, but all my plans for covert orgasms have been shot down. He's been kind and supportive, like always, but has shown no interest in private time with me.

Did I do something wrong?

His one-eighty turnaround started right after I woke up in his bed. Sure, I turned him down for sex, but that was because he was bleeding. Did I offend him? I can't imagine that. Did my tears scare him off? I doubt it.

The only thing I can come up with is that real life has crept in, and his attention is divided between calls from the MC, meetings with Tag, and proving to Doc Kelvin that he's fit to be out of bed and back on his bike.

I know he misses patrolling the streets with his Devil brothers, but the wall he put up between us is personal.

Doesn't matter. Our ill-advised affair was bound to end, so it's good that we gain some distance and perspective before I leave.

And no matter what, I loved our time together.

Best week of my life.

"I seriously suggest you give it a couple more days, Sean." Doc Kelvin is fighting a losing battle on that.

Sean insisted this exam take place in the living room downstairs because he's tired of lying around in bed. "Aye, your medical opinion has been heard and is appreciated, Doc."

"And will promptly be ignored." Doc closes his medical bag. "I don't know why I patch you Quinn brothers up some days."

"Because you love us." Finn cups his fingers against his chest in the shape of a heart.

Doc rolls his eyes. "No. It's definitely the money."

Finished with Sean, the good doctor turns his attention to me. "And how are you feeling, lass?"

"Much better, thank you. My ribs are still tender, but the cuts and bruises are fading. Instead of eggplant purple, most of my body is now a sickly yellowish green."

He gently slides his finger under my hair and examines the damage left by Vladimir's ring. "I'm sorry I couldn't do more with this. Once it heals, I can refer you to a couple of talented plastic surgeons that could minimize the scar."

I step back and let my hair cover the raw flesh left behind by my Bratva betrothed. "I'm thinking of keeping it. I know it's gnarly, but it's a symbol of survival, right?"

"A true battle scar." The look Sean gives me warms me deep

into the marrow of my bones. And the husky tone lacing his voice tells me he's proud of me.

Doc Kelvin steps back and gathers his bag. "Then my work is done here. Until the next clusterfuck, I bid you farewell."

Finn chuckles. "You've been spending too much time at the theater with your wife."

Kelvin shrugs. "If watching men tromp around a stage singing puts me in the woman's good graces, it's a win."

"Happy wife, happy life," Laine says.

"Aye, that's the truth of it, isn't it?"

Laine and Finn walk Kelvin out, and the two of us are alone at last.

When he looks at me, he holds up his hands. "Don't listen to Doc. I'm fine. Quinns are too tough to keep down for long."

"Or too stubborn."

"Both work."

I roll my eyes, but there's no heat in the look I give him. He's too damned ornery to care, even if I were actually annoyed.

And really, what right do I have to voice an opinion?

Our time together was the collision of two worlds—a perfect storm of fate and injury.

Sean's gaze narrows on me. "Where'd you go just then? And why do you look so sad?"

I glance around to ensure our conversation is still private and sigh. "This week has been incredible, but Ryan's wake is tonight and the funeral's tomorrow. Like it or not, it's time to get back to my life."

"That doesn't mean you need to go back to that house. I can have you escorted to the wake and the funeral. Then, if your father tries anything, you can get out and be brought back to the north side where you'll be safe."

I reach up and cup his jaw, running my thumb over the scar on his lip. "I'll be fine. I'm stronger than I used to be and see things clearer now."

"And how do you see this playing out?"

I pat his arm. "Da will be furious with me, but he won't upset Mam while she's grieving. I'll apologize that having choices in my life jammed him up, but be clear that I'm not sorry for refusing the Bratva. It was a cruel and cold misjudgment on his part."

"I don't like it, P. Your father isn't firing on all cylinders lately. What if it goes bad and he turns on you?"

I shrug and take a step back, putting some distance between us. "Your brother called the Bratva boss in Russia, right? He's soured the deal with Da?"

"Aye, Tag's negotiating an agreement, but your father made big promises about how much product he could move. The terms the Russians expect to be met mean more weapons than Ireland can handle."

"But Da isn't part of that, is he?"

"Not that we know of, but nothing is locked down. If the Russians decide to go with your father, there isn't much we can do about it."

The concern lacing Sean's words melts my heart, but the reality is, Russian deal or not, I can't hide in Quinn Castle for the rest of my life.

"I'll pay my respects to my family, pack my bags, and then, after everyone leaves the reception tomorrow, I'll walk out the door."

"And go where? You're not planning to stay on the south side, are you?"

"No. I have a couple of girlfriends who share a flat up in Cabra. I'll stay there while I figure things out."

My plan to live on the north side seems to ease some of his anxieties, but not all. "What if your father doesn't let you leave?"

"Sean, I'll be fine. The important thing is that I know who my father is and what he's capable of."

Sean runs his fingers through his ebony waves and exhales. "I don't like this one bit."

"That's you being overprotective."

"No, it's my instincts screaming that you need to stay here until we figure something else out."

"I can't. Tag's been decent about me being here, but I agree with him. I'm kerosine to the open flame of your already dangerous lives. Nothing can change the fact that my last name is McGuire, and having me here threatens to pull Dublin into an all-out war."

Tag hasn't been welcoming, but I get it.

His father is dead. His girlfriend is pregnant. And he's in charge of keeping people safe.

I see the affection in Sean's gaze and understand why he pulled back. This is hard enough as it is.

One week wasn't enough, but one month or one year wouldn't be either.

"We had a good run, Mr. Quinn, but it's time I face my life and start picking up the pieces." I extend my hand, and he grips my palm and pulls me forward.

He takes what I intend as a platonic parting and claims my mouth for a kiss. His tongue runs along the seam of my lips, and I submit without hesitation.

It's embarrassing how easily I succumb. I make a mental note to at least attempt to play hard to get, but even as I do, I resign myself to the truth.

There's no resisting Sean Quinn.

The kiss is aggressive and his hand slides under the front of my shirt. He palms my breast, and I groan, arching into his touch. "I thought we were parting as friends. You're not playing fair."

"Didn't you hear? I'm a very bad man."

But having a very bad man in my corner has been a very good thing. I end the kiss and try to stop wanting things I shouldn't. "I'll let you know when I'm back and settled. Maybe you can take me for a ride on your bike."

"Or you can ride me on my bike."

And just like that, my core is weeping for him and I'm sliding my hand over the bulge in his jeans. His hips flex and he presses his cock against my palm.

"Oh, shit. Sorry."

The two of us break apart and I find Finn standing in the doorway holding a red and blue box. "Sorry. Your rice was ringing, Piper."

My what? It takes a moment for my mind to catch up with what he's saying. "Oh, thanks."

Sean steps between us and points at Finn. "You saw nothing. You say nothing. Got it?"

Finn hands Sean the box and holds up his hands. "How could I see anything? I wasn't even here."

Finn rushes out of the living room like his ass is on fire and Sean hands me the box with my cell in it. "Will he tell Tag? Will this come back to bite you?"

Sean shakes out his hands and exhales. "No. Finn's a smart kid. He won't piss Tag off or fuck me over. He'll keep what he saw to himself."

Good. I don't want Sean to suffer because of our crash of fate any more than he already has.

I pull my cell free from the rice and brush off the layer of white dust. "I guess it finally dried out."

"I guess so."

Swiping my finger across the screen, I tap in my code and unlock it. There are sixteen texts and a dozen missed calls from Rory and Brody, a couple of calls from Mam, and one from Da.

One? Is that all my disappearance was worth to him?

I delete it without listening to it. Why should I? He called once, late on the night of my dinner with the Russians. He likely heard from Vladimir and Arkady and left me a scathing rant about how useless I proved myself to be and how I needed to fix it or consider myself cut off and cast out.

A week ago, that would've destroyed me.

Now it barely registers.

"Are you okay?" Sean asks.

I draw a deep breath and do a gut check. "I am. Or, at least, I will be. I'm Piper-fucking-McGuire. No one can make me feel weak and insignificant unless I allow it. From now on—I won't allow it."

Sean winks and pulls me in for a hug. "That's my girl."

I love the sound of that, but we both know I can't be.

As amazing as this was—and it really was—it was temporary. My father would burn down their lives if he found out I was with a Quinn.

I can't repay their kindness by bringing violence down on their family—especially when their family is expecting a new addition.

"Put your number in my phone. I'll text you an update later. You'll see. Everything will be fine."

His thumbs glide over the screen, and then he hands it back. "I'll be waiting for the text. I mean it, Piper. If I don't hear from you, I'll be crossing the river and out for blood."

"That's not your job anymore. I'm not your problem."

Sean leans close and lifts my chin with his fingers. "You were never a problem, kitten—a complication, yes—but never a problem."

His breath dust across my cheek and sexual energy hums over my skin. "That's a fine distinction, Mr. Quinn."

One corner of his deliciously full lips lifts into a cocky smirk. "I meant what I said about not letting anyone hurt you again. If anyone lays a fucking finger on you, I will cut them off with garden shears. And if anyone dares to make you cry, I will put them in the fucking ground."

I hear the threat in the growl of his voice and see it in the storm darkening his emerald green eyes. "I'll text you. I swear." I press one last kiss on the scar of his cheek. "Thank you for being my black knight. I will always cherish you as my first. Be safe, Mr. Quinn."

Sean

From the moment Brendan and Bryan leave to take Piper to the bridge closest to her home, I'm climbing out of my fucking skin. Her going back to Mad Mattie is a mistake. I feel that to the depth of my soul. It's why I couldn't take her myself. I knew I could never let her go.

The McGuires don't deserve her.

Mattie doesn't understand the meaning of family, loyalty, or basic decency, for that matter.

He's a greedy fucker with delusions of grandeur.

Da's larger than life presence and power always kept him in check. With Da gone, the truce isn't worth the paper it's printed on. Tag wants to believe he can earn that level of obedience from him, but it'll never happen.

There's no stopping a runaway train.

My bike roars to life the moment I give her some throttle and the throaty rumble soothes some of the rage burning like wildfire in my blood.

No, it's not all rage. There's a lot of panic, too.

I respect how far Piper has come in a week, but she still doesn't know how petty and twisted Mattie can be.

My mind is a whirlwind of fury and not even the wind pulling at my hair and my leather cut flapping against my chest can soothe the beast within.

Gearing down, I lean into the turn to take me to the clubhouse and slow down as I approach the ten-foot steel door that keeps wandering eyes from prying into our business.

My boots have barely touched the asphalt of the driveway when the mechanics of the door kick in and my way is clear. Keefer Gallagher is standing on the porch of the clubhouse with the gate remote and closes things up behind me.

Once I've parked my ride, I dismount my girl and unbuckle the strap under my chin. I leave my helmet and gloves on my seat and shuffle my way over to the porch steps.

"You look like shit, boss."

"And you're a fucking pageant queen?"

Gallager chuckles. "Fair enough. So, Kelvin let you out of bed, did he?"

"Didn't have much of a say in it. Three days of fucking around in bed is about all I can take."

I mean that in the sense of not being able to ride or work, but my subconscious mind takes that as a cue to revisit every erotic image of what three days of fucking around in bed with Piper could've looked like.

Shit. I've gotta get a grip. "So, what did I miss? Give me the highlights."

"I'm sure Tag's told you most of it. We've had five separate fires and lost two trucks."

"Aye, Tag told me. He said we managed to salvage most of the warehouse contents, so it was only about a ten percent loss."

"What's this 'we' you speak of? I don't recall you being there while we sucked in smoke and hand the hair burned off our arms."

I arch a brow. "I'm not in the mood for your lip today, K-man. Keep it up and you're liable to get your balls twisted off by a pair of gardening shears."

My VP laughs and opens the door. "Come on in, boss. I'm not sure why, but the guys missed you."

"Sean!" The boys rally around and welcome me back, one of

them offering me a beer, and several of them asking to see the damage.

I accept the beer and decline the show and tell.

Shuffling over to the bar, I lean against the rail and twist the top off my drink. "Where's Kieran? I need him to do something for me."

Frenchie throws a thumb over his shoulder. "He's working in the paint shop. You want me to get him?"

As much as I hate the idea of moving, there's no sense in fucking up Kieran's artistic genius. The guy has a gift and whatever bike he's working on, it'll be better without the process being interrupted.

"Nah, I'll go to him. Thanks, man." Pushing off the rail, I head down the hall toward the side door. The paint shop is a two-bay garage that the boys sealed off and pimped out so that Kieran could have a studio to work his magic. The boys know better than to get into his space.

And that means the conversation I'm about to have with him will remain private.

CHAPTER SEVENTEEN

Piper

$\mathcal{I}$ knock on the wide, brown door of the modest stone house overlooking the canal. *Be home, Clare. Please be home.* Clare Malloy has been my partner for half a dozen projects in college and is the only one I can think of that my parents might not know about.

When the door opens, I breathe again. "Hey, Clare. Sorry to drop in unannounced—"

"Sweet mother, Piper, what happened to you?"

I tilt my head and pull my hair to cover the side of my face. I'm still sporting the remnants of a black eye and the gruesome scabbing of Vladimir's Bratva branding. "It's a bit of a long story. Can I come in? I need your help."

"Of course, come inside."

I follow her down the cramped hallway, and she blocks the entranceway to the living room. "A friend from school popped in. We'll be in my room."

"What kind of friend?" her Da asks.

"The girl kind, Da. Don't get your knickers in a twist."

"Hello, Mr. Malloy," I call out, to back Clare up.

"Hello, lass."

With that settled, Clare escorts me to the back of her house, where she shares a room with her younger sister. "Come in. Sit down."

I sit on her bed and before she can bombard me with questions, I tell her a watered-down version of the story that I thought up on the way here.

It's vaguely true—more like truth adjacent—but covers all the bases.

"So, I haven't talked to my Da since last week, but I want to go to Ryan's wake."

"Of course you do."

"And I thought that if I borrow a dress and you help me fix my makeup to cover most of the bruises, he might not cause a scene."

"But if this big client of his hurt you, don't you think he'll want to know?"

"I'll tell him, but tonight is about Ryan and our family. I don't want bad blood to affect the wake, and I figure having all our friends and family around will help keep things civil."

She looks me over and I can tell she's concerned, but I force my best smile. "Please?"

"Of course, I'm just worried about you."

"And I appreciate that, but this will work. It has to."

The Donnybrook Pub has been one of my father's favorite hangouts since before he was a made man. It's where he met his first wife, Aimee, when she was working as a barmaid, back in the late eighties.

It's where he and Mam used to come to play darts on Saturday nights.

It's where Declan was remembered a couple of weeks ago and now it's where Ryan will be remembered tonight.

Two brothers in one month.

I'm not sure I'll ever forgive Da for what he did to me, but there's a tiny part of me that's grateful it happened. Seeing the monster my father can be freed me from my delusion of needing his approval.

It taught me a lot about myself and how strong I am, with or without the McGuire name.

"Piper?" Rory is standing on the front step of the pub, an unlit cigarette hanging from his lips. "Where the fuck have you been? We've been worried sick."

He's about to wrap his arms around me when I press my hand against his chest. "I'm pretty battered up. Be gentle, please."

"Battered up? What the fuck does that mean?"

I step closer and give him a one-arm hug, turning my body so the embrace doesn't affect my bad ribs. "Later. Tonight's about Ryan."

Rory shifts the hair cascading over my bad cheek and frowns. "Who the fuck did this to you, Piper? I swear to God, I'll end them."

I grip his wrist and kiss his knuckles. "You can't end them. I'll explain everything tomorrow. For now, let's get inside. And if you want to stick close to me and run parental block, I'd appreciate it."

"Whatever you need. I've got your back."

Rory puts his cigarette back in the pack and leads the way into the pub. Seeing him shocked and outraged means more to me than he could possibly know.

At least someone in my family loves me.

Maybe it's not as bad as I imagined.

Maybe it was just Da losing his grip.

"There's my sweet lass. Piper girl, I've missed you." My

grandmother is going deaf, and her announcement of my arrival is louder than I would've liked. She's drawn the attention of both of my parents and Billy Gravely.

"Hello, *Maimeó*." I kiss her cheek and wonder if I can wedge myself between my brother and my grandmother all night and avoid the fight storming toward me.

Judging by the look in Da's eye and the speed at which he's cutting through the crowd, that seems unlikely. But right before he gets to me, Mam grabs his arm and stops him. She leans close to his ear and my father's fire seems to extinguish.

Billy Gravely is another story altogether.

"What the fuck did I miss?" Rory whispers in my ear.

"If I'm still breathing at the end of the night, I'll tell you the whole horrible story."

"Were you high when this happened?"

I take in Rory's disbelieving expression and roll my eyes. "Please don't joke. Not one bit of what happened is funny."

"No, it's not, but you have to admit a tale where Da sells you to the Bratva and Sean Quinn rescues you and nurses you back onto your feet sounds like something that might happen in a topsy-turvy mirror universe."

"And yet it's true. Vladimir waved the contract in my face and Da's signature was right there at the bottom."

"He's fucking lost it."

"I know. And there's no way Mam didn't know about it—at least after the fact—but she didn't seem relieved to see me tonight at the wake. If anything, she seemed as angry as Da."

Rory flops backward onto my mattress and stares up at the ceiling. "What are we going to do?"

"We? You don't have to be dragged into this mess. I'm going

to go to the funeral tomorrow and after we come home, I'm going to pack my things and move out."

Rory props himself up on his elbows. "No way will they let you just move out. Besides, how do you rent a place without a job or references or money?"

"I'll crash with friends for a bit while I pull that together." In truth, I have a private bank account where I've been stashing my shopping allowance and any loose cash I found lying around.

I've got almost eight grand to make a new start.

But that's not something I'll share with anyone—even Rory. I love him to death, but I've seen how Da manipulates the boys to bend to his will.

"How much are you going to tell Mam and Da?"

"All of it. If they want to pretend the Quinns are the source of all evil and the ruination of our lives, that's on them. I know better. Tag wants the truce. He has no interest in a power war. It's all Da."

"But they already killed Declan."

"That was Tag's right-hand man finding out Declan was sleeping with his girlfriend and using her to spy on them."

"But didn't they send her to spy on *us*?"

"Aye, Sean said Aiden fell in love and genuinely lost his head when he realized he was being played."

Rory exhales. "And that was the curvy redhead with the tits?"

I frown at him. "All women have breasts, Rory. Maybe find another way to describe her."

"The curvy redhead with the rocking, big tits?"

I roll my eyes at him. "All right. You better get clear of me. Mam and Da may have stayed late at the pub, but I have a feeling the first thing they'll do when they get home is storm up here to grill and berate me."

Rory sits up and shakes his head. "I'm sorry, sis. This is all kinds of fucked up."

"I know, but at least I know what they're capable of and

won't be caught unaware again. After the service tomorrow, I won't be here to play the part of their pawn."

Ryan lifts his fist for a knuckle bump, and I lock my door behind him when he leaves. Then I pull out my phone and rush over to my bed.

Where did he put his number?

I scroll through my contacts. He's not under Sean or Quinn, but that's smart. He wouldn't want my father gaining access to my phone and finding him in there. I start back at the top under the A listings and scan my contacts one by one.

When I get to B. Knight, I laugh and hop onto my bed.

> So far so good. The wake was tense but civil.

I wait while the little dots bounce as he texts his reply.

> You won't be safe until you're clear of them and back on the north side. Don't let your guard down.

> I won't. I've got this.

> I love that you think so, but trust me, you don't.

His lack of faith stings a little, but it's less about me and more about his perspective based on his experiences. We're all a product of our past.

> Better go. Big day tomorrow. Need my beauty sleep.

> There's no improving perfection.

> Sweet dreams, Mr. Knight.

> Sweet dreams, P. Be safe.

~

I don't sleep much. I lie in bed for hours, listening for the sounds of my parents returning from the pub. It's after two when they come in and then I'm on full alert.

I don't want to have our confrontation when they're upset and drunk, but like everything else—I don't have a say in that.

Despite lying awake and listening for them to come—they don't. I wake hours later, still dressed and lying on top of my covers.

I unplug my phone and check the time. It's just after eight in the morning. Deciding I want to be fully awake and prepared for what's to come, I grab some clean clothes and have my shower.

I don't put makeup on to cover the bruises. They need to see what Da's plotting came to. To that effect, I put my t-shirt away and grab a crop top.

Might as well go for maximum impact.

Before I go downstairs to face the firing squad, I send a quick text to Mr. B. Knight.

Heading into the lion's den. Wish me luck.

Call if you need help. River or not, I'm there.

It means a lot that he'd brave the hostilities of breaching rival territory to help me.

I tuck my phone into the pocket of the pants I'll wear until it's time to dress for the funeral and draw a steadying breath.

After everything I've faced this week, why am I so afraid to face my parents? Whatever they say can't be as bad as what was done to me.

Outside my bedroom, I stand in the upstairs hall and listen

to the mumbled voices and clinking sounds of my family in the kitchen.

How can they be down there having breakfast as usual? Were they like this while I was gone for the past week? Did life just carry on?

Oh, our daughter was almost raped and murdered by the Russians, pass the sausage.

And the more I envision it, the more likely it seems.

Did I ever matter to them, or was I simply the end of the lucky streak of Da making boys? Looking back on my life and viewing it through that lens clears up so many moments in my childhood.

They always said I was naïve. They were right.

Only my *naïveté* wasn't about the business and the workings of the world, it was about my value within the world they created.

I descend the stairs with a fire in my heart and the knowledge that this is a 'them' problem. My arrival into the kitchen brings a rush of silence.

My parents are sitting in their usual seats, looking disdainful and cold. Rory and Brody are eating and keeping their heads down. Darcy is standing at the counter in front of the toaster. And Niall is blessedly absent.

"Good morning, everyone."

My mother looks up from where she's worshipping her coffee mug at the table. "What's so good about it?"

"Nothing at all." I reach into the cupboard to get a glass. "I was simply trying to be civil."

"Och, *now* you try. You could've used some of that civility last week when you were sent to charm the Russians. Do you understand how important that was to our family?"

I'm ready for the comment, so I don't even flinch. *Point to me.* "You mean while those hairy brutes pinned me down and to rape me? I'm sorry Da's plan didn't work out, but I wasn't expecting to be gifted to strangers like a party favor. I'm a McGuire—I fought back."

"You're no McGuire," Da snaps. "McGuires know what it means to sacrifice for the business that keeps us in power—a business that keeps a fancy roof over your head and a bank account full of money so you can go shopping every ten minutes."

I pour myself a glass of juice and lean on the center island, facing them. With a subtle finger swiping over my ear, I move my hair, so they get a good look at the black eye and the raw flesh of my cheek.

"You asked me to entertain them through dinner and then show them to their suite. You asked me to be charming and ensure they had a good time. I did that. What you *didn't* ask me about was an arranged marriage, or being whored out, or being shipped to Russia as a trophy for a bunch of rapists and killers."

Da's gaze narrows. "Watch your mouth, young lady. You don't know enough about things to stand there and judge me."

"Maybe not, but I saw the contract. Vladimir shoved it in my face as he blackened my eye and ripped up my cheek with his Bratva ring. My eyes may have been watering at the time, but I saw you offered your virgin daughter as a signing bonus, and I saw your signature making it official."

"Marital alliances are made between powerful families all the time, little girl. You know this."

"I know it happens and maybe something could've been worked out if I was consulted and had a say about who it would be and where I would live, but you can't just give me away to secure a gun deal."

"I can and I did."

Rory's spoon falls into his bowl and he pushes away from his place at the table. "Seriously? I've been sitting here waiting for you to explain to Piper that she misunderstood, or that the

Russians made it up. Are you honestly saying you sold her virginity to secure weapons? That's cold, Da."

Thank the stars for Rory.

At least one person in my family truly loves me.

Da throws Rory a hard stare. "Enough from you, boy. I am the head of this family and don't answer to any of you. Securing an alliance with the Russians is tactically necessary to push out the Quinns and claim what should've been ours from the beginning."

"Why should it be, Da?" My glass clanks on the granite countertop and orange juice swishes over the rim. "The Quinns live by a code. They were committed to the truce you signed with Cormack decades ago."

"Cormack Quinn is dead, as is the truce. And with him gone, we have our opening to rule all of Dublin."

"Why does that matter?" I ask. "We have millions of dollars, houses, and a thriving business. You're a powerful and feared man. Why do we need more? What was so wrong with coexisting with the Quinns? Going after them is going to start an all-out war."

Da shakes his head. "You disgust me."

"Then we finally have something in common."

He's out of his seat and storming toward the island in the next heartbeat. I grab a knife out of the butcher block and my fingers tighten around the handle with a death grip. As strong as the urge is to back away and shrink in the surge of his anger, I hold my ground.

The surprise in Da's eyes is only a flash before it's replaced by fury. "You dare raise a knife against me?"

"To defend my life? Aye, I dare."

His gaze grows dark, and I feel Darcy moving into position behind me.

"Don't fucking try it, D. I've been manhandled enough this

week that I'm liable to forget you're my brother and add another McGuire boy to the funeral listings."

"Piper!" Mam gasps. "How dare you speak of our dead with such disrespect?"

Da lifts his chin, makes eye-contact with my brother, and tilts his head to wave him off. When he meets my gaze, there's nothing left of the man I once considered my father. "You're the reason Ryan's dead, Piper. If he hadn't been sent to find you, he'd be alive and maybe you'd be dead."

"Sorry to disappoint you, Da."

My father glares at me. "Ryan is dead because you let yourself be taken by a Quinn. Where was your fight and survival instinct then?"

I scoff. "Sean scraped me off the sidewalk bloody and beaten. The Quinns were kind to me. They got me a doctor and when I felt ready to leave, they wished me well. They value the truce. They don't want war. They don't want to see innocents killed in their streets."

Da shakes his head. "You're as stupid as you are useless."

There it is. "That's what I'm used to—just with a little more venom because you stopped hiding your true colors."

"You're lucky I'm a forgiving man, Piper." Da takes another step forward and then glances at the knife and stops. "Billy told me you'd be brainwashed by the Quinns, so I'll let you live despite your disrespect. Get upstairs. Consider yourself confined to your room until I decide what is to be done with you."

I blink. Does he actually think I'm still his approval-seeking little girl? "Sorry, Da. I came home to pay my respects in the wake of Ryan's death and to look you in the eye to tell you I know what you did with the Russians. I won't be confined in my room, and you won't decide what's being done with me. I'm leaving after the service, and I won't be back."

I cast a glance at my mother. Her expression is unreadable, but she's not talking me out of leaving, so that says something.

"So insolent." Da's gaze narrows on the blade of the knife. "How long do you think you'll survive in the world without the McGuire name to protect you? Where will you go? How will you feed yourself?"

"None of that is your concern anymore. You lost the right to be my father the moment you traded my virginity for guns. The funniest part is I'm not a virgin, so I'm not sure if I even qualify as your party favor."

Da's expression blanches. It's the most emotion I've seen in him since this confrontation began. His gaze shifts to my mother. "What is she saying? You assured me she was a virgin."

"She *is*. She's lying."

I laugh. "I'm not lying. Why would you think you know better than me? I'm not a virgin. Despite your hovering, I've had amazing sex and countless orgasms, and there's nothing you can do to change that. Does that make your contract fraudulent? I wonder what the Russians will think about that. I'm sure they won't appreciate you lying to them."

Da looks like he's about to have an aneurysm, and I take that as a win.

My mother is standing now, and she looks like she might faint. "Shut up, Piper. Get upstairs to your room."

Apparently, I've struck a nerve.

In my head, I hoped that my mother might still side with me once she found out what was done to me.

Now I'm more certain than ever that she knew the plan and went along with it. The pain of that realization is numbing to the point of dizziness.

Mam points at the stairs, and I consider that my cue to take my leave. I don't rush. I take my time climbing to the top of the stairs, go into my room, and close the door quietly behind me.

When the lock clicks into place, I take my first deep breath in the past ten minutes. The knife is still clutched in my hand, and I make a concerted effort to release my fingers and allow the circulation to begin again.

I did it.

I didn't plan to draw such an aggressive line in the sand, but when he came at me, I grabbed the blade purely on instinct.

A few deep breaths with my back against my bedroom door and the shakes settle. I'm fine. I stood my ground and had my say.

I'm on the other side of it.

All I need to do now is to attend the funeral and then walk away. I scan the room that has been my personal space for two decades. Everything looks exactly the way I left it last week, but nothing is the same.

This will be the last time I set foot in this room.

With my bridges burnt to a crisp, it's time to plan for the next phase of my life.

I head to my closet to grab my suitcase, but it isn't there. Fine. They can't stop me from leaving just by taking away a suitcase. I stride across the hall to Rory's room and grab one of his sports duffle bags from under his bed.

Once I'm back in my room, I start to pack.

CHAPTER EIGHTEEN

Sean

$\mathcal{I}$'m sitting in the back room of the Dublin Devils' headquarters, the air thick with the smell of oil and leather. My phone lies on the table in front of me, its screen too dark for my liking.

I'm waiting for a text from Piper, hoping she's safe, especially since it's been over an hour since she said she was off to confront her father.

She's tough—I know that—but she's also innocent and very breakable.

I tip my tumbler back in a greedy gulp, the images of her beaten and bleeding forever etched into my mind's eye. Never again.

I will gut anyone who ever lays a fucking hand on her.

Piper doesn't understand the lengths I will take to keep her safe. I will slaughter anyone in my fucking path to get to her.

I'm already counting the days until I can hunt down Vladimir Volkov and Arkady Sidorov and string them up from the nearest bridge with their cocks cut off and shoved down their throats.

Mattie McGuire deserves the same fate.

But as angry as Piper is at her father, I doubt it would earn me any favors in the romance department if I emasculate her father like that.

How about a good 'ole 9mm round through the skull?

That might go over better.

I stare at the clock on the opposite wall. With Ryan's funeral in a few hours, it feels like the city is holding its breath, waiting for a spark that will ignite the chaos.

The phone vibrates, and I'm quick to grab it, but it's not Piper. "Hey, Tag. What's the craic?"

"That's my question, brother. First off, how are you?"

He's not asking about my mental state. There's no reason why he would be worried about that. He has no idea I've fallen for the enemy and am about to be sick knowing she's out of my reach.

No. He's talking about the hole in my side.

"I'm sound as a pound. How are things on your end?"

"Quiet. Maybe too quiet. I don't like it."

I glance around the dimly lit room, the maps of Dublin on the walls marked with our territory and notable incidents over the past weeks. "Calm isn't a bad thing, but I hear what you're saying. Maybe the McGuires are taking the day off to mourn, or maybe they'll strike out."

"Exactly. There have been no fires, and no attacks. It's making me jumpy."

"What are you thinking?"

"I want twice the normal number of riders patrolling along the river and watching over the Quinn properties."

My fingers tap against the wooden table as I watch the arms of the clock stretch around their circle again and again. "Aye, I'll

JENN MADORE & CAROLINA MAC

get it done. Anything else? Have you heard anything more from the Russians?"

"Nothing from the two in the city, no, but I have a call scheduled with the big boss, Anton Volkov, later tonight."

"Have you figured out how to satisfy their expectations and keep them out of Dublin?"

"Not yet." Tag sighs on the other end of the line. "We can't handle the volume of product Mattie negotiated for without tipping the balance of our entire operation. I want more legitimate businesses in the future, not less."

"You'll think of something—you always do."

"Thanks for the vote of confidence, but if you get any big ideas, throw them into the ring. The hours are ticking down, brother. We need a plan."

"All right. I'll give it some thought today, and we can talk over dinner."

"You're coming for dinner? I figured once you were back on your bike and Piper was gone, you'd be back to your flat."

"Aye, well, maybe I'm not ready to give up Cora's cooking just yet."

Tag laughs. "Whatever it takes. You know she loves it when we're all under one roof."

"Aye, she does at that."

I end the call and stare at my phone again, willing it to light up with Piper's name. Today, of all days, I need to be focused, but I can't help but worry.

Mattie McGuire is a venomous snake.

If Piper's not careful, she'll get a nasty bite.

The silence of the headquarters feels more oppressive than ever, each tick of the clock hands taunting me.

I stand to rally my army, to throw myself into the work. It's the only way to keep the worry at bay, focusing on what I can control. Not waiting for a text that may not come or for the night to unfold.

We're in the eye of the storm. All I can do is prepare myself in the silence and wait for the chaos to unleash.

I step onto the front porch of the clubhouse, pulling the door shut behind me with a solid thud. The air is crisp, carrying a sharp chill that's uncommon for Dublin at this time of year. Where has the summer gone?

I fish a cigarette from my jacket and light up, taking a long, slow drag. The nicotine hits, but it doesn't do much to ease the knot of worry that's locked in my chest.

Flicking ash off the end, I pull out my cell and dial Kieran, my sergeant at arms. He picks up on the second ring. "Have you got an update from the south side?"

"Yeah, boss," Kieran's voice is steady, reliable. "My guy's on it. He watched over Piper at the wake last night, made sure she got home okay. He's stationed outside her house now. Says three black limos just pulled up. He'll tail them to the funeral and keep me posted."

That information helps settle some of the restlessness stirring inside me. "Good. Keep me updated. And make sure your guy stays sharp. If anyone moves on Piper, I want to know immediately."

"Got it. Anything else?"

"Aye, Tag wants to double up on patrols. He's not sure if the funeral will inspire Mattie to take the day off or come at us. He wants to be prepared. Where are you now?"

"Frenchie, Tig, and I are at the staging warehouse, replacing the loading bay door."

"Okay, you three stay on that, I'll get Keefer and we'll work the patrols."

"Let me know if anything fun starts. We'll be there."

I chuckle. "Don't worry. I'm sure we'll all get our fill of bloody battles in the days to come."

"Promises, promises."

I end the call and slide the phone back into the side pocket of my leather vest. I take another drag of my cigarette and scan the lines of bikes in the yard.

It's a fucking beautiful sight.

I wonder if Piper would ride. I could get her a Low Rider or maybe a Nightster, and have Kieran paint it up all sexy and spank. Thinking about Piper in leathers does powerful things to me.

I groan as my cock hardens and I realize I have no right to fantasize about a future where the two of us can break the sound barrier together.

She's not for me.

She's a McGuire.

Still, she's packing it in with her family and that gives the little ember of warmth kindling in my cold, dark heart an ounce of hope.

Her plan to live on the north side with friends means I can at least see her and know that she's doing okay.

Looking out across the yard, I allow myself a moment to breathe. I exhale and watch as the smoke curls up into the gray afternoon sky.

Before heading back inside, I pull out my phone again and type out a quick text to Piper.

> Thinking of you today.

It's not much, but it's generic enough that if anyone questions it, the context is easily explained on the day of her brother's funeral.

I hit send, hoping it offers her a sliver of comfort on a day that's bound to be filled with grief and tension.

Crushing the cigarette under my boot, I decide there's not much more I can do here for now. I open the door and lean inside. "Saddle up, boys. We're on the move."

While boots and chairs shuffle against the wood floor inside, I walk over to where my bike is parked. The familiar weight of the keys in my hand grounds me, and though my side hurts when I swing a leg over, I settle onto the seat and wait for the pain to ease.

When my boys are present and accounted for, I fire up the engine, the throaty roar rumbling through the quiet, echoing in the fenced property around us.

I can't do anything more for Piper right now, so I might as well keep Tag happy. The road is a sanctuary for me anyway, the rhythm of the ride a meditation.

Mickey rides to the gate and opens our way and the boys roll out. As my tires take hold, I shift gears and fall into the stream of bikes spilling onto the street like a river of steel and leather.

"Keep it tight, Devils. Today, more than ever, we need to watch each other's backs."

CHAPTER NINETEEN

Piper

*T*he service ends and as funerals go, Ryan gets a lovely send off. Only the members of our family and of Da's inner circle come to share a toast at the gravesite.

I stand in front of the lowered casket with Rory on one side of me and Brody on the other. All afternoon, my protective brother bookends kept me isolated from our parents, Darcy, and Niall.

Which works for me.

After having my say this morning, all the fight drained out of me. I'm still angry—I doubt I'll ever get over that—but I don't have the energy to waste on people who don't respect me.

Once the bottle of whiskey has been passed around and everyone has their sip, Da raises his glass. "To Ryan. May the sun shine warm upon your face, and the rains fall soft upon your fields. And until we meet again, may God hold you in the palm of his hand, my boy. *Suaimhneas síoraí air.*"

"*Suaimhneas síoraí air,*" we all repeat, wishing him eternal rest.

With that done, Rory and Brody walk me back to the limos parked along the cemetery trail.

"Are you sure you won't come back to the house for the reception?" Brody asks.

"Not this time. I wanted to be here for Ryan, but I'm ready to take my things and go. I was half afraid Da would lock me in my room and not let me leave. It's best if I get out while I can."

Rory hugs me and kisses my forehead. "Well, we'll miss you, little bug. Call us and let us know how you are. And if you're ever on our side of the river…"

I ease back and shake my head. "I don't suppose that will be for a long while. But if you're ever on the north…"

Brody laughs. "Equally unlikely."

I wonder if it has to be that way. If I told Sean I wanted to have lunch with my brothers, he'd let them come across without hassle, wouldn't he?

In my heart, I know he would.

The boys might not believe me, but the Quinns aren't the horrible monsters Da makes them out to be. That's his paranoia getting the best of him.

"Rory, Brody, come here, lads." Da is standing with Billy Gravely, Niall, Darcy, and a handful of his men.

They check with me, and I nod. "Go ahead. I'm just going to grab my bag and go. It's probably easiest if you keep the old man away from me, anyway."

Brody kisses my cheek. "Text us."

"I will."

I watch them leaving and wonder if I can make a world for them that doesn't involve the insanity of my father's violent reign. It's too late for Niall and Darcy, and possibly even Brody…but Rory could be spared.

I open the door to the limo and reach in to grab my duffle off the seat where I left it.

A strong hand grips my wrist and yanks me inside.

173

Adrenaline spikes as I'm yanked across the wide seat by Arkady Sidorov. My ribs send a searing pain through my side, and I let out a scream of terror. *"Help!"*

My plea is cut off by the slamming of the door as Vladimir settles onto the seat opposite us. "We meet again, firesnapper."

I pull at my arm, but Arkady's too strong. With a knock on the opaque privacy glass, the car pulls away from the cemetery.

Twisting to look out the back window, I see Rory and Brody being held back by Niall and Darcy, as my father laughs and waves.

The fucking asshole.

I'm in shock.

My cell rings and Arkady finally releases his hold on me. "Answer phone."

If it means he's not manhandling me, gladly. I pull my cell out of my purse and shrink as far away from the Russians as I can get.

Vomit burns at the back of my throat when I read the caller ID. "You are some kind of fucking monster, Da."

The old man is still chuckling. "Och, such a mouth—so disrespectful."

"Respect is earned, not a given."

"And you thinking so has brought us to this impasse. You set my deal with the Bratva on unsteady ground, now you will make it right. Whether you like it or not."

Bile twists in the pit of my belly and there's a good chance I'm going to throw up.

"To put us back on working terms with our friends in Russia, you will become a doting wife to Vladimir and fall in line for his friends."

I scoff. "Never going to happen."

"Then your mother will mourn another of her dead children."

"But not you, right, Da? You won't mourn me."

"Your actions killed Ryan. You were dead to me the moment he stopped breathing."

The breath leaves my body as the truth of his words sinks into my battered heart. "Only McGuires born with a cock mean anything to you, is that it?"

"Aye, you're finally catching on. You've caused insurmountable loss, and you will pay for your shortcomings."

"My shortcomings? Refusing to be raped and gifted away like a whore is not a shortcoming—it's my right."

He laughs again, this time his voice is full and booming with amusement. "You live and die by my order, Piper. You have no rights. It's a pity you didn't realize it sooner. Maybe all this ugliness might've been avoided."

The phone goes dead and my mind spins.

I study the evil glint in the eyes of the two Russians taking me captive and wonder how the hell I'm going to get out of this.

"You understanding now, da?" Vladimir takes my cell, rolls down the window, and tosses it out of the car. "Your father made promise. Now negotiation can resume."

Blindfolded in the back seat of the limo, I chastize myself for being in this position. Why did I insist on respecting the loss of my brother at my expense? I wasn't even close to Ryan.

Part of me—the last bit of the little girl in me—wanted to be there for my family in our time of grief. I didn't want to add to my mother's heartache as she mourned the death of Ryan.

But she wasn't worried about me. She was angry that I stood up for myself and refused their plan.

Ashamed and furious, I lay on the back seat, wishing I had listened to Sean when he told me I wasn't out of danger. He warned me I didn't grasp how vile my father could be.

He was right.

If I *had* listened, we could be eating Pop-Tarts in my lovely new flat. We couldn't be a couple, but I would be safe, and I could start over.

The limo stops, and Vladimir removes the fabric covering my eyes. "We're here—home away from home. After wedding, I take you to mother Russia. You be good wife. You see."

I shudder as thoughts of wedding night horrors flash through my head. Tears burn behind my eyes, but I refuse to let them fall.

Arkady gets out and extends a hand. "Out."

I don't move to comply, and Vladimir places a firm hand on my arm. "Obey Arkady, Piper. Don't make him hurt you again."

As if he cares. It's not like I've forgotten the evil glint in his eyes as he pommeled my face and tore the flesh off my cheek with his ring.

He didn't care about me being hurt then.

I can't see a way out of this, and they won't hesitate to rough me up, so I comply. I slide along the leather seat and get out without touching Arkady or letting him touch me. We're parked at the back of a house, but I can't see anything beyond that.

Salt hangs heavy in the breeze, so we must be near the bay. South of the city, maybe? I need to get my bearings so I can plan my escape.

Vladimir leads the way, and Arkady remains within striking distance, so I follow. They escort me through a mud room entrance and up a narrow corridor. Arkady stops before a closed door and then ushers me inside.

It's a standard guest bedroom setup: a bed flanked by night-stands, a chest of drawers with a mirror over it, and nothing in the way of personal items or finishing touches.

Homey.

I turn to say so but my comment dies in my throat. Arkady is right in my face and before I know what's happening, he's got my wrists bound with wide plastic tie wraps. "What the hell?"

I fight his hold, and he shoves me with both hands. The contact knocks me back onto the bed and then he's climbing over me, grabbing my bound wrists.

"Get off me!" I'm about to lose my mind when he releases my wrists and rolls off the bed. My arms are stretched above my head and my shackles are locked onto the headboard.

Vladimir grins and moves to the side of the bed. "We leave you now, firesnapper. Arkady and I will check on wedding preparations. Tonight is big night."

"Tonight? I'm not marrying you."

Vladimir grips my jaw and squeezes until tears burn behind my eyes. "I have papers. Your parents give you to me. You are mine."

"I'm *not* yours. Your papers mean nothing. This isn't legal. Nothing about this is legal."

"Legal? We are Bratva. Legal is nothing to do with anything." He leans in, still gripping my jaw. "We should celebrate. Arkady, bring vodka...and the dress."

The dress? Is he seriously so delusional that he actually thinks he can force me to marry him?

"I'm not marrying you," I repeat.

"So you say."

Arkady returns with an unopened bottle of Russian vodka and hands it to his boss. Then he hangs a dress bag on a hook on the closet door.

He can't seriously have a wedding dress in there, can he? Even as my brain stumbles to make sense of any of this, I know he does.

He's just that crazy.

Vladimir breaks the seal of the vodka and holds up the bottle. "To Vladimir and Piper." He knocks back a couple of long swallows of vodka and then puts the bottle in my mouth and tips it back.

I choke, swallowing and sputtering as the alcohol burns its way down my throat.

"Good girl. Tonight we transform you into magnificent Russian princess."

He takes another swig of vodka and then strides over to the closet. After unzipping the garment bag, he pulls a god-awful mass of white lace free of its confines. "So beautiful. My mother sent dress from Russia. It belonged to first wife."

I blink. "How many wives have you had?"

"Four. You will be youngest and most beautiful. Special in your own way."

Is he implying that he's gone through multiple wives, or that he has a harem stashed away back in Russia? I'm not sure, but I have no intention of finding out.

Somehow, I have to get out of here.

Somehow, I need to get back to Sean.

"Rest now, firesnapper."

I roll my eyes. "It's firecracker, not firesnapper."

He grins. "See? Already we make good for one another."

Vladimir leaves the room and after the door closes, a dead bolt slides into place.

I want to scream but need a plan of escape more.

I pull at the restraints binding my hands. There's no give to them and without something sharp, I'll never break their hold.

I won't be getting out of here until I'm let out.

And that will be when either Arkady or Vladimir comes to get me for the wedding. I clamp my eyes shut as hot tears escape.

I can't marry into the Bratva—I won't.

My heart belongs to another crime family. I would gladly give up my McGuire name to be a Quinn.

Mrs. Sean Quinn.

CHAPTER TWENTY

Sean

It's four in the afternoon, and I'm losing patience with the fucking world. Tag has had us patrolling up and down the river, watching the warehouses all day, and not one damned thing has happened.

Whether Mattie took a day off to honor his family—which I highly doubt—or he's fucking with us, today was nothing but wasted hours and wasted gas.

"Am I keeping you from something, brother?" I glance to the head of the meeting table and meet Tag's scrutinizing gaze. "You've checked your phone ten times in the last ten minutes. Is there something I should know about?"

I can't very well tell him I've lost all focus because I'm waiting for a text from Piper. She's still the enemy in Tag's eyes and I'm supposed to understand that and put the family first.

Besides, she probably got caught up after the funeral and is just meeting up with those girlfriends who share a flat up in Cabra. The fact that I haven't heard from her doesn't mean she's in trouble.

I might have a serious protector complex developing. Piper is a smart girl just beginning to assert her independence. She doesn't need me hovering.

"No. Nothing. The day is just wearing on me."

Tag leans back in his chair and pinches the bridge of his nose. "Aye, I'm well acquainted with that feeling, but I need you to focus. My call with Anton Volkov is in three hours and I still don't have a workable plan about how to unseat Mattie in this gun deal."

"Ask and ye shall receive, brother." Finn has a spring in his step as he bursts into the meeting room, laptop in hand, followed by Laine.

The moment Tag sees his fiancé, he launches to his feet. "What's wrong? Why did Finn bring you here?"

Laine waves away his concern and points to where Finn is setting himself up on the table. "We have an idea—a good idea about how to handle the Russians."

I stride over to the door and shout down the hall. "Brendan and Bryan, family meeting."

Finally, maybe we can end this.

Brendan and Bryan hustle in a moment later and I point to the door. "Close that."

Bryan gets the door, and then we all move to stand behind our baby brother.

"All right, Finny, what have you got?"

He meets my question with a smile. "The biggest problem we've been having trying to overtake the McGuire gun deal is the volume, right?"

Tag crosses his arms. "Aye, we could accept their first shipment, but we have no use for that number of weapons on a regular basis."

"Not to mention it would pull funding from our legitimate businesses," Laine adds.

When did everything Quinn become *'our businesses'*? It irks me a bit that Tag has opened us up to the woman so quickly, but she's smart and he's happy, so I let it go.

"Well, worry no more, brothers, because we have the answer." Finn grins and opens the files Laine gave us from the Tessiano Outfit.

She smuggled a thumb drive out of the states, hidden in the urn of her mother's ashes. It contained a dozen folders filled with detailed operational information from the Chicago crime family.

"The Tessianos want guns. The Russians want us to buy their guns. Why don't we act as middlemen and either connect the two or take a cut of the transaction fees to handle shipping?"

I pat Finn's shoulder. "The idea has bite to it."

Tag doesn't look so sure. "But if we approach the Tessianos, knowing what we know, there's a good chance they'll realize Laine is alive and living here with us."

Laine flashes him a sweet smile. "Which might happen anyway at some point. Better we address the situation and clarify that I'm not a risk. The Tessianos are businessmen first and foremost. I have no interest in causing them trouble or in hiding for the rest of my life. If you explain that we're together and make them see the benefit of an alliance, it might solve two problems."

Tag doesn't seem convinced, but by the looks Brendan and Bryan are flashing me, the rest of us are loving this idea. Which is why they're all looking at me.

I'm Tag's voice of reason.

"It's a solid plan, T. It would also ally us with two strong powers elsewhere in the world."

"Never hurts to have more friends in low places," Brendan adds.

Bryan tips his glass back and sets the empty on the table. "And it would shut down Mattie in a big way."

"That in itself is reason enough to do it." I meet Tag's gaze and make sure he's really paying attention. "The truce is over, brother. Despite wanting to keep Da's legacy of peace alive, the McGuires have other plans. If we don't start fighting back, the violence will escalate."

He frowns, but I read the resignation in his eyes. He knows I'm right. "Fine. Let's brainstorm the different scenarios of how it could work."

My brothers and I take a seat around the table and Tag pulls Laine into his lap. Two weeks ago, I thought it was crazy that he always needs to touch her.

Now...I would give anything to have Piper holding my hand or sitting in my lap while we work out how to take down her father.

Am I as far gone as Tag? Am I in love with Piper?

Even as I ask myself the question, I know the answer. I began falling in love with her from the moment I picked her up from that sidewalk. It didn't matter that she was beaten and bloody—she stole my breath as quickly as she stole my heart.

A half an hour later, we've decided how to proceed. If the Tessiano Outfit agrees to leave Laine in peace, Tag will get them the guns they need to secure their interests in Chicago and the surrounding areas.

It'll take some finesse to get the guns inland to them, but Finn has some ideas about how we can eliminate Tag's transportation concerns.

"You nailed it, Finny." Tag pats Laine's thigh and kisses her cheek, urging her to get up. "You both did. Now, give me a few minutes to jot down my ideas of how the conversation should go. My call with Volkov is in two hours and I want to be home and in my office for that."

"I guess that's our cue to clear out." Finn closes the laptop, and we all stand.

My phone buzzes in my hand and I draw a deep breath as I answer it. "Kieran. What can I do for you?"

"I've got bad news, boss."

I step backward and sit on the edge of the table. "Tell me."

"Piper got grabbed by the Russians after the cemetery. They were in one of the limos and drove off with her."

"Drove off where, Kieran? Where the fuck did they take her?"

"To a house down by the bay. My guy stayed on them until she was unloaded and taken into a house south of the city."

"Does he have eyes on her?"

"No. Not her, but he says she hasn't left. In fact, he said there have been trucks in and out over the past hour delivering food, flowers, and chairs. He says it looks like they're getting ready for a party."

"A party? They fucking kidnapped her from a funeral and they're throwing a fucking gala? What is wrong with these people? Didn't anyone try to stop them?"

My guy said the only ones who tried were the two youngest McGuire boys. They were held back while Mad Mattie laughed and waved goodbye.

All the blood drains from my head and I can't tell if I'm going to pass out or go ballistic. "Mattie laughed? He fucking laughed as his daughter was taken by the same fucking animals that beat her and tried to rape her?"

"Sorry, boss. I'm just reporting the news."

It's not his fault I need to kill someone. "Text me the address. Where are you?"

"In my paint shop."

"If you're in the building, why the fuck aren't you telling me this in person?"

"Because I'd like to keep my face pretty and my insides right where they are, fuck you very much."

I roll my eyes and rein in my urge to kill. "Fine. Pull one of the trucks into the front and start loading it up. We're going across the river."

I hang up my cell and fight the urge to throw the piece of shit technology against the wall. I would...except Piper might need to call me.

"You can't move on the Russians." Tag's voice is stern and when I whip around to meet his gaze, his expression is uncompromising. "We've spent the past hour planning an alliance with Volkov. You can't storm into McGuire territory and kill his cousin."

"The fuck I can't!" I move to storm out of the room, but Brendan and Bryan block my exit. They're standing in front of the door with their arms crossed like fucking bouncers at a club.

I turn back to Tag, feeling more like a trapped wolf than a man. "Those animals have Piper and after what they did to her the last time, how long do you think it'll be before they have her pinned to a mattress or bleeding because she won't stop fighting?"

Even as I say the words, my stomach tightens.

Tag's gaze softens. "I know you got attached to her when she was in your care, but she's a McGuire, Sean. She's not our problem."

"Not our problem?" I close the distance and have my hand around Tag's throat before I register I've moved. "I'm more than *attached* to her. I fucking love her. She's mine and I let her go because you'd never let me keep her. She's in danger because I couldn't give her what she needed—a home and a new name."

The surprise in Tag's gaze would be funny if anything about this was funny—but it's not. It's heartbreaking that Piper was betrayed once again and that now she's alone and scared.

"Ease up on the breath play, Sean." Brendan's hand is over mine as he tilts his head into my field of vision. "Choking out Tag won't get your girl home any faster."

"Did you have sex with her?"

Laine's question cuts through the testosterone-infused fury filling the air and I release Tag and turn on her. "Excuse me? That's none of your fucking business."

She's not the least bit intimidated by my attention. "I'm not being nosy. I'm looking for a way to help you. Mattie McGuire guaranteed that his daughter was untouched. It was a stipulation of the agreement. If the two of you were intimate, that changes things."

I don't know what to do with the violence wreaking on my sanity, but I try to focus. "Yes, we had sex."

Tag curses behind me. "She's a fucking child and was in your care."

"She's an adult, and it was her idea. She wanted to retake control of her life. It started out as a way to flip off her father but became more."

"The two of you spent a week together. That's hardly enough time to throw around the word love."

Laine scoffs. "And how long was it before you said you loved me, Tag? You kidnapped me and claimed me as yours to protect an hour after we met and moved me into your home an hour after that."

Tag grunts. "That was different."

Laine shakes her head. "If her last name wasn't McGuire, we wouldn't be standing here. If Sean told you he fell for a girl from the south side who was kidnapped and at risk of being raped or killed, you'd be loading the trucks and planning a full-on rescue."

Tag glares at his girl. "But she *is* a McGuire, and the people who kidnapped her could be allies or enemies, depending how we handle this. We have to think about our family."

"Piper *is* my family," I snap, running my hand through my hair. "At least, she could be. I ignored that and tried to play by the rules, but I love her, Tag. I can't just leave her at the mercy of the men who beat the shit out of her when she wouldn't allow them to rape her!"

I see that he's warring with his emotions, but I don't have time for him to figure things out. "I've got to go."

Tag curses. "Okay, here's what we're going to do..."

CHAPTER TWENTY-ONE

Piper

*B*y the time the deadbolt slides free and the door opens, my fear has morphed into an eerie calm and my world is buzzing with a low hum. I might be losing my mind. Either that, or maybe this is what it feels like to be homicidal.

As crazy as it sounds, I'm relieved it's Vladimir and not Arkady that comes through the door.

Vladimir may be delusional to think I will ever be his blushing bride, but he's mostly a scary brute and wants me to stop fighting him.

Arkady is a mean fucker who wants to hurt me.

Vladimir strides over to sit on the edge of the bed. He reaches up to my face and moves my hair to see the hamburger he made of my left cheek. "Time to get dressed. Guests are arriving."

My brain can't even process that. I've heard the trucks and the people coming and going all afternoon, and despite Vlad telling me the wedding is tonight, I didn't think it was possible.

How can this be happening?

"I can be good friend with powerful family. My cousin says if I am happy, he is happy. Then your family is happy, too. Your father gets guns."

"My father is a liar and a monster. You can't believe anything he says."

Vladimir frowns. "Last week you say your father is upstanding man and powerful businessman."

"Last week I didn't know he had signed me up for an arranged marriage. It won't hold up. I'm not a child bride that has no say. I'm an adult and I don't agree to any of this."

Vladimir frowns. "I have papers."

Yes, yes. He seems to think that's his answer for all of this. Not the brightest bulb, Vladimir.

"The papers are a lie. I'm not an innocent virgin, Vladimir. I have a lover and my father knows it. He's playing you for a sucker because he wants your cousin's guns. You can't believe him."

There have been few moments when I've gotten through the testosterone fog these Russians live under, but the moment I say I'm not a virgin, Vladimir stiffens. "You lie."

"No. It's the truth. I'm not an innocent. I won't be your good girl virgin. I'm in love with another man—a powerful man who has an army at his command. He'll be coming for me."

The words come out of my mouth as an attempt to gain my freedom, but as they hang in the air between us, I acknowledge how true they are. I love Sean.

I'm in love with Sean Quinn.

Just as I think I'm getting through to Vladimir, Arkady joins us. He looks at the two of us and says something to Vladimir in Russian.

Vladimir stands gesturing to me lying there. "She says she's not innocent—not untouched."

Arkady's gaze darkens as he scowls at me. "Lying to Vladimir Volkov is dangerous. His cousin very dangerous man."

"I'm not the one who lied to you. My father lied. When I found out he sold me off as a virgin, I told him I'm not. I made it clear he had to fix this and tell you the truth."

Vladimir frowns. "He said nothing."

"One of you lies." Arkady flicks his hand toward Vladimir, motioning him toward the end of the bed. "Time to find out who. Grab her legs."

Without hesitation, Vladimir's meaty hands clasp around my ankles. The breath rushes out of my lungs as Arkady climbs over me and lifts the skirt of the dress I wore to Ryan's funeral.

I fight to kick my feet, but Vladimir's too strong.

I fight against the plastic binding my wrists, but that only serves to make the cuffs bite harder into my flesh.

"Get off me," I screech, bucking my hips. "Don't fucking touch me."

With a violent grab, Arkady snaps the crotch of my underpants and sticks two fingers in me. He's rough and I'm the farthest thing from turned on, so the digits feel like sandpaper as he penetrates me.

I scream and then it's over.

Arkady pulls his hand back and spits on me. "Not a virgin."

I turn my head to the side, wiping his saliva onto the pillow. "How is this my fault? My father is the one who lied to you."

"McGuires are liars," Vladimir shouts, scowling at me. "When I tell Anton, no guns for you. And no wedding. I want an innocent, good girl, not a whore."

I take the insult because it doesn't faze me. The important points in Vladimir's rant are that the wedding is off, and I've screwed over my father. Technically, I was a virgin when Da drew up the marriage contract, but no one needs to know that.

See, I can fight dirty, too.

Now the question is, will they let me go or kill me?

Sean

The sound of the waves slapping against the side of the boat syncs with the pounding of my heart as we approach Vance's Harbour. The night is dark, only the distant lights of south Dublin and the soft glow of our equipment lighting our way.

The salt in the air mixes with the adrenaline that courses through my veins, each breath tasting of the bay and imminent danger.

Beside me, Brendan checks his gear for the umpteenth time, his movements precise and methodical. The guy is an adrenaline junky, but I wouldn't want anyone else by my side.

"We'll get Piper back for you, brother." Brendan lays his AR-15 across his knee. "Whatever we need to do."

"Without killing Russians." Bryan gives Brenny a knowing look. "Tag said this won't work if we kill the Russians."

That will be a challenge.

If they hurt her or violated her, they will be put down.

It's been hours since she was taken, and we're only just launching our assault. It was hell waiting for the sun to go down, but Tag needed time to work his magic, and we needed the cover of darkness to get into McGuire territory without tipping anyone off.

Thanks to Kieran's informant following the limo from the cemetery, we know where Mattie McGuire moved the Russians after we snatched them from the Nyx Hotel.

It's a private estate home that backs onto Vance's Harbour in the neighborhood of Blackrock. It's also a stone's throw from several of the McGuire warehouses.

Location, location, location.

"Almost there," Gallagher whispers into the comms from the lead boat.

Bryan scans the shoreline with a night vision scope.

I tap my earpiece and wait for the beep. "Everyone ready?"

We've got two dozen Devils across the three boats, all of which are equally focused on getting back my girl and fucking up Mattie McGuire's plans at the same time.

"Remember to be quiet as we move up the beach. We need the element of surprise and don't know if this party they're having has spilled out onto the grounds."

The boats slow as we near land, the outline of the mansion glowing against the starlit sky. It's a fortress, but many of my guys are ex-military and know how to breach a target.

The important part is that Piper is inside and no one in her life is looking out for her. The betrayal of her parents is unforgiveable. They will pay for hurting her.

"Arriving in two."

Gallagher's voice, barely audible over the comms, brings me back to the moment at hand.

I'm coming, kitten. Hold on.

Everyone checks their weapons one last time, securing silencers, and patting the extra mags in their vests. The hull of the boat gently grinds against the gravelly beach. We disembark swiftly, and fan out, taking cover behind the natural brush and rocks dotting the landscape.

Gallagher's team finds shelter behind an upcropping of rocks. "Good luck, boys. Safe home."

"Safe home," I say, watching as ten silhouetted shadows stalk up the beach. "Light up the skies, boys."

When they're on their way, I refocus on our part of the plan. The mansion looms above a small crest ahead, garden lights dancing against the darkness, its party guests unaware of the storm about to hit.

Brendan moves up beside me, his gaze scanning the perimeter. "The guards on patrol are McGuire men, not Russian. Tag has no problem with us taking them out, right?"

"None at all," I respond, adjusting my grip on my rifle. "Kieran, take your team to the west and front, silent takedowns of any and all McGuire guards you come across."

"Copy that," Kieran responds.

"Brenny, your team has the east and the back of the house to secure our exit."

"Got it."

"Bryan, you're with me."

It's nods all around and then we're jogging off in a crouched run, dodging from shadow to shadow as I close the distance between me and my girl.

As we stalk closer, the mansion's opulence seems strangely out of place for Mattie McGuire and his Bratva contacts. There's a woman playing a fucking harp and an ice sculpture, for fuck's sake.

What the hell kind of party are they throwing?

And then it clicks. The rows of white chairs leading to an arbor weighed down and choking with flowers. The long, red carpet leading from the house to the podium set beneath the arbor.

"It's a fucking wedding."

Bryan stops scanning for danger and takes it in. "Is this Mattie making sure Piper can't get out of his contract?"

My world tilts and my vision flips. Everything around me is tainted red. It's like a lens of savage hatred and the need to kill falls over me like a fiery film.

Mattie McGuire will die for this.

It's a truth I know, down to the depth of my aching soul. He will bleed for this, and it will be by my hand.

I crouch low, moving from shadow to shadow, the cool night air carrying the promise of revenge.

We pass Brendan and Duke dragging a downed guard into the bushes and position ourselves in view of the side entrance.

There are catering trucks parked along the side of the house and party workers moving in and out.

I tap my earpiece. "In position. Ready for our diversion, Gallagher."

"Then get ready for the fireworks, boss. In three, two, one..."

There's a beat of silence when I wait for the night to erupt, and then it does. Just down the beach, a fiery burst of explosion lights up the sky and then another. By the time the third goes off, party guests are flooding out of the house and into the backyard.

That's our cue.

Like ghosts, Bryan and I surge forward. Anyone hired for the event back away when they see us racing up the corridors.

The first guard we come across doesn't have time to sound the alarm. Brendan is a crack shot and with his silencer in place, the guard is down, a silent heap sliding down the golden damask wallpaper, before he can react.

Adrenaline surges as we push deeper into the house.

The chaos of the warehouses exploding down the beach has drawn almost everyone out of the house. Men are shouting furiously in the back, and as much as I'd love to see the look on Mattie's face as he's watching his warehouses burn, he's not my priority.

"That looks promising." Brendan points the barrel of his gun down a side corridor to where two armed guards are standing outside a door.

Their focus is locked on a window to the back of the house. They have no idea we've got them in our sights.

"Shoot first, ask questions later?" Brendan asks.

"Not with the possibility that Piper could come out that door. Wing them, but keep things low."

"A challenge. I like it. You've got left. I'm right." Brenny strides forward, letting off two shots in quick succession.

I plug the guy on the left in the thigh. With any luck, I caught his femoral artery, but I don't care. The only thing I care about is Piper. "Finish them up close and personal."

"Roger that." Brendan lets his assault rifle fall to his side on its harness and pulls out his Glock.

As he closes the distance on the two bleeding on the floor, I storm through the chaos and kick the door open. Wood splinters as the slab swings on its hinges, but the only thing I see is Piper.

She's wide-eyed and bound by her wrists to the frame of the bed.

She's alive.

That's all that matters to me—until I see blood staining the inside of her thighs.

CHAPTER TWENTY-TWO

Piper

*H*e's here.

When the explosions started, Vladimir and Arkady ran out of here like their asses were on fire. I hoped—no, I prayed—Sean was coming for me.

But even as I did, I reminded myself not to be so naïve. The Quinns don't come across the river. If he did, Sean would be breaking the truce his brother so desperately wants to preserve.

But he's here.

"What the fuck did they do to you?" Sean's voice is warbling with fury and I'm not sure what set him off until I track his gaze.

There's a thin trail of blood on the inside of my thigh. "I'm all right. Sean, listen to me. They didn't rape me."

"Then why the fuck are you bleeding?"

I could say it's my period and avoid telling him the humiliating truth, but I don't think I can lie to him. I don't *want* to lie to him. "I told them I wasn't a virgin and Arkady verified that with two fingers. It wasn't pleasant, but it isn't worth dying over. Now, untie me and take me away from here."

As if to punctuate the urgency of my request, automatic gunfire sounds off outside the house.

Sean stalks closer. "Aye, we'll leave, but everything about you is more than worth dying over, Piper. Don't ever doubt that."

My wrists burn as Sean slices through the plastic ties that bind them. The relief of being freed is immediate, but the fear and adrenaline that have been clawing at my insides don't subside.

Sean pulls me into his arms, the reality of my rescue not settling in yet.

"Thank you." My voice is as unsteady as my hands. "I wasn't sure you'd come."

Sean eases back, his scowl intense. "I will always come for you, kitten. But from now on, I won't need to because you're never leaving my fucking side."

I like the sound of that.

I'm not sure how that will work, but it's a nice thought for a terrible moment.

"Hate to break this up, but it's time to go." Brendan is leaning into the room with urgency written all over his face. "Hey, Piper. Glad you're not dead."

"Thanks. Me too."

Sean grabs my hand and leads me out of the room. We rush through the mansion, dodging people fleeing the chaos that the Quinns have unleashed.

Anxiety twists hot in my guts as we step over the bodies of dead men—men I recognize. They work for my father, so why would they be here? Are they guarding the Russians?

The truth is much simpler than that, and the realization sinks in with each hurried step. My father's men are here because this wedding is all part of his twisted plot to marry me off to the Russians. The entire event is a lovely farce meant to bind me to a life I never wanted.

My father is behind all of this.

We burst out a side door and sprint along the stone wall of the house. The backyard sprawls before us, a scene of shattered elegance.

The wedding preparations—a grotesque reminder of what was meant to be my future—lie in ruins. Draped tables are overturned, gorgeous flower arrangements are trampled... It's the backdrop of Vladimir's delusional plans for me.

"Almost there." Sean glances over his shoulder to send me a reassuring gaze and I scream.

Just as the beach is in sight, Vladimir and Arkady step into our path, guns raised.

We stagger to a halt, the cold night air prickling my skin. Vladimir's face is twisted, his gaze burning with a mix of madness and betrayal.

Arkady stands beside him, his loyalty to Vladimir unwavering despite the chaos.

Time stands still.

My heart beats so loudly I can hear it in my ears.

Sean tightens his grip on my hand, a silent promise that he's here, that he won't let them take me.

But facing the men who see me as nothing more than a pawn in their power games, I realize how quickly that could change.

Vladimir and Arkady embody the chains I've been fighting to break all my life, and now, on the precipice of freedom, they threaten to drag me back.

Arkady aims his weapon, his intent clear in the set of his jaw and the lethal calm in his eyes.

Sean raises his hand. "Not a good idea, gentlemen. If you call your boss, Anton will tell you to let us leave without conflict. A deal has been struck. We're not your enemy."

Is that true, or is he bluffing?

I can hardly comprehend how Sean orchestrated a deal with Anton Volkov. My gaze flits between Arkady and Vladimir, gauging their reaction.

With a grunt that sounds more like a growl, Arkady pulls out his phone and dials. The conversation in rapid Russian slices through the tense silence, his voice terse. After a brief exchange, he hands the phone to Vladimir.

Vladimir's conversation is clipped, his tone betraying a flicker of surprise and annoyance. When he ends the call, his eyes pin me with a glare that chills. "Fine. You go. You not my innocent bride, anyway. Filthy whore."

Sean's muscles tense beside me, and I squeeze his hand. Before he loses his composure and escalates the situation, I tug at his arm. "Let's go. Please, Sean. Take me home."

Something in my plea breaks through his anger because he nods to Brendan and then pulls me into motion.

We make our way toward the edge of the harbor, my bare feet sinking in the sand. The darkness of the bay beckons. Safety is almost within our reach.

"Get the boat started, Brenny."

Brendan races ahead of us, wading into the water to where two boats are bobbing in wait.

Bang. Bang.

Sean's body jerks with the impact of gunfire, and his hand tears from my hold. He face-plants into the sand and doesn't move.

"Sean!" Panic seizes me as I drop to my knees beside him. "Sean."

Before I can roll him over to assess the full scope of horror, I'm hauled backward and thrown to the ground.

I twist around, rising to my feet to face Billy Gravely. His eyes burn with madness as he reclaims a vicious grip on me and pulls me away from Sean's body.

The world spins as I'm dragged along the waterfront, further away from Sean and my chance at freedom.

"You're a fucking menace," Billy grumbles more to himself than to me. "Do you realize the fucking damage you've done? First by pissing off the Russians, then by taking up with the Quinns?"

His questions are rhetorical and with Sean shot and likely bleeding to death, I don't have the energy to answer them even if they weren't.

I'm lost in the anguish of losing Sean, the chill of salty spray and shock working in harmony to make me shiver.

Until a roaring heat hums over my skin.

I glance up the beach as we approach the remnants of what used to be three of my father's warehouses.

Flames lick the night sky, the structures reduced to fiery skeletons. The sharp, acrid smell of burning wood and melted plastic assaults my senses.

The distant explosions I heard when I was tied up in that room make sense now. The Dublin Devils weren't just here to rescue me—they were also attacking my father's empire.

Good. I hope his losses are unrecoverable.

As we get closer, the heat from the fires becomes almost unbearable. The light from the flames casts eerie shadows across Billy's face, making him look more monstrously unhinged. He's muttering under his breath, his words lost in the crackle and hiss of the inferno.

My father's legacy is going up in smoke, and a part of me feels vindicated. He brought this upon himself with his endless greed and his cold disregard for anything other than power.

I strain against Billy's hold, wrenching my arm, but it's no use. His grip tightens, his nails digging painfully into my skin. Between my ribs, my raw wrists, and the way he's handling me, pain sears me inside and out.

We stop at the edge of the warehouse property, close enough

JENN MADORE & CAROLINA MAC

that the heat dries the tears on my cheeks and makes my skin feel tight and oversensitive.

I look back down the beach, my heart hammering against my battered ribcage. Is Sean still alive? I squint against the brightness of the fire, searching the darkness beyond the swirling smoke and flickering flames.

Movement ignites hope, but when I see who's approaching, that hope is stomped out.

It's not Sean—it's my father.

His face is contorted with rage, his eyes burning not from the fire's reflection, but from something consuming him—insanity maybe.

He's been known as Mad Mattie for years, but seeing him now, I'd say he's living up to his moniker.

"You ruined everything." Spittle sprays over my face and he screams. "Look what you've done."

"Me? I was locked in a room. This is on you, Da."

His swing is fast, his backhand brutal. The force of the blow connecting with my face spins my head and knocks me to the ground. Blood runs hot from my nose, the sting of the hit mingling with the heat from the fire, overwhelming and suffocating.

I'm on my knees, disoriented, my ears ringing, when I see him draw back his hand again. I brace myself for another hit, closing my eyes against the imminent pain.

Gunshots ring out, startlingly loud and close.

I flinch, expecting pain, but when I open my eyes, it's my father who falls. He collapses onto the sand, a startled look of confusion etched on his face.

Billy Gravely takes the next hit.

The force of the shot to his shoulder spins him. He staggers back, and the gun in his hand drops close to me.

I launch to get it, and when I raise it, he's already on the run. I point and shoot, firing every round he has left in the magazine.

When the gun silences, I stay there, frozen. I can't move. I can't think. I can't breathe.

Is it over? Will more of my father's men come?

But no one comes.

The only sounds are my ragged breath, the roar of flames, and the crash of waves. I don't know who fired those shots, whether it was one of Sean's men, a disgruntled ally of my father, or someone else entirely.

But in this moment, I don't care.

I glance down at my father lying in the sand and feel nothing but profound relief.

I can finally be free of him.

CHAPTER TWENTY-THREE

Sean

My lungs are burning, each breath a raspy, painful struggle as I stagger down the beach toward Piper. Sand sticks to my sweat-drenched face, the coarse grains mixing with the salt of my sweat.

Each step is agony. My back screams with the damage from bullets hitting my vest, but none of that matters.

Piper is all that matters.

Gravely's shots knocked the wind out of me, and for that haunting moment, while I laid face-down in the sand, half-conscious, I thought the worst.

I thought he'd close in and finish me.

Thankfully, Brendan was quick to race back and Gravely ran like the piece of shit opportunist he is.

My brother and my vest saved my life.

In turn, I got here in time to save Piper's life.

She's kneeling on the beach, a small, trembling figure against the sprawling backdrop of chaos and fire. My heart pounds harder with each step I take towards her. "Piper!" I call out, my voice rough.

As I drop to my knees beside her, the relief at seeing the rise and fall of her chest is overwhelming. She's bleeding, but she's alive.

I let my gun fall to the sand, and ease the Beretta out of her hand. It's empty. She unloaded the magazine at Gravely and sent him running into the darkness.

I know I hit him. Hopefully, Piper added even more lead to his diet.

"It's over, kitten. I've got you."

She stares up at me and I see the fog of shock and loss clear. Her cool blue eyes widen and a sob breaks in her chest. "I thought you were dead."

She launches herself at me and between my knife wound and the bullets I just took in my back, the impact of catching her is beyond painful.

And nothing has ever felt better.

I stroke her hair, soothing her even as my body protests every movement. "I'm alive, and I've got you, P."

"But how? I heard the gunshots. I saw you go down."

I press her hand against the tactical vest I'm wearing. "I came prepared. Now, we need to leave."

Her eyes, wide and filled with tears, follow my gaze to where Brendan is standing over her father. The old man is lying motionless in the sand, but Brenny will ensure that he stays that way.

And watching us plug him in the head isn't something I want seared into her memory. "I'm sorry if him being dead hurts you, beautiful, but I couldn't let him beat you. I killed your father."

She meets my gaze as I help her to her feet. "You killed him?"

I swallow, studying her reaction as I dip my chin. "Aye, it was me."

If me killing her father repulses her, I don't see it. Maybe it'll take time to sink in. Maybe she'll resent me for it, despite me trying to keep her safe.

He was her father, after all.

"He stopped being my father a week ago. I'm glad he's dead." The coldness in her words chills me, but I understand and I'm proud of her.

She saw what her father was capable of, the lengths he would go to in order to get his own way.

If his death meant her freedom, then so be it.

Urging Piper toward the darkness of the shoreline, I keep one arm firmly around her waist and signal Brendan to make sure Mattie McGuire never gets up. The silencer on his AR-15 absorbs the sound of the shot and the three of us leave the chaos and death of the night behind us.

As Bryan drives through the gates to our family compound, the long, winding driveway stretches past the light of the headlights. I know every tree standing sentinel along our path, every dip in the expansive lawn, every flowering bush in every flower bed.

Mam took such pride in making this our home and when I look at the manicured boxwoods and the fieldstone walkways, I think of her.

The love she held for each of us.

The fierce protective instinct she and Da both surrounded us with. We were their children—the living legacy of their love.

I want that with Piper.

I want our children to grow up playing with Tag's kids and for the twins and Finn to be bad examples and teach them all the crazy and dangerous things we did as kids.

I want it all.

I understand why Tag brought Laine here instead of to his loft in the city. He wants those things, too.

Piper is beside me, her body tense, her eyes haunted by too many ghosts. I want to say something to ease her, but words fail me. What do you say to a girl who's been thrown away by her family?

Even if I knew what to say, with Brendan and Bryan in the front seat, now is not the time.

Tag and Laine are waiting for us on the driveway. The relief on Laine's face when she sees us unload is palpable. It eases a tightness in my chest. She always seems genuine with me and my brothers, but there's no mistaking her concern.

I'm grateful she cares as much as she does.

Tag deserves a good woman.

"Everyone intact?" Tag asks.

"Drake has a broken hand and Frenchie caught shrapnel in his leg, but that's about it. Kelvin was waiting at the clubhouse to take care of any injuries."

Tag studies us one by one and then nods. "All right. We'll recap the night in the war room and then you boys can get cleaned up."

"I need to see to Piper first." My tone is harsher than I intend, but it's been one hell of a night. "She's been through hell. The debriefing can wait."

Tag frowns. "Not your call."

Laine steps forward, her expression softening. "I'll take Piper up to your room and run her a bath. I swear I won't leave her side. And if she needs you for any reason, I'll call you right away."

Everything in me is screaming not to let her out of my sight. It's crazy, but after the past week, I've learned to expect the worst when it comes to her.

Piper touches my arm lightly, her gaze meeting mine. "Go

with Tag and your brothers, Sean. It's important. He needs all the details to prepare for retaliation."

Her voice is steady, stronger than I expect from someone who's just been pulled from the brink. When I study her gaze, it's there too. Undeniable strength.

Tag's expression tightens. "How bad is it going to be?"

I take a deep breath, the weight of my next words settling like lead in my stomach. "Mattie McGuire is dead. Things went sideways, and I caught up to them while he was beating Piper. Gravely was there to put her down. I opened fire on both of them."

Tag's gaze widens. "Mattie's dead?"

"Definitely," Brendan says.

"What about Gravely?"

I sigh. "I winged him for sure and Piper unloaded his Beretta at him as he ran away, so if we're lucky, he's following Mattie straight down to hell."

"When have we ever been lucky?" Tag absorbs the news and then turns to Piper. "It wasn't our plan to kill your father, and I'm sorry you lost him, but please know we will do anything to protect our family. Sean tells us you're his family now, so that makes you ours as well. I'm sorry if that puts you in a tight spot."

She shakes her head, a bitter smile touching her lips. "It doesn't. After the past week, I'm severing all ties with the McGuires. I will miss Brody and Rory, though. Rory isn't deep in the business, and I'm hoping after seeing what happened, he'll walk away, too."

Tag nods, understanding and respect mingling in his gaze. "If any of your brothers walk away, I'll hold no grudges. They'll be safe from us. I give you my word."

"I appreciate that, Tag. Thank you."

I appreciate that too. "Thanks, brother."

Tag's word is good, and it eases a sliver of the worry

gnawing at me about my family and Pipers being in a bitter war until the end.

If she thinks we can save Rory, we will certainly try.

With that settled, the six of us move into the house. I walk with my arm around Piper's hips and when we arrive at the bottom of the stairs, I kiss her temple. "I'm downstairs if you need me."

"I'll be fine. Take your time."

Piper

Warm water envelops me, soothing some of my aches and washing away the grime of the night's harrowing events. Sean's tub is a vast soaker that could fit three people comfortably. It feels like a sanctuary after the chaos of the day.

I close my eyes, letting the heat seep into my bones, losing myself in the tranquility of the moment.

I'm safe.

Sean and his men came to get me.

My father is dead.

My mother has another funeral to plan, but this time, I won't be attending.

The sound of the door opening and closing softly pulls me back to reality. I open my eyes as Sean enters the bathroom, a tea tray in his hands.

I chuckle. "Don't let your leather-clad biker gang catch you being a tea granny. It'll ruin your street cred."

He sets the tray on the tile shelf behind the tub. "I think my street cred can handle it. How are you feeling?"

"A little numb. The adrenaline has worn off, leaving a hollow emptiness in its wake."

"I know how that feels." He tests the water, dragging a finger through the layer of bubbles. "Reality will set back in at its own pace. Don't rush it."

Despite the humidity in the room, my skin tingles with goosebumps as his finger brushes over the rounds of my breasts. "And I'm not just a tea granny. I brought some of Cora's chocolate cake. I know you like it, and the sugar will help with shock and stress."

"You're a very thoughtful man."

"I enjoy making you happy."

"Do you know what would make me happiest right now?"

"What's that?"

"For you to get naked and join me in this big, beautiful tub. I might even share my cake with you."

He arches an ebony brow. "Are you sure? You've been through an ordeal. We don't have to get naked. You're mine now. We can take things as slowly as you need."

"What I need is you—all of you—and the cake."

"Naturally." He pops the first button of his vest free from its mooring and then the second. At first, I think his unhurried movements are him being seductive, but when he winces, taking off his shirt, I realize it's more.

"You're hurting."

"I'll be bruised for a few weeks from Gravely's shots to my back." He drops his shirt, toes off his boots, then undoes his belt. "Cowardly fucker. There's no honor in shooting a guy in the back."

"There's no honor in Billy Gravely."

Sean moves slowly, but it's worth the wait. When his boxers hit the floor, he lifts his leg over the side of the tub and joins me in the water.

The addition of his body sends a rising wave across the tub, the heat of the water climbing up my skin.

"Fuck, this feels amazing." His eyes roll back in his head and his entire body seems to sag.

"Except you're too far away." I shift forward, straddling his muscular thighs, meeting him chest to chest. Oh, and what a chest he has. "That's better."

"Aye, much better." His hands slide up my back as he leans forward to kiss me. He pauses just before our mouths touch and then tilts his head to kiss my split lip. "I saw your father hit you and I lost my mind. I'm sorry I wasn't there to stop him before he hurt you."

I roll my eyes. "You'd just been shot twice in the back, so I'll forgive you. Besides, you made sure he didn't hit me a second time."

He dips his chin. "Are you sure you aren't angry about that? I would understand if you were."

I reach between us and wrap my fingers around his stiff cock. "I swear on the perfect cock of Sean Quinn, that I have no resentment or anger about him saving me from the nightmare of a man who was my father."

"Is my cock a bible or a talking stick in this scenario?"

"Does it matter?"

"Not in the slightest. In fact, if you have anything else you want to get off your chest, have at it."

I raise up on my knees, shift forward, and sink down, taking him into my body. My chest swells as I draw a steadying breath. "And all is right in the world once more."

Sean reaches to the side and lifts the plate with a generous slice of chocolate cake sitting on it. "And we have cake, too." There's a warmth in his eyes that makes my heart flutter.

Sean feeds me a bite of the cake, the rich sweetness of chocolate melting on my tongue. It's absurd, almost surreal, to find such a moment of peace and normalcy after everything.

"Did you really tell Tag I was your family?"

"When I heard you'd been taken, I lost my mind. Tag said I got too attached to you and I set him straight. I told him I fell in love with you and that giving you up to live a life free from me and the battles of our families was the stupidest thing I've ever done."

I chew my next bite of cake and swallow. "You weren't wrong to try, though. If things had gone differently today, I could've ended up at my friend's place and I could've had a life outside of our families."

Sean pauses with my next bite of cake hovering at my mouth. "Is that what you want?"

I take the delicious offering and flex my hips, feeling him inside me. "It was never what I wanted—only what I thought was realistic. And don't kid yourself. I was already plotting ways to get you to visit me, so I could seduce you."

He chuckles. "Seduce me? I thought I seduced you."

I swallow and let the chocolaty bliss work its magic on my taste buds. "It was me who suggested we have sex to make a woman out of me and take me off the bargaining table. It was me who took advantage of you when you were too weak to get out of bed after being stabbed."

"Aye, that's true. You were *very* dedicated to nursing me back to health."

I grin. "Orgasms release dopamine and make you feel better. That's a fact."

Sean chuckles, his hands gentle but firm on my hips. "Then let's see if we can make each other feel better, shall we?"

I answer him with a kiss, and by winding my arms behind his neck. His lips are soft against mine, and he tastes of chocolate decadence. The kiss deepens, and I groan into his mouth.

If this is what life with Sean could be, sign me up.

My world has narrowed down to the here and now—to him and me—the warmth of the water splashing in the tub as I ride him, the taste of chocolate on our tongues as we kiss, the solidity of Sean's protective determination.

Everything else—the danger, the fear, the uncertainty—

melts away under the heat of his touch, the sweetness of his kiss.

In this moment, nothing else matters but the feel of him, the strength of his arms, and the fact that when everything I thought about my life blew up in my face, he was the one to help me gather up the pieces.

Here, in Sean's arms, I find not just solace but a fierce, protective love that promises to hold back the night, to keep the shadows at bay.

As we lose ourselves in each other, in the simple joy of being together, I realize that this is what I've been searching for my entire life: a chance at happiness, at peace, at a love that allows me to be seen and valued.

That's all I've ever needed.

CHAPTER TWENTY-FOUR

Sean

*P*iper and I arrive late to the dining room, but everyone is still milling around the table drinking coffee or, in Bryan's case, eating what is likely a third plate of protein.

Seriously, the guy's a beast.

There's an unspoken tension in the air, heavy and foreboding, but thankfully Tag, Laine, and my brothers give us a chance to make our plates and sit before getting into the drama of the day.

I know it's coming. There's no way, after me killing the head of the opposing crime family last night, that Tag can relax. He'll be stressed out for months.

I'll have to apologize to Laine. Tag can be broody AF when stress levels are high.

Not that I'm much better. My attention will be largely focused on the MC and security until the McGuires make their play of retaliation.

Piper and I sit with our plates and when she points to the apple juice, I pour.

The usual morning chatter has a somber tone today and once I have swallowed a few bites, I give Tag a nod. "All right, let's hear it."

Tag's expression is grave as he stirs his coffee, his eyes meeting mine across the table. "I understand the necessity of what happened, but am concerned about the repercussions. Mattie's loss could destabilize not just the McGuires, but all of Dublin."

Brendan nods. "If they take it out on us, innocents could well get caught in the crossfire."

Bryan wipes his mouth with his napkin. "If they had any insights into how to hurt us, they'd bypass us all together and go straight at our citizens."

"But they don't have any insight," Tag says. "They've never understood our commitment to the people and likely never will."

"At least not yet." Piper catches herself and throws my brothers an apologetic look. "Sorry. Am I allowed to speak up?"

Tag's expression softens. "Are you here as Sean's girlfriend and not as a McGuire?"

"I am. Sean is my family, not them."

"Then, if you've truly cut ties and are part of this family, your insight could be invaluable. Feel free to speak."

Piper looks between us, her face calm, but I see her confidence waning. "I was going to say that while my father and my oldest brothers are or were mindless brutes, my mother and Darcy are a great deal more strategic. With Da gone, depending on who has a say in what comes next, things might take a different direction."

Tag smiles. "Something to keep in mind, for sure. Do you have any idea what your father's succession plan was?"

"He never said—because honestly I think he was arrogant

enough to think himself invincible—but Niall and Declan were always favored to handle things if he wasn't around. With Declan gone, maybe my mother?"

Tag sits with his coffee mug in both hands. "Aye, Samantha being in charge going forward would stir things up. With your father, it was always about brute force, power, and money. Your mother would be a wild card."

"Do you think you could find out more about how things might play out?" Brendan asks.

The idea of Piper going anywhere near the McGuires again makes my blood run cold, but before I protest, she speaks up. "I could go to my father's funeral, but…"

She hesitates, her gaze meeting mine.

The last McGuire funeral was where they ambushed her. I reach under the table to touch her leg, a hot rush of protectiveness blooming in my chest. "It's too dangerous. They might use you as leverage against us or take out the loss of Mattie on you. No. I don't like it."

"Agreed. I won't pretend to mourn that man. He deserves everything he got." She sits quietly for a moment and then sighs. "I could get information another way."

"How's that?" Tag asks.

"If I had a phone, I could call Rory. He's not deeply involved in the business, but he's the closest to me. He'll be worried and will tell me what he knows."

Tag considers this and then leans back in his chair at the end of the table. "We'll get you a new phone, Piper. Anything you can find out from Rory could help us prepare for whatever comes next."

Piper's expression is composed, but her eyes reflect a storm of emotions. Whatever she's afraid of, I'll protect her. It's my honor to be the one who loves her, and I will never let her down.

"Are you sure you're okay with this?" I ask, searching her face for any sign of hesitation.

Piper reaches up, her thumb tracing my scar from my lip up my cheek. "I'm sure. I may not be a McGuire anymore, but I'm not willing to give up Rory. Not if there's any chance we can still be family."

That's fair. I don't want her to give up everything for me. I want to be her sanctuary, not her jailor.

"Then I should meet with him and talk to him, too."

Her gaze narrows on me. "And say what?"

Her protective instincts flair and I smile, imagining Piper protecting her brother from me. She would, too.

My girl's got fire in her blood.

Not that she'd ever have to. I will never betray her trust if Rory remains good to her.

"I would say you are safe and free to start a new life on the north side that could include him. I'd assure him I won't let anything happen to him as long as he doesn't come at us directly and put us in that position."

The tension in her body eases, and she leans over to kiss me. "Thank you."

"We're in this together now, kitten. We're a team."

Her eyes become glassy, and I press my palm against the damage on her cheek. All she ever wanted was to be considered equal and useful to others.

The McGuires were too stupid to see her value.

I will never make that mistake.

The bell above the door to Eddie Rocket's Diner jingles and Piper looks up from where she's dipping one of her fries. It's not Rory entering the restaurant, and the excitement in her gaze dims.

I pop an onion ring into my mouth and send her a smile. "He'll be here, P. He's only a few minutes late. We told him to be careful. He's likely just making sure he's not being followed."

I glance over a line of red vinyl booths at the new arrivals walking over the black-and-white tiled floors. It's mid-afternoon, so the place isn't busy, but it isn't empty either.

Rory had been hesitant about meeting north of the river, so I picked this place because it's right at the corner of the O'Connell Bridge. Technically, it's Quinn territory, but I guaranteed his safety and assured him that coming to us is the only way he gets to see his sister.

It'll take time for him to trust that the Quinns aren't the villains their father painted us to be.

It'll take time to trust him, too. Even though I assured him it would just be the three of us, I've got a couple Devils discreetly patrolling the area.

Not that I'm expecting trouble, but after everything that's happened, I won't take chances with Piper's safety.

Not ever again.

The bell chimes again, and Rory steps inside. He scans the diner until his gaze lands on Piper. Relief washes over his features as he quickly crosses the room and envelops his sister in a tight hug.

"Are you okay? Like really okay?"

"I am now. Thanks for coming." Piper clings to him, burying her face in his shoulder. It's clear she needed this, needed the assurance that not all her family ties are poisoned.

"Niall will skin me if he finds out, but I had to see for myself." Rory pulls back slightly, his eyes narrowing as he notices the bruise on Piper's face. "Who did this?"

His gaze turns on me and I'm pleased to see the flare of protective violence igniting in his eyes.

"Da did it." Piper's voice is steady despite the stormy emotions swirling in her eyes. "He was about to do a lot more, too. He and Billy were going to kill me, Rory. I have no doubt about that. Thankfully, Sean got there in time."

Rory's gaze is still locked on me, and I let him look. I'm the man who rescued his sister, but I'm also the man who killed his father. There's a lot to unpack there.

I remain relaxed as he scrutinizes me, a mixture of anger, resentment, gratitude, and then reassessment passing over his face. "Thank you," he says, extending his hand. "For saving my sister...again. I wish I had done a better job of it myself."

I accept his thanks and appreciate him admitting his failing. "Your sister is an extraordinary woman. She deserves to be happy. I know you know that."

"Aye, I do."

"So, when I tell you I love her and will never allow her to be hurt like that again, believe me."

Rory is only twenty-one, embarking on his journey to becoming his own man. It's important for him to see the world for what it is and not what he's been told it is.

The Quinns are not his enemy—not unless he draws a line that puts us on opposite sides.

"Piper is under my protection, and by her request, so are you. As long as you don't come at us directly, the Quinns will consider you part of our extended family."

Rory seems to consider that. He smiles at Piper and then looks back at me. "Would you mind if we talked privately?"

I expected as much and am prepared to give them space. "Of course. Take your time."

I grab my tray and move to a seat by the window. From here, I can keep an eye on them, but am out of earshot, so their visit is private.

Seeing them together, the bond they share is obvious. Thank fuck she had at least one person who loves her.

Powerful families can have different dynamics. Thankfully,

our family was always rooted in love and respect of one another.

Piper's life has been indifference, control, upheaval, and betrayal. That's over. Her new life is just beginning.

As I sip my milkshake, watching them, I decide that if Rory continues to be good to Piper, I'll make it my business to ensure the kid doesn't get consumed by McGuire violence.

He's young, and with the right influences, maybe he can escape the life that's already claimed too many.

Piper deserves that much.

It'll take time to prove to him that we're not the monsters he's been bred to believe, but if he's willing, maybe there could be a different life for him, too.

CHAPTER TWENTY-FIVE

Piper

*I*t's been five days since Sean rescued me on the beach and my father's control over me ended. Five days of adjusting to the fact that my life is budding to life, and I can make choices. Five days of tension in the air on a business side, but love in the air personally.

And those are the moments I treasure most.

Sean Quinn can be violently protective—I acknowledge that. He will kill to keep me safe, but he's also endlessly romantic and giving.

He kisses me before he leaves the house, lets me know if his plans change over the course of our time apart, and texts to ask if I need anything on his way home.

He shows me more consideration than anyone ever has— and I love him for it.

Soul deep, heart hammering, love.

"You're quiet tonight. Is anything wrong?" Sean squeezes my hand and smiles down at me.

We're touring the grounds and he's leading me toward the

gazebo by the pond. A gentle breeze stirs the leaves of the trees around us. It's a little chilly, but summer is still trying to stay with us.

Today was my father's funeral, and Sean hasn't left my side. He's been attentive and didn't even bat an eye when I said Rory sent me the virtual link to watch remotely, if I wanted to.

I didn't, but I gave the link to Tag in case it could help him in any way, in his quest to keep the family safe.

The setting sun casts long, dappled shadows across our path, its warmth waning as the day succumbs to evening.

"Nothing is wrong. I was just committing the moment to memory: the beauty of your family estate, the unconditional acceptance you've shown me, and the excitement of the future expanding before me."

Sean sends me a sidelong glance. "Before *us*, kitten. I intend to be included in your future, however you imagine it."

I lean against his shoulder and hug his arm. "You have the starring role, Mr. Quinn."

"As I should."

The champagne sunset reflects off the man-made pond and the water sparkles around the dark silhouettes of a group of ducks floating on its surface.

"It's lovely out here."

"Aye, it is. Da put the pond in for our mother when we were kids. We wanted a swimming pool, but she thought that would take away from the atmosphere of the castle, stables, and grounds. They compromised on a pond."

"You and your brothers swam in there?"

"All the time. As soon as it was warm enough—and often before that—we'd swim while Mam oversaw the shenanigans from the gazebo and read her travel books."

A nostalgic smile warms his face as he looks out onto the waters. I squeeze his hand, grateful to witness a glimpse of his childhood and learn a bit more about the life that made him the man he is.

As we arrive at the gazebo, my breath catches in my throat. It's transformed into something from a dream.

Delicate gossamer sheers flutter gently in the breeze, the soft fabric catching the pale, tangerine light. It creates a glow that seems to capture the warmth of the sun.

Inside, a plush mattress is lain out, piled with fluffy blankets and pillows that invite us to forget the world. A tray laden with snacks—cheese, fruit, and a bottle of wine—sits nearby, promising a sweet interlude to our evening. And above it all, laced along the inside edge of the structure, is a string of white fairy lights.

"It's beautiful, Sean," I whisper as I step inside.

The sheers billow around us, enveloping us in a soft, ethereal world apart from the rest of the estate. I run my fingers over the blankets, the textures rich and comforting under my touch.

Sean watches me with a smile, his eyes reflecting the colors of the fading day. "It's a bit cool, but I intend to keep you plenty warm under the covers."

The chill in the air is noticeable, but the thought of curling up with Sean under the blankets warms me from the inside out. "You're too much, Mr. Quinn."

He grins. "You like it, then?"

"Och, no. I love it. Almost as much as I love the man who did all this for me."

"Connor?" His gaze narrows. "You do know he's married to Cora, right?"

I laugh. "So, you're saying you didn't do this?"

He chuckles and gives me a squeeze. "I'm teasing. I hung every light and set up every pillow. Cora made the snack tray, but I told her what I wanted. I also brought these."

He holds out a box of frosted cherry Pop-Tarts and waggles his ebony brows.

I reach up and cup his face in my palms. His skin is cool from the breeze, but his smile is warm enough to keep any cold at bay. "It's perfect. Thank you."

Sean pulls me close, his arms wrapping around me as we stand at the entrance of the magical space he made for us. "I think the fabric dancing around us, is inviting us inside."

"I think you're right."

He lifts me off my feet, and I wrap my legs around his hips. "I hope you mentioned to your brothers not to come down to the gazebo tonight."

He laughs, his warm breath washing the skin on my neck. "Don't worry. They have been warned."

Our night in the gazebo is glorious and true to his word, Sean keeps me warm all night. In the morning, I don't want to face the day, but today is the reading of the will and the Quinns need to know the outcome to prepare for the next stage of preparations.

Hidden under the blankets, the two of us stare at one another like kids huddled under a blanket fort.

"I don't want to go inside."

Sean frowns. "I'll be right beside you for whatever happens."

"I wasn't talking about the reading of the will. I was talking about leaving our cocoon and having to put on cold clothes after being so toasty all night."

"Then we don't get dressed."

I roll my eyes. "And how does that help us get to the house? By the time we get to the back door, my nipples will be hard enough to poke someone's eyes out and your cock will have retreated so far up inside you, it may never come out to play again."

"A vivid picture, but I wasn't suggesting that we go full

monty and streak our way across the estate. I was suggesting we slide our shoes on and keep ourselves wrapped in blankets."

"That sounds cozy."

"That's my girl, always up for a little adventure."

I am...and finally, someone sees me.

The two of us pop up, get ourselves bundled, and then slip our feet into our shoes. The awkward run back to the house is filled with laughter and I hope with everything in me, that no one is watching us because we must look like drunken lunatics.

Still, five minutes later, we've made it to Sean's room without running into anyone. We drop our microfiber warmth and exchange it for the warmth of each other.

"Shower," Sean says around my kiss. "We can continue this and get ready for our day."

"Mmm, my man the multitasker."

Sean sweeps down and throws me over his shoulder, spanking my bare bottom as he strides toward his private bathroom. "Time to clean you up. After how many times I lost myself in you last night, I'm surprised my cum isn't still running down both of your thighs."

Sean is relentless.

"I'm surprised you're not faint from dehydration."

He laughs and I'm not complaining because I've got an up close and personal view of Matunos, the Celtic bear god inked into Sean's back. I've always loved bears and the two flanking the god are incredible."

High on the dopamine rush of sex with my mafia man, I lost count of how many orgasms we shared. I entered the sexual arena later than I would've chosen, but Sean has certainly made up for lost time.

And I love everything about that.

After he has me breathless in the shower and crying out his name in the steamy bathroom, he wraps me in a towel off the heated rack. "Are you all right? You're not too sore, are you? I didn't hold back much last night."

I arch a brow at him. "That was you holding back?"

The grin he flashes me is pure sin. "When I'm healed and I'm sure your ribs can take it, you'll have your answer to that question, but not a moment sooner."

"I can't imagine."

He wraps me in his arms and kisses the tip of my nose. "I will sex you so good, I will sear your soul and ruin you for any other man but me."

"Yes, please."

He chuckles. "But not until we're both at our best."

I sigh and stick my bottom lip out in a pout. He catches my lip between his teeth and gives me a little nip. "Now, be a good girl and put some clothes on so we can get out of this room. You know I can't resist you."

I do know that—and I love it.

I feel the heat of his gaze follow me as I hurry to the walk-in closet and shut the door. Surrounded by a rack of dresses, cashmere sweaters, designer blouses, and more jeans, slacks, and yoga pants than I could possibly wear, I pick an outfit for today.

I still can't believe he gave me the entire closet. He swore he didn't need it. Other than his suit hanging against the wall by the door, he insisted his clothes were fine folded in the dresser drawers.

Who am I to argue with logic like that?

And so, for a new life, he bought me a new wardrobe. I told him I could buy my own clothes, but he insisted. It makes him feel good to take care of me.

It makes me feel good too.

CHAPTER TWENTY-SIX

Piper

Sean's family is waiting in the sunken living room after we grab a quick bite of breakfast and eat it standing at the island in the kitchen. When we arrive, all eyes turn toward us.

Tag folds his newspaper and sets it on the antique coffee table. "Good morning, you two. How was your camping adventure?"

Sean brushes the back of his finger over the blush on my cheek and chuckles. "I wouldn't try fishing anytime soon. Piper's cries of pleasure likely scared them all away."

I blink and my mouth falls open. "I can't believe you said that."

He laughs. "You might as well get used to my brothers razzing us because teasing is our love language."

Thankfully, Finn takes pity on me and changes the subject. "I have the laptop set up for the reading of the will. If you sit at the desk behind the sofa, you'll be able to see them, they will see you, and no one will see us, sitting here and listening."

That works for me.

"You're still willing to let us listen in?" Tag asks.

"I am. It's just…my family isn't like yours." What will they think if my mother or one of my brothers sinks their filthy fangs into me? "They might say things about me or about you. I need to apologize beforehand."

Sean lays a heavy arm across my shoulders and pulls me to his side. "You don't have to apologize for them, P. And trust me, they won't say anything we haven't heard before. Consider us five little ducks, letting everything roll off our backs."

I look at his brothers and take in the scars and the tattoos and the 'fuck with me and die' vibe they give off. That metaphor cracks me up. "You five are the furthest thing from five little ducks I've ever seen."

He grins. "But I made you laugh."

"Aye, you did."

My phone rings and I check the caller ID. "It's my mother."

Cue a round of frowns and pursed brows.

"Did you give her your number?" Tag asks.

"No, and Rory wouldn't have either. I'm not sure how she got it."

"But she did," Sean says.

"Should I answer it?"

The guys all shrug. Which is no help at all.

Sean gives me a gentle squeeze. "That's up to you, kitten. We aren't here to tell you what to do."

That in itself seems so bizarre to me. In my household, everyone always told me what to do.

I stare at my phone a moment longer and it stops ringing. "Problem solved. She hung up."

Sean kisses my temple. "Why do you think she called?"

"Likely to fill my head with sob stories about me needing to come home and how sorry she is that Da's plans drove me away."

"It could have something to do with the will," Finn suggests. "It's almost time for the reading. She might want to talk to you beforehand, to get you in line or something."

I don't even care. "Then I'll sign into the video call, and she can talk to me in front of the lawyers if she wants to. Odds are she won't, though. She won't want to air our dirty laundry in public."

I leave the Quinns sitting in the living room and round the couch that sits opposite a dark chestnut desk. Stepping between the desk and the window wall, I sit in the soft leather executive chair.

Finn stands on the other side of the desk and points to where I need to click the mouse. I'm on the corporate website of Simpson, Jones & O'Brien, the firm my father used for all his family law issues.

When I click to join the meeting, a pop-up tells me the host has been notified, and then the screen opens to show me the interior of an elegant meeting room.

"Good morning, Ms. McGuire." The woman who opens the call smiles at me, and then begins setting out vases of water and boxes of tissues on the conference table. "I'm Connie Flaherty, Mr. Simpson's assistant. I'm terribly sorry for your loss."

I fight the urge to say it's no great loss. I could tell her my father was a cruel and unfeeling mobster and that thinking of him dead and lying in his coffin gives me a warm, satisfying glow in my tummy, but I spare her the family drama.

She's just doing her job.

"Mister Simpson stepped into the corridor to greet your mother and your brothers, dear. I'm sure they'll be in shortly and we'll get started."

"That's fine. Thank you for making it possible for me to connect remotely."

"Of course, dear. You're not the first to be out of the country when something like this happens. We're prepared for any contingency."

Little does she know that I'm less than twenty minutes from their office, but I don't trust my mother not to try to kidnap or kill me if I were to step foot on the south side of the river.

"I appreciate that. Thank you."

"Not at all." Connie finishes setting out seven black folders around the table and smiles at me. "Have you ever been to a reading before?"

"No. This is my first."

"Well, there's nothing to do but listen. Mr. Simpson will read out your father's wishes and will explain anything that is unclear. It's as simple as that."

Lloyd Simpson has been one of Da's lawyers since I was a kid. He's smart, efficient, and I've always liked him—even if I don't trust him one bit.

By his very position, he's spent decades ensuring that my father got what he wanted. He might be a nice guy, but his loyalty to a man like Matty McGuire is telling.

Mister Simpson sweeps into view of the camera and smiles at the screen. He's a distinguished-looking man with salt and pepper hair, tortoise-shell glasses, and an expensive suit. "It's wonderful to see you, Piper. I'm glad you could make it for the reading. You're looking as beautiful as ever."

"Thank you, Mister Simpson. Kind of you to say so."

I watch as my mother, Niall, Darcy, Brody, and Rory each take their seats. When Mr. Simpson sits and flips open the front of one of the black folders, I stare at the empty seat.

Who is supposed to be sitting there?

They knew I wasn't coming, so who gets that folder?

And then, he comes into view and takes a seat.

Billy Gravely.

Sean is standing out of view and I'm not sure what he sees in my expression, but his gaze hardens.

What's wrong? He mouths.

I write on a notepad and hold it up for him to see.

Billy's not dead. Why is he there?

There's no time to come up with an answer before Mister Simpson clears his throat. "All right. Let's get started, shall we?"

He picks up a stapled document and reads aloud. *I, Matthew Terrance McGuire, being of sound mind and body...*

I bark a laugh and then cover my outburst with a cough. "Sorry. Carry on."

I hit the button to mute myself and make eyes at Sean. "Sorry. The whole 'sound mind' thing caught me off guard. I suppose the will wouldn't be valid if it started: *I, Matthew McGuire, being fucking nuts...*"

Brendan and Sean chuckle, and I go back to listening to Mr. Simpson. He's droning on, listing the assets and holdings of Da's companies and corporations.

And as the lawyer's deep baritone waffles on, my mother plays the part of the heartbroken widow and weeps into a wad of tissues.

All the times I've heard her screaming at my father and threatening to leave him, maim him, or even kill him, makes it hard for me to believe she's so broken up over his death.

"There is an exhaustive list of McGuire holdings in your packages, but if I read them all, we'll be ordering in dinner before I finish." Mr. Simpson adjusts his glasses and carries on. "Now to the allocations of assets. The house on Pleasant Street, five-hundred thousand dollars, and a monthly stipend of ten thousand dollars go to his beloved wife, Samantha McGuire."

My mother looks up as if she's confused.

"All facets of the McGuire family business will pass jointly into the hands of Niall Matthew McGuire and William Connor Gravely."

What? Da left half ownership of the McGuire business to Billy Gravely?

"Niall and Billy will assume joint ownership of all properties listed other than the family home and will run the business with equal rights. Mathew McGuire's living sons will assist in the running of the business to be eligible for their monthly stipend of twenty thousand a month."

A flicker of dizziness passes through my brain as I hear Mister Simpson roping Brody and Rory into the business.

So, if they don't join the business, they get nothing?

At that moment, I hate my father more than ever.

Mister Simpson keeps on talking and his words jumble in my head like popcorn in a popper. "There are also a list of bank accounts, trust funds, mortgages, stocks, bonds, vehicles, and real estate holdings that will be divvied up between the boys."

He turns to the screen and offers me a sad smile. "I'm sorry, dear. There is no mention of you receiving anything from the estate."

"That's more than fine, Mr. Simpson. I wouldn't want it even if it were offered."

Mister Simpson turns his attention to Niall. "You and Mr. Gravely will be given a detailed copy of everything when you leave. I'd like the two of you to make an appointment with Connie, to come in one day this week to go over all of it. There is too much involved in the estate to read it over once and presume you have a grasp on it."

Niall presses his palm on the folder in front of him and forces a tight smile. "I understand, Mister Simpson. We'll set an appointment before we leave."

Did Niall know Da's plan about partnering up with Billy Gravely? Given the anger in his eyes, I don't think so.

"And with that, the reading of the will is complete," Mr. Simpson says.

My mother gets to her feet and presses her hands against the table. "This is bullshit, Lloyd. Niall and Billy get the business and are supposed to run it together? Billy isn't part of this family. If anyone should be added as a co-owner with my sons, it should be me."

Mr. Simpson takes off his glasses and sets them on the folder before him. "It's not up to me, Samantha. Your husband gave strict instructions when we drafted the will. We went over the problem of Mister Gravely not being a McGuire, and Mattie assured me Billy was entitled."

My mother shifts her anger to Billy, smiling smugly on the opposite side of the table. "You did this, you snake."

Billy chuckles. "I can't help that he liked me more than you, Sam. Maybe you should've put out a little more."

There's a rush of bodies and the scramble knocks the camera free from wherever it was positioned. Over the next few minutes, I'm looking at shoes shuffling on the carpeted floor of Mr. Simpson's office and voices shouting as all hell breaks loose.

What a fucking mess.

But honestly, I'm glad I signed on, because seeing my mother lose her shit was too funny.

Payback is a bitch—*bitch.*

Sean

Gathered in the living room, the shock of what we just learned is still ringing in my ears. Mattie McGuire dropped a grenade in our laps—Niall and Billy Gravely will now steer the ship for South Dublin's operations.

I glance around at Tag, Piper, Laine, and my brothers, seeing a mix of skepticism and concern etched on their faces.

Piper looks particularly disturbed. "Niall holds no affection for Billy or the way he handles things. This will make things difficult for him and my brothers."

Bryan shifts forward in his seat. "It's crazy. Your mother got frozen out of the business after all these years by Mattie's side. Wow, she must be pissed."

Piper grunts and wraps her arms across her chest. "Women had no value in business in my father's mind. He made that very clear."

"Your father was wrong about that," Laine says. "I've dealt with misogynistic alpha-holes for the past decade, Piper. That kind of thinking is their shortcoming, not ours. It's a weakness I've enjoyed exploiting many times."

Tag's scowl softens when he looks at his fiancé. "I don't know how Niall feels, but Billy shared that sentiment with Mattie. Maybe it'll be something we'll be able to exploit in time."

Piper doesn't look convinced. "Niall isn't as brash as our father or Billy, but he was groomed by Da for a long time. He never questioned the way Da did things like Darcy did. But Billy Gravely? He's a wildcard, unpredictable and violent. The prospect of him having any significant power is terrifying."

Tag leans forward, his fingers steepled in front of him. "How Niall and Billy work together will dictate a lot going forward."

"It could work to our advantage," Brendan says. "If there's a power struggle and the two of them are locked down in a pissing match for control, they might implode."

"Billy won't let that happen." Piper rubs her arms as if warding off a chill. "Billy has never respected my brothers. Declan could get him to stand down, but he'll run right over Niall and Darcy. If they stand up to him, I wouldn't be surprised if he simply killed them to eliminate the conflict."

"Then let the implosion begin," Brendan says.

I throw him a scowl. "Brenny. They're still her brothers for fuck's sake. A little compassion would go a long way here."

Brenny's amusement dissolves, and he flashes Piper a look of apology. "My bad. Sorry."

I rub the back of my neck, feeling the weight of the weeks

and months to come. With Billy Gravely at the helm, even partially, the fragile peace Tag's managed to maintain feels more tenuous than ever.

"Any way you look at it, it's a clusterfuck." I pull Piper against my chest, the warmth of her against me a balm I'm becoming addicted to. "With Billy in a position of power, things will get bloody. It seems Mad Mattie is screwing us over, even from the grave."

"Which was likely part of the reason he did it." Piper looks up at me. "I'm sorry."

I hug her closer and kiss the top of her head. "There's nothing for you to apologize for, Piper. None of this is on you. We'll figure it out. We always do."

The room falls silent, each of us lost in our thoughts, strategizing for what comes next.

EPILOGUE

Piper

*a*s dawn creeps through the curtains, Sean's bedroom— *our* bedroom—is cast in a soft glow. I wake, cocooned in dreamy warmth, nestled in the tattooed arms of my Black Knight.

He's home.

After the reading of my father's will, he said he had something that needed to be taken care of, and he'd be out of the country for a few days.

He didn't tell me where he was going, and I didn't ask. I know how to skirt the dangers of our families and am relieved that at least for now, there have been no new threats coming at us from south of the river.

He's sleeping next to me, his features softened by rest, the usual stern intensity that marks his expression replaced by a rare, unguarded peacefulness.

I study the chiseled beauty of his face, following the line of the scar that mars his cheek and lip. It's a silent testament to the violence of the life he's led—a life vastly different from my own, yet intricately entwined.

How many times did I glimpse Sean over the years at public events or, on the rare occasions, when Cormack Quinn met with my father?

Each encounter left me more fascinated by the tattooed man, who seemed shut off and unreachable. He has always carried the weight of the world on his shoulders, a silent warrior in a world of chaos.

Yet, when we're together, he keeps the chaos of mafia life at bay. He was right when he told me we couldn't be together because I had the wrong last name.

I was a McGuire.

That association carried too much weight, too much history, and too much bad blood. But I'm not a McGuire any longer. I've finally broken free of the shackle of my father and his control.

When Sean killed my father to save me, all ties to my old life were severed at last.

Maybe, in a few months or even years, he'll give me a new last name. The thought sends a thrill through me, a flutter of excitement at the possibility of truly claiming my place in his world.

I would be proud to be a Quinn, to be part of the family he belongs to, to stand by his side not just in love, but in name.

And who knows? Maybe I could even get my motorcycle license. The idea makes me smile, and I imagine riding alongside Sean, sharing in the freedom and exhilaration he finds on the open road.

It's one part of his life he treasures, and the prospect of sharing it with him sparks a warm glow in my heart.

Or maybe, once I finish my PR program, I can help the Quinn family by managing their optics, ensuring they remain in the good graces of Dublin's people.

I told my parents my skills could be a useful way to

contribute to the business, but they never supported the idea. I bet Sean will take my interests more seriously.

Lying here, with Sean's steady breathing as a comforting backdrop, a frisson of potential hums over my skin and raises the hair on my arms.

I shiver and Sean stirs. His eyes open and it's so cute as the haze of sleep clears and then his eyes light up when he sees me. "Hey, you're awake."

"And you're home."

He closes the distance between our mouths and gives me a quick kiss. "I got in a few hours ago and didn't want to wake you."

"Was your trip successful?"

"You could say that." Sean flips back the covers and strides over toward the window.

I don't know if I'll ever get used to seeing my man strutting around naked. The way he moves, with the flex and release of his inked back and butt muscles, is mesmerizing. He's a walking work of Celtic art, chiseled by the fae gods.

He catches me staring and chuckles. "You ogling me, kitten? See something you want to pounce on, do you?"

I take in the glory of full-frontal Sean and sigh. "If paying my dues in my first twenty years earned me twenty more in Sean Quinn heaven, I say it was time well spent."

Sean arches a brow and kneels on the mattress. "If you think you're getting away from me in twenty years, you're delusional. You're mine, kitten. All mine. Forever. The end."

"If you insist."

"I do." His easy smile dissolves a little as he runs his hand over the wooden box he picked up off the desk. "And you know there are no lines I won't cross to keep you safe and make you happy, right?"

"Aye, I do."

"And you understand the kind of man you're sharing your body with, right?"

I press my hand over the Celtic cross on his heart. "And I wouldn't change a thing about you."

He's studying me as we talk, and I sense that he's measuring my resolve.

"Sean, you're scaring me. What's this about?"

His gaze softens and my heart melts. This man owns me, and he knows it. "It's about you, kitten. It's only ever about you."

My gaze drops to the wooden box in his lap. It's a little smaller than a box of tissues and stained so dark brown it's almost black. "What's in the box, Sean?"

He swallows. "Justice."

Oh, dear. My heart takes off in my chest. "What did you do?"

"I kept my promise to you."

"What does that mean?"

"Open it and find out."

I close my eyes and draw a deep breath. Justice. What does that mean? My hands are trembling when I lift the lid of the box and then I'm staring at two fingers lying severed in a small patch of congealed blood.

How is what I'm seeing justice? These are definitely fingers from a man...a big man with hairy knuckles...

The memory of Sean's words hits me... *If anyone lays a fucking finger on you, I will cut them off with garden shears.*

I blink. "You severed Arkady's fingers?"

Sean's gaze has grown impossibly dark. He meets my gaze, and his lips quirk up into a cruel smirk. "He had no right to touch you the way he did."

"But won't this cause trouble with Anton Volkov and your gun deal?"

Sean frowns. "It wouldn't have changed things even if it did. I made you a promise, and I kept it."

"But Tag worked so hard to make things work."

Sean shrugs. "Thankfully, Anton is a man of vengeance himself and agreed that since Arkady violated you after he and Tag had come to their agreement, I was free to exact my act of justice."

Justice. I have no sympathy for Arkady, but this seems extreme. Then again, Sean is staking his claim and setting a precedent. Anyone who hurts me will pay a price.

"Thank you." I lean forward and kiss him. "It's not a conventional girlfriend gift—and I never want to be a collector of body parts—but you're right. It balances the scales, doesn't it?"

"I think so, and Anton threw in a taped apology from Volkov as a bonus, if you want to see it."

I think about that and close the lid on the box. "No. I don't need it. From now on, we focus on the horizon. Our future is in front of us, not behind."

Sean takes the box and puts it on the floor on his side of the bed. "Sounds good to me. Now, back to bed. We've got a few hours before sunrise, and I was having the sexiest dream."

"I hope I was in it."

"You had the starring role, kitten."

"As I should."

He chuckles, kisses my neck, and pulls the covers over us as he snuggles me closer. The house is quiet, and he succumbs to the pull of sleep even as he tucks me in.

And that is why I love him.

Protecting me and ensuring my well-being is instinctual for him. He doesn't pretend to care for me or force himself to consider my needs.

He loves me.

And I love him right back.

AFTERWORD

Thank you for reading Dublin Devil. If you enjoyed the story, and as a favor to us, please leave a quick rating or review on Amazon.

Do you want to spend a little more time with Sean and Piper? Maybe check another item off Piper's sex wish list? Sign up to my newsletter for an exclusive bonus epilogue Here

If you're ready for more of the Quinn brothers, read on or claim a copy of Book 3 of the Emerald Isle Mafia series and see what happens when Brendan falls for the woman who's not afraid to take on the Dublin Brute.

DUBLIN BRUTE – SNEAK PEEK

Brendan

The past year has been a bitch for Clan Quinn. Cormack Quinn —a man above men and our Da—passed suddenly of a heart attack last October, leaving Tag to assume leadership of the family business—running organized crime in North Dublin.

It took months for each of us to find our place—the spot where we could do the most good.

Tag is our leader—there was never any question about that. He's the oldest of the five of us and is smart, strategic, and good under pressure. He is also a champion in good standing with the citizens of our fair city.

Sean's the second born and runs the Dublin Devils MC. He's always been more of a doer than a talker, so putting him in charge of a leather and steel army with over a hundred men with bendable moral compasses keeps him busy.

Finn is the youngest. Aside from a bad spell when he was sneaking out at night and coming home with bloody knuckles and black eyes, he's more of a behind the scenes member of our mafia family. He's got a knack for computers and isn't hindered by little things like security protocols and firewalls.

And then, there's me and my twin brother, Bryan. We sit at the table with the MC and are muscle for Sean when he needs us. We're handy with sniper rifles, love a good torture session if there's an interrogation, but for fun, Bryan and I have another passion.

We cage fight for charity.

"Earth to Brenny." Sean snaps his fingers and tilts his head into my field of vision. "What are you daydreaming about over here, B?"

I accept the Guinness he's holding out for me and cast a gaze around the interior of the clubhouse. It's cleared out while I wasn't paying attention and now Sean and I are the only two here. "I was thinking about the fight on Sunday night. I have a first-round pairing with that fucker, Paddy the Predator."

"Och, that's a shitty draw. He's a tough one. I see why you're worried. Have you been watching his fights?"

"Aye. I've studied him a bit. He's got a few moves on him, but I'm not worried."

Sean arches an ebony brow. "Then maybe you're not as smart as I thought you were."

"Fuck you."

Sean chuckles and leans back on the couch opposite me. "You'll be fine. Just don't let him snap anything. I need you here with me on Monday. Remember, the fights are for charity. It doesn't matter who wins."

I press a hand against my chest. "You wound me, brother. It matters a helluva lot. I've got a following to inspire, a reputation to uphold."

Sean laughs. "They're called groupies. Don't get your nuts in a tangle over the long lineup of ladies who are hot for you. If you lose, they'll be just as eager to nurse you back to health."

Rude. "They're not all horny women. I have some male fighting fans, too."

"Point one out to me on Sunday."

"Fuck you."

We both laugh.

The two of us sip on our beers for a bit and I marvel at my older brother. Since he got with Piper, he's a lot less broody and ready to hang people from bridges.

Tag's the opposite. Now that he's got Laine and a baby on the way, he's glaring at everyone as if they're a potential threat.

"Any news from across the river?" I ask.

Sean swallows. "Piper's brother mentioned that Billy Gravely has nerve damage on his left side and is meaner than ever. Another inch or two to the right and I may have put the fucker down."

"Better luck next time."

"Aye, if I hadn't just had my bell rung, taking two to the vest, I might've been able to save us a lot of trouble in the future."

"Niall McGuire might've sent you a thank you bouquet for saving him from having to partner up with the asshole."

Sean nods. "From what we've heard, Gravely is as testy as a wounded wolf and goes against Niall's orders at every turn."

"Do the lads think Gravely will make a move against the McGuires when he's strong enough?"

"If he had the men to do it, I wouldn't put it past him. Gravely's a snake."

I take another sip of the dark ale and frown. "He might not be far off. Kieran is following up with one of his street rats, Petey, about that tonight."

"About what exactly?"

"Apparently, this kid heard that Gravely is gathering his own band of rogues. With Mad Mattie leaving him half the McGuire organization, his popularity among the cutthroats on the island is rising."

"Does Tag know this?" Sean raises a dark eyebrow.

"It's speculation so far. Kieran said the kid got something solid and they're meeting tonight at the Confession Box to go over it."

"If that's true, we need to be ready for a power shift. Text Kieran and tell him you're joining that meeting. We need to know if this rumor is smoke or has merit.

I upend my beer and stand. "Yes, boss."

I leave the MC clubhouse, hop on my Harley, and head out to meet up with Kieran, the Dublin Devil's Sergeant at Arms. The russet-haired rogue has a silver tongue and a way with people that makes him unbeatable as a handler for the network of informants that keeps us abreast of Dublin activity on both sides of the river.

Sean was smart enough to recognize his gift early and put him to work.

The Confession Box is a gem of a historic pub, away from typical tourist traffic, located next to Mary Pro Catholic Church. It's owned and operated by two sisters who offer great service and an authentic atmosphere.

My family generally lands at the Jimmy Francis Pub if we're going out for a steak and a pint, but I've been to the Confession Box a few times.

Gotta support local industry.

A gust of icy air burrows down the collar of my leather jacket, and I shrug my shoulders up toward my ears to block against the wind.

Fucking hell.

Summer ended like the flick of a switch this year.

It doesn't seem to bother the tourists or the locals. The night is vibrant with the buzz of Dublin's energetic heart.

I swing my bike into a parking spot farther from the pub than I'd like, but the crowd from the Abbey Theatre just let out, and theatergoers are flooding the streets.

As I dismount, I adjust my jacket and check my watch. It's time for Kieran's meeting, and I scan the area.

The thrum of the crowd carries a mix of accents and laughter, and I make my way towards the pub. My boots click against the pavement in a steady rhythm as my mind wanders to what Petey might tell us tonight.

Is Gravely really going to make a play and go for control of the south? Will he stop at the south or will he try for all of Dublin?

There's no question. If he seizes the south, he'll be gunning for us soon after.

Just ahead, I spot Kieran. He's leaning against the wall of the pub having a smoke and lifts his chin in greeting when a teenager in skinny jeans and a hoodie comes over to meet him.

My sightline is interrupted by two beautiful ladies as they pass between me and my destination. Before I can refocus, the night erupts into chaos.

Gunshots split the air, sharp and sudden, slicing through the hum of the crowd.

The kid standing with Kieran is spun by the impact, and instincts kick in.

Kieran grabs the kid, and I go for the beauties. One of them is already on the ground, so I grab the blonde and tackle her, rolling to shield her with my body.

We hit the pavement, my arms caging her in, protecting her the best I can as we roll behind a stone planter. Her phone clatters away, skidding across the sidewalk.

"I've got you, beautiful. Stay still." I scan the sightlines for the shooter but can't see a damned thing.

The woman under me is trembling, her breaths coming in sharp gasps. I can feel her heartbeat racing against my chest. "Shh...just breathe. You're safe. We're just going to wait things out here for a bit."

"What about Tanya?"

Her friend is down and by the amount of carnage on the sidewalk around her, she won't be getting up. "Sorry, luv. There's nothing I can do for your friend."

The girl looks up at me and I'm struck stupid. I've seen more than my fair share of stunners in my life, but she puts them all to shame. Pulling her a little closer, I run a comforting hand over the sleeve of her cashmere jacket. "What's your name, beautiful?"

"Nora...Nora Kelly."

"It's good to meet you, Nora. I'm Brendan. I'm not going to let anything happen to you. I've got you."

If you're ready for more of the Quinn brothers, see what happens when Brendan finds out who Nora is and why they can't be together in Dublin Brute.

ALSO BY THESE AUTHORS

While Jenn Madore is a new pen name, moving her into contemporary romance, she isn't new to writing romance. With over ninety titles in Paranormal Romance and Fantasy Romance as JL Madore and Urban Fantasy Adventure as Auburn Tempest, there are plenty of stories to read if you're interested.

Likewise, Carolina Mac has over two-hundred titles in pulp fiction and crime thriller.

You can find all these titles on Amazon and thank you for reading.

Made in the USA
Las Vegas, NV
02 April 2025

20455171R00148